Other John Dickson Carr mysteries
available from Carroll & Graf Publishers

THE NINE WRONG ANSWERS

JOHN DICKSON CARR

Carroll & Graf Publishers, inc.
New York

Published by arrangement with Clarice M. Carr

First Carroll & Graf edition 1986
Third Carroll & Graf edition 1995

Carroll & Graf Publishers, Inc.
260 Fifth Avenue
New York, NY 10001

ISBN 0-7867-0174-9

Manufactured in the United States of America

CONTENTS

For Val Gielgud

My dear Val:

I dedicate this book to you for three reasons. First, because I think you will like it. It has been called "a novel for the curious" because there seems no other way of classifying it. It is a novel of character combined with one of very fast action, yet always underneath—without police investigation—runs a fair-play duel of wits between reader and writer.

Second, because I have such pleasurable memories of wartime days when I worked under your direction at the B.B.C. In these pages you may find one or two wartime characters faintly reminiscent of real persons. But they were such pleasant people (as, in fact, was everybody I knew at Rothwell) that I do not think they will be offended. And, as you are aware, no such regrettable goings-on ever occurred at Broadcasting House.

Third, because of Sherlock Holmes's and Dr. Watson's sitting room at the Exhibition in Baker Street last year. The background is authentic, since I was taken behind the scenes by my friend Mr. C. T. Thorne. But soon, if plans mature, you as producer and I as adapter will begin a new series of radio plays about the stout-hearted doctor and the greatest detective of them all.

Yours as ever,
John Dickson Carr

VILLA MIMOSA
TANGIER, MOROCCO
JANUARY, 1952

1 OVER THE THRESHOLD

WHEN he heard those odd words through the open transom, Dawson sat up straight in his chair.

He sat in the large, rather dingy library of the law office, ten floors up in a building in Lower Broadway. It was an old building. Outside two open windows, their Venetian blinds drawn up, the air pressed in a hot stuffiness from the canyon. It was deathly quiet. Walls of calf-bound books exhaled a fragrance which almost turned Dawson's head. Only the immense table, of dark mahogany on which burned a low-slung desk lamp in a green glass shade, seemed new.

Bill Dawson, fidgeting in the deep leather chair, clutched a copy of yesterday morning's *Times*. Dawson was still young, despite six years of war and six of peace. His suit was very shabby for all its cleaning and pressing. His carefully laundered shirt was frayed at the neckband; and, he kept uneasily pushing up his cuffs.

In his pockets Bill had his British passport, a few letters addressed to him, a match folder, an empty pack of cigarettes, and exactly sixteen cents.

Amberley, Sloane & Amberley.

In the library, facing his chair, was a high door with a ground-glass panel. Discreet black letters on the glass said, "Mr. Amberley." The door was closed, the old-fashioned transom stood open for air. A light shone behind the panel.

And Bill Dawson's thoughts rushed on.

'Why the devil did I come down here?' he reflected desperately. 'Nothing else to do, probably. Only to stand outside the building and look at it, and wish it were nine o'clock tomorrow morning so that I could go in?'

This was where he sat up straight.

For some moments he had been conscious of three voices beyond the open transom. They seemed to belong to a middle-aged man, a younger man, and a girl. But, since they were not speaking loudly, Bill had deliberately refused to hear them.

Now, however, two of the persons had reached a perplexity boarding on anger. The heavy voice of the middle-aged man, urbane and kindly, spoke out.

"Forgive me, Larry, but I don't understand all this."

"And I'm afraid *I* don't either, Larry," said the girl.

1

Her voice was English. No mistaking that. Bill Dawson, who was all imagination, instantly began drawing a mental picture of the girl. The voice was low and pleasant. And yet . . . She gave a small, affectionate laugh.

"Please, Larry! I'm awfully sorry! But it *is* simple. Isn't it, Mr. Amberley?"

"Perfectly simple," the urbane and hearty voice assured her. "Now let's be reasonable, Larry. Here are two tickets for the B.O.A.C. plane to London tomorrow afternoon. Idlewild, five o'clock. One ticket for you, one for Miss Tennent. Take them!"

"I'll take them," said the girl. "But do you know, Mr. Amberley, I'd much rather you called me Joy. Thank you."

Mr. Amberley laughed.

"Don't mention it—Joy." He spoke like an indulgent parent. "Now here," he went on with sudden solemnity, "I have ten thousand dollars in cash: large and small bills. They're yours, Larry; your uncle's instructions were to give them to you in person. What about it?"

The silence stretched out.

"My dear Larry," exclaimed Mr. Amberley, losing some of his suavity, "will you kindly tell me what ails you? It's hot tonight; it's late. Why won't you take the money? *Why?*"

Still the younger man called Larry did not speak. But a fist suddenly crashed down on a desk top: a wild gesture, as of one who despairs of being understood.

Bill Dawson sprang to his feet.

Despite what he believed to be his man-of-the-world's air at thirty-two, Bill had heard more than enough. His impulse was to hurry away from there, and forget his own business until tomorrow. Bill was not at his best. He didn't mind being so hungry that it cramped him; he had been hungry many times before; but how he wanted something to smoke! His hand slid for the dozenth time to the cigarette pack in his pocket. It was still empty.

And so sheer perverseness, as well as a biting curiosity, kept him there. Still gripping yesterday morning's *New York Times*, Bill sat down again. His fortune, three nickels and a penny, rattled.

"Larry! Darling!" coaxed Joy Tennent. "Honestly, aren't you being rather ridiculous? All you've got to do is sign that paper or document or whatever it is, and your uncle will make you his heir. I don't want to sound mercenary. And of course we—we hope the dear old boy will be spared to us for many years. . . ."

"Naturally, naturally!" agreed the lawyer.

"But," said Joy in an offhand tone, "let's not be utterly

2

stupid either. The poor man *is* filthy rich. Darling, he'll make you his sole heir on the smallest of conditions. Isn't that so, Mr. Amberley?"

Paper crackled.

" 'Laurence Hurst, nephew of the said Gaylord Hurst—' " he intoned, and stopped. "There are only two conditions, Larry. You must go back to England at once. Every week you must pay your uncle a visit, either at his apartment in London or at his house in Hampshire. That's not much to ask, is it?"

"After all, darling," laughed Joy, "you're not going to be murdered."

The younger man spoke at last. *"Stop that!"* he said.

It was as though the lighted door vibrated, sending ripples over wavy glass. The dim light of the inner office mingled with the dull shine of the green-shaded lamp on the table in the law library, creating a sort of suspended dusk.

Like Joy's, the voice was British. But Bill Dawson, who had been expecting to hear some weak character, was surprised at its tone and quality. It was strong, virile, almost dominating.

"Tell you what," said Hurst, who spoke like a telegram. "Give me a few days. Think it over. That's all. Where's the harm, George?"

"I'm sorry," said Mr. Amberley, "but I can't. Your uncle wants an immediate yes or no, immediate action. . . . That's why we're here at this unholy time. Larry, give me just one good reason why you won't accept his offer!"

"All right. I'm afraid," said Laurence Hurst.

Laurence Hurst did not sound frightened in any cowering way. His speech was that of a man who sees before him a calculated, deadly risk, a hundred to one against him, and shies back. The astonishment of Joy Tennent and George Amberley could be felt palpably.

"Afraid?" echoed Joy. "You, of all people? What are you afraid of?"

"Death."

"But, darling!" protested Joy, after a pause. "Who on earth is going to kill you?"

"Ever met my uncle, Joy? You, George?"

"I think I may say," Mr. Amberley replied smoothly, "that I am well acquainted with Mr. Gaylord Hurst. I haven't actually met him, no. But we've handled his business affairs in America for a good many years. And his reputation! He is a well-known philanthropist. . . ."

"Yes," the nephew said flatly.

"A patron of art and letters . . ."

"Yes. Tchaa!" snorted Hurst, with a powerful contempt.

3

"And a very admirable man. I think he has the true spirit of charity."

" 'Spirit of charity.' Good God! If you knew——!"

Once more Joy Tennent uttered her small, affectionate laugh; but this time (Bill felt) it was brittle with faint cruelty.

"Do wipe the sweat off your forehead, Larry! Poor darling! And to think," she murmured, in a puzzled tone, "you've shot tigers, and climbed mountains, and fought deep-sea fish —oh, everything!"

Startlingly, there was now a note of complacency in Hurst's voice, upsurging with vanity and arrogance. But vanity and even arrogance were frank and childish, like a schoolboy trying to be modest.

"Yes. Done a few things in my time, maybe."

"And now," said Joy, "you're afraid of a poor old man with one foot in the grave."

All the complacency was swept away.

"Look here," Hurst began with suppressed violence. He hesitated. "Look here, Joy. Does this mean you've chucked me?"

"Oh! darling, of course not!" cried Joy. "No, no, no! But you see . . . well, if we're to be married, *I'm* the one who's supposed to be protected. It may be very old-fashioned, but I like to be protected."

"George!"

"Yes, old man?"

"Where's that blasted paper? Give it me. And a pen."

Bill Dawson, listening absent-eyed, found himself looking fixedly at a small desk calendar on the table near the lamp. Tuesday, June 12th, 1951. But he scarcely saw the figures.

"Now that's better," said Mr. Amberley. "I shouldn't have persuaded you, of course. But frankly, Larry, I think you're doing a very wise thing. No, don't sign it yet! We must have a witness."

"I'll witness it," offered Joy.

"Yes, my dear. But you're Larry's fiancée; it would look better if someone else signed. My secretary will do." Amberley raised his voice. "Miss Ventnor!"

There was no reply. Evidently Mr. Amberley must have pressed some button; distantly, amid the labyrinth of dark offices, a faint buzzer twitched to life.

"Everything seems strange tonight," complained the lawyer, abruptly fretful. "That girl promised to be here. —Miss Ventnor!"

A shadow appeared on the wavy glass, growing to a huge grotesque as it approached. Mr. Amberley flung open the door.

4

"Miss Ventnor!" he shouted.

Bill's mental picture had been not far out. George Amberley was tall and easy of manner. His rich dark-gray suit had been carefully tailored to hide his growing stoutness. Smooth gray hair, brushed flat, was polished to silver by the light behind him. Yet his round, heavy face, set off by fretful blue eyes and a broad mouth, was much younger than his voice suggested. A professional half smile vanished when he saw Bill.

"Excuse me," he said loudly; "but who are you?"

Bill got up and went over to him.

"My name is Dawson. William Dawson."

"Dawson?" Mr. Amberley gave a start.

"Yes. I believe you wanted to see me. Do you mind looking at this, please?"

Opening out his copy of the *Times,* Bill folded it and pointed.

In the office behind Amberley's back, there was a startled stir and feminine whisper as Bill spoke. Still he could see neither Joy Tennent nor Laurence Hurst. He supposed the stir and whisper had been caused by still a third British voice. But he did not guess everything.[1]

Mr. Amberley took the newspaper with reluctance, and glanced briefly at the item. Bill knew every word by heart.

> *DAWSON* [it began in capital letters, continuing as formally as would have a solicitors' advertisement at home]. *If William Dawson, grandson of Lady (Alice) Penrith, of Restvale, Bedfordshire, England, will communicate with Messrs. Amberley, Sloane & Amberley, 120 Broadway, he will learn something to his advantage.*

"I saw that only this morning," said Bill. "I had to borrow . . . I thought it was best to come in person. So I got here by train from upstate New York. Did you put that advertisement in the paper, sir?"

Mr. Amberley seemed to wake up.

"Yes. Yes. I remember now." Suddenly his bulbous blue eyes sharpened with suspicion. He looked up at the open transom. "But isn't this a rather unusual time to come? How did you get in here?"

"I was standing down in the street, looking at the building. . . ."

"Why, please?"

[1] The astute reader will already have wondered whether the preceding scene was not a corporate conspiracy directed at Bill Dawson himself, who was intended to overhear the conversation. This idea is wholly wrong. Discard answer number one.

"I don't know. There was nothing else to do, I suppose. In any case, there was a little bald elevator man. He came out and said, 'Want anything?' I said I wanted to see Mr. Amberley, but I didn't expect he'd be there. Then he said you were expecting me."

"Didn't that strike you as peculiar?"

"Yes; ruddy peculiar! But I didn't say anything. He took me up here, and pointed to your office. The door wasn't locked, and there was a light in the reception room. I blundered into this room."

Suspicion began to fade from the round, heavy face.

"Yes, that's Joe." Mr. Amberley blew out his cheeks. "I happen to be in conference with some English clients, and Joe must have thought . . . Have you any identification, Mr. Dawson?"

From his inside breast pocket Bill took the passport. After a quick examination, George Amberley handed back both passport and newspaper.

"That's fine, that's fine!" he declared, with absent-minded briskness. "Now I'm all tied up in a conference, and I know you'll excuse me. Er—suppose you phone tomorrow? And arrange an appointment for one day next week."

Bill's eyes moved round to the desk calendar: Tuesday, June 12th. "Very well," he said, with a sick knowledge that it wasn't very well. "I didn't mean to intrude. But it would take only a moment to tell me," he tapped the newspaper, "what this means."

Mr. Amberley frowned. Yet, in the act of turning away, for the first time he really looked at his visitor.

He saw a pleasant-faced, medium-sized young man, with heavy shoulders despite the slender build. Bill's light-brown hair contrasted with his dark-brown eyes, round which fine wrinkles of amusement had deepened. The face was sharply intelligent, too fine-drawn; it might have seemed weak except for the jaw.

Amberley's covert gaze ran over his companion's clothes, the tie, the frayed collar. Amberley's expression changed. He moved out into the library, softly closing the door. "Mr. Dawson, I beg your pardon."

"Not at all, nót at all! It was only that—"

"I understand. I am sorry to tell you that Lady Penrith is dead."

Bill nodded. In a sense he had expected this, since the item mentioned her name; on the other hand, Gran's title might have been used merely to attract notice. But he had been very fond of old Gran.

"You see, Mr. Dawson, it's a question of a legacy."

"Legacy?" exclaimed Bill. "To tell you the truth, I'd been hoping for something like that. But from Gran? She's as poor as they've made all the decent people in England today."

"Well, at least your view of Lady Penrith makes my job easier. It isn't a large legacy, I'm afraid: a hundred pounds in your money, something under three hundred dollars. But it'll get you back home, if that's what you want?"

"No. I like it here."

Mr. Amberley looked still more pleased. Then, thrusting his hands into his trousers' pockets, he grew fussed.

"Now see here, young man!" he snapped. "Don't take offense where none is intended. Here's a couple of tens; it's all I've got on me except some change. Take these as a little advance."

It would have meant a bed, meals, cigarettes. That was why Bill never understood the words he spoke then.

"No, thanks," he said hurriedly. "Thanks very much; but I don't need it."

"Sure?" the other asked quietly.

"Yes! Absolutely! But if I could meet you before one day next week . . . ?"

"Ah, I forgot!" Mr. Amberley snapped his fingers. "Would tomorrow morning suit you? Fine! At half past nine? Fine!" He extended his hand. "Good night, my dear sir. It's been a pleasure."

Hurst's powerful voice struck at them over the transom.

"George! Don't let our friend get away!"

"Get away?"

"Got to have a witness, haven't we?"

"But Miss Ventnor can sign as witness! She must be somewhere; I'll find her."

"Unless," laughed Joy, "she's been murdered and hidden in the library."

Again Bill was conscious of a shock.

"This," muttered Mr. Amberley, "has got to stop!" Once more he glanced up at the transom, and afterward at Bill. "Tell me, Mr. Dawson. Did you . . . ?"

"Hear what was said in there? Yes. I heard nearly everything."

"What's the odds, old boy?" Laurence Hurst shouted back. He sounded feverishly genial. "We've just heard your story too. George, bring him in!"

Mr. Amberley opened the door.

IN one corner of the office, heavy with old-fashioned luxury, stood a massive desk. A lamp had been pressed down so close to the large pink desk blotter that light spilled out only across packets of banknotes on the blotter. The room was shadowy.

"Hello," said Joy Tennent, rather awkwardly.

She stood behind one side of the desk. Joy's heavy, sleek black hair was parted on one side and fell to her shoulders, where it curled up. Her large eyes, dark blue, looked ingenious and friendly. So did her half-smiling mouth. She was not tall, and rather sturdy. Wearing a sensible but costly tailored suit, she seemed, like many English girls, to be almost in too good training until you remarked the excellence of her figure.

"Oh, dear!" she said. "It was rather awful of us, wasn't it? I mean, talking like that?"

"No, Miss Tennent," smiled Bill. "I shouldn't have listened."

"You shouldn't have, should you?" Joy made it a very small severity. Then she returned his smile.

To the lapel of her dark-green jacket was pinned the tiny figure of a leopard in small diamonds. Round her neck hung a discreet diamond pendant. Joy lifted one hand and touched the pendant. As though by instinct, she twitched her head round and looked across the desk.

Laurence Hurst sat in a heavy chair on the other side, his long legs stretched out.

"Nonsense, my pet! Rot! Bilge!" Hurst stood up, and considered Bill. "Pay no attention, old boy! Here, let's have a look at you."

But already he had been studying Bill: with intensity, even with a growing inspiration. Hurst noted Bill's tie.

"You were at Harrow, I see," he began heartily.

"Right. And you were at Stowe."

"Not long, old boy. Ran away to sea when I was sixteen. Fact! You could still run away to sea then: just like the stories. Board of Trade's stricter now. Never regretted it, though. —Been in the States long?"

Hurst had charm. Though he was a couple of years older than Bill, and two inches taller, they had much the same build because of the latter's heavy shoulders. And both had light-brown hair and dark-brown eyes.

Hurst's handsome face, with long head and indrawn cheeks,

and a narrow line of mustache, resembled that of what used to be called the strong silent Empire builder. His clothes were as conservative as those of Amberley. Yet Bill suspected that his clipped speech, almost comically in the old tradition, was affected to conceal emotionalism.

"Been in the States long?" he repeated.

"Three years. No, that's not quite accurate: nearer four."

"Why'd you come here to begin with?"

"Well," Bill answered wryly, "I suppose you could say I was looking for adventure."

"Were you, by George!"

Larry held out a pack of Pall Malls. Bill had to steady himself not to snatch at one like a toper at a drink. But his empty stomach almost betrayed him. Larry snapped on a lighter. Bill, drawing smoke deep into his lungs, discovered that his head and eyesight were swimming. Though he could not help coughing, he was steady in a moment; and nobody had noticed.

"Now, then!" said Larry. "Did you find it here in the States?"

"No, not much."

"Working here? Or traveling for pleasure?"

"Oh, drifting from job to job all over the country. At garages and filling stations, mostly. They taught us something about motors during the war."

"Ah, the war. Motors! In the Raf, were you? Ground crew?"

"Not so important. Fighter pilot."

('By the gods,' thought Bill, 'I'm talking exactly in his own 1920 style of speech. It's insidious, like saying "Aye" in Scotland.')

"Were you, by George!" said Larry. "How long?"

"Six years."

"Six . . . Look here! Don't tell me you were one of the original Battle of Britain pilots?"

"Well—yes," Bill admitted guiltily. "But keep it to yourself. There are too few of us now; and nobody ever believes."

Joy Tennent dropped her suspicious scrutiny of Larry. She turned toward Bill.

"And so, of course," she said gently, "you never had any adventure."

"All I can tell you, Miss Tennent, is that it didn't seem like that at the time. It was much too . . . I don't know."

"H'm," murmured Joy. Her dark-blue eyes, accentuated by her faint pallor, grew deeply human. "May I ask your real profession, Mr. Dawson?"

"Nothing, actually. I wanted a fellowship at Caius. But the war interrupted things at Cambridge."

"Books!" snorted Larry. "Like my uncle!" But his tone altered. "Give you a little tip, old boy. Never opened a book in my life, except maybe stories I like. Never mind books! Study people!"

"Never mind people," said Bill. "Study books."

Larry ignored this.

"You're one of these nervy, strung-up blokes, aren't you?" he demanded in his powerful voice.

"Here!" protested Bill, resenting this as all men do. "What makes you say that? No! I don't admit—"

"Never mind! Often heard Raf men say your kind made the best fighter pilots. All nerves beforehand; steady as a rock when trouble came. —Can't understand it myself. Never had a nerve in my body."

Joy's large eyes opened wide.

"There's different kinds of fear. Can't you understand? I was in that war too, my pet. Never been afraid in my life of anything I could see and fight."

"Darling!" murmured Joy. "Do you think your uncle is going to chase you with ghosts?"

Larry lifted one fist; but repressed this tendency toward the emotional, and the fist dropped. Yet, so far as Bill could see in the dim light, the Empire builder's face had become pale.

"Once," Larry began, "when I was a kid . . ."

"Larry, for the last time!" interrupted Mr. Amberley.

Mr. Amberley had been studying a typewritten document, backed with stiff gray-brown paper. Something on the final page seemed to trouble the lawyer, but he stood up, pushed the document across toward Larry, and removed the cap of a fountain pen.

"Let's either finish this," he said sharply, "or else forget it. Which is it to be, Larry?"

"Curse it all, I told you I was willing!"

"Good. Then sign here, where I've made a cross in pencil."

Pulling the chair to the side of the desk, Larry Hurst took the pen, sat down, and steadied his hand before signing. Joy Tennent hardly seemed to breathe.

The pen moved down to the signature line—and stopped.

"By the way, Dawson!" said Larry. "Are you married?"

Mr. Amberley uttered a groan.

"No, I'm not married," replied Bill.

"Engaged? Girl friend? Any close friend in this country?"

"As for the first, no. The second, only the usual thing. The rest, no; I've drifted too much. But why all this about me?"

"I wish *I* understood!" said Mr. Amberley.

But Joy seemed to understand. Her gaze flashed from

Larry's hair and eyes to Bill's hair and eyes, as well as their equal shoulder breadth. At last she seemed to find the answer to her study of Larry. "No!" she burst out, almost at a scream. "No, no, no!"

Mr. Amberley lowered his head as though to cool it.

"Do I understand, Miss Ten—er—Joy," he said, "that *you* now have some objection to this agreement?"

"Oh, no!" yearned Joy in her sweetest voice. "Do please forgive me. It wasn't that at all. But moods are so horribly contagious, aren't they?"

"Right!" agreed Larry, and signed with unsteady haste. He wagged the pen at Bill. "Your turn, old boy."

Bill leaned over and signed: for a different reason, with almost as much of a scrawl as Larry. Amberley had evidently seen nothing but more difficulty in Joy's outburst. Bill believed he could see what was in the girl's mind. But it was so grotesque that he almost laughed.

Amberley was beaming again.

"That's fine!" he said, taking back the fountain pen. "I'm a notary public, and I can take care of the rest. Mr. Dawson, I have some final instructions for our young friends here: addresses, hotel reservations, and so on. I know you'll excuse us. Until tomorrow morning, then!"

"Best of luck, old boy!" muttered Larry, though he breathed hard.

"All the best," murmured Joy. "Awfully sorry I—we probably shan't see you again. Ever again."

Closing the door behind him, Bill walked slowly across to the far door, and finally to the reception room and outer door. His heart beat heavily, and he felt light-headed. He was still half hypnotized not only by the scene in the office, but by all that money on the pink blotter.

Ten thousand dollars. Tomorrow he would have a hundred pounds. His sixteen cents would at least buy him something to eat, and a bed did not matter. Yet the sight of all that money on the desk had altered his vision.

Crazy longings crawled through him. And for the first time Bill really looked into his own heart. He knew that what he had said a while ago was not the truth, though he had believed it to be. Much as he liked America, he had not come here for adventure. That was his unconscious defense against the defeated hope of an academic career.

His father, a Sussex clergyman, could not have sent his son to Cambridge without that scholarship. Now . . .

Ten thousand dollars once was two thousand pounds. Now it had become one and a half times greater. With that sum, Bill could dissolve his debt to his father and mother. He could return to Cambridge, get his fellowship. If he were careful (though in money matters Bill was never careful) he could . . .

"Ah, well!" he said aloud, and sauntered into the passage.

"S-st—! Dawson!" hissed the voice of Larry Hurst.

Bill whirled round.

Though the passage was dark, the glow from the library partly illuminated Larry as he stood in the doorway. It showed his crisp, short-cut brown hair, the faint horizontal wrinkles in his forehead, the brief case in his right hand.

"Yes?" said Bill.

"Can't stop a moment," gabbled Larry in a low voice. "Told 'em I was going to the gents'. Look here: if you had an opportunity for adventure, would you take it?"

"Yes!" shouted Bill.

"Sh-h! Steady!" Larry glanced over his shoulder. "Like to earn ten thousand dollars for six months' work?"

It was seconds before Bill could answer. His throat was too dry.

"What work?"

"Danger. Haven't you guessed? You're to go back to England and take my place for six months."

Bill had guessed, but he had thought it too nonsensical to be considered.

"That ought to please you!" said Larry. *"That's* out of books!" He uttered his rusty laugh; but very briefly. *"The Prisoner of Zenda. The Masquerader. The Great Impersonation.* Read 'em all when I was a boy. Only it all depended on two men looking exactly alike: same face, height, voice, everything. Rot! Wouldn't happen once in a hundred years. You and I don't look very much alike. Don't even think alike. Eh? No. This'll be a new kind of impersonation."

"I don't doubt it," said Bill, staggered. "Listen! Are you serious?"

"Serious! My God!"

"All right, all right. But . . ."

"Mind you," warned Larry, "this isn't whatd'yecallit?—ah, altruism. Not by a jugful! Sort of test, that's all. I'll come to claim my rights in six months, if you're still alive."

"It won't work," said Bill. "We couldn't get away with it."

"If I prove to you it will work," said Larry, with toiling emphasis, "will you agree? Got to trust you. Will you agree?"

"Yes!"

Larry's tall silhouette writhed in the doorway.

"But fair's fair," his nature compelled him to say. "Can't do this with your eyes shut. Just dying—well! That never

12

seemed so bad. But there's different ways of dying, or even living. Got it?"

"Frankly, no," said Bill. "But that's the point. There's something I'm bound to know, first of all. This uncle of yours: what's he like?"

"Smallish old swine. Not as tall as you, but fatter. Bad eyesight. Even in the old days used to wear bifocal glasses that . . ."

"No, no, I don't mean his appearance. Put it like this. If he offers to make you his heir, why do you think there's a booby trap attached to it? And why should your father's brother want to do you any harm?"

Hesitating, Larry craned his head round. His right hand tightened on the handle of the brief case.

"Got to get back there," he insisted. "No time to explain now. Steady, steady! Whole story in five minutes. Tell you what: go down to the floor below this; wait beside the lifts. It'll be dark there. Joy and I will get away as soon as we can."

"Joy?"

" 'Fraid so, old boy. Think she knows already; got to tell her. Devilish fine girl, Joy. Ought to see her with no clothes on. Only one fault, Joy: tries to manage me for my own good. How'd *you* like to be managed by a woman?"

"As a matter of fact, it's the one thing I won't put up with." Bill's tongue slipped. "Marjorie never once tried to . . ."

"Who's Marjorie?"

"Only a girl I once knew in England."

"Oh. Not here? That's to say, if anybody in America began making inquiries after you'd gone—?"

"Don't worry. Nobody will."

"Good! Only one thing more."

With impatient fingers Larry opened the brief case, swinging it round so that the gilt letters *L.H.* glimmered. He put the case on the floor. From it he scooped out the bundles of banknotes, picked up from Amberley's desk a few minutes before.

"Bargain's a bargain," Larry said mildly. "Here's the damn money. Take the lot now."

"Wait a minute, Hurst! You haven't told me how we can get away with this impersonation!"

Larry did not even reply. Sweeping away objections in his bulldozer fashion, he unceremoniously stuffed bundles into Bill's pockets.

"That's the lot," he declared, patting the effect as he might have patted an impressive snowman. "Count it while you wait. Got to go now: George might suspect."

"But—!"

13

"Whole story," insisted Larry, "in five minutes!"

Silently Larry turned back and crossed the library. He stopped only long enough to fasten the catch of the brief case, so that Amberly should not notice the banknotes had gone.

Bill stood motionless. All the money for which he had so hopelessly longed, which would fulfill every dream except Marjorie, now filled his clothes, made him bulge like a straw dummy. Presently he began to laugh.

"Whole story," he said, "in five minutes."

3 THE SOFTNESS OF A LEOPARD GIRL

EXACTLY fifteen minutes later, while Bill waited in the corridor of the ninth floor, he heard the soft footsteps scraping down the stairs.

With a next-door building gone, moonlight penetrated the windows and lay bloodless on a floor of speckled gray tile.

As she descended the stairs, however softly, Joy Tennent's high heels rapped. Larry's big shoes had a distinct whack. Since both spoke in low voices, neither could have imagined the words would carry along the corridor.

"You fool," said Joy. "You fool!"

"Heard enough of this, old girl," said Larry. "Now chuck it."

"Darling. What's the good of saying, over and over, that you liked him and therefore he's all right? *I* rather liked him myself. But lots of pleasant people are crooks. And—oh, dear! You must go and give him all that money. He could be *miles* away by now."

Larry's footfalls halted on the stairs. So did Joy's.

"Never thought of that," Larry admitted blankly.

Bill felt vaguely surprised. 'Neither did I,' he thought.

"Please understand, darling," Joy's voice drifted down. "I'm not saying he's a thief. But he is hard up."

"Hard up? Didn't you hear George offer him a loan? And he refused it?"

"Yes, Larry. I also heard his—his tone when he said it. Mr. William Dawson," Joy pronounced the name with care, "is as damn-your-eyes as you." Her voice wavered. "I'm positive he hasn't had anything to eat all day, and you must have seen how he pounced on that cigarette. He must be desperate. Don't rave like a lunatic, if he isn't waiting for us."

"He'll be there. Bet you anything you like. Now come on!"

The footfalls descended in echoes to this floor.

Bill turned round and stood with his back to the moonlit window.

"I was wondering what had happened to you," he called. His voice rolled down the corridor. "Have you still got that brief case, Hurst? I feel like a scarecrow stuffed with money."

Joy and Larry stopped dead. They looked at him across the long carpet of moonlight. It is to Larry's credit that he did not crow with triumph over Joy.

"Here you are," he said, extending the brief case when they had reached the window—Larry quickly, Joy slowly. "Now let's clear out and find a bar. Quick!"

"Not just yet," replied Bill, putting bundles back into the case.

A rakish soft hat was pulled down on Larry's head; he wore the hat with an air, as he wore his blue double-breasted suit.

"But George Amberley's still up there, old boy! We don't want him to come down in the lift and find we haven't gone."

Bill, putting the last banknote packet into the brief case, looked casually at Joy and smiled. He did not·comment, or intend to comment. He could sense from her physical presence that she was furious with him.

Nevertheless, Joy returned his casual smile. She opened her handbag, brought out a pack of Chesterfields, and held it out.

"Cigarette, Mr. Dawson?"

"No, thanks. Not at the moment."

The diamond leopard glittered in hard, tiny flashes as Joy moved. She put the cigarette in her own mouth. Fumbling for his match folder, Bill struck a light for her.

"Thank you so much."

Larry, like heavy armor on a battlefield, crashed into the silence.

"You want to know," he demanded, "how I'm dead certain we can get away with an impersonation? Right! Told you, didn't I, about running away to sea when I was sixteen?"

"Yes; well?"

"That was in '33. I haven't been back to England since. Fact! Haven't set foot in England, haven't seen or spoken to one person I used to know, for over eighteen years. At sixteen I was a kid. . . . If somebody even near my age went back as Larry Hurst, and if he'd got the same color hair and eyes— got it? He could be any height, any character, anything. And who'd notice? Nobody!"

Now Bill could understand Larry's clipped, old-style phrases.

"Well?" prompted Larry.

"Away from home for eighteen . . . wait! You said you were in the war."

15

"Right. Landed in Australia in '39. Joined up with the Diggers; fought in Burma."

"But your parents, your relatives, would be bound to recognize an imposter! I might fool your friends; but nobody could fool your family."

"Parents both dead. Look here: how'd you think I've been living since I was twenty-one? Costs a packet to shoot heavy game. Costs . . . never mind. Inherited my mother's fortune." Here Larry, darting a sudden quick glance at Joy, went on rather too loudly. "Spent most of it by this time. Admit that."

"Yes, darling," said Joy absently. "You have."

"Still got twenty-two thousand, though. Joy knows. Anyway, both parents dead. No living relative except old Gaylord."

"That's the odd uncle?"

" 'Odd.' Yes, rather. You call him 'Uncle Gay.' " Larry made the sound of one revolted. "Told you about his bad eyesight, eh? Wouldn't matter in any case, unless I'd got a big beak, or ears that stuck out: follow me? But I haven't. Neither have you."

"No. If you had time to brief me thoroughly, I could avoid too many snags. Suppose your uncle begins questioning me about your youth?"

"Just say you don't remember. Say it as if you didn't *want* to remember." Larry's voice went up. "By God, that's true! He'll understand, right enough."

"Again," pursued Bill, "you seem to be rather a fabulous traveler and sportsman. What if your uncle—or anybody else —wants to hear my reminiscences?"

"Invent 'em!"

"H'm. Yes. Something tells me," declared Bill, though not unhappily, "that my description of a tiger hunt will make the curry fly off the table. But it's a beauty of a challenge."

"Good for you, old boy!"

There was a red-glowing flash as Joy dropped her cigarette on the floor.

"Now the next obstacle," Bill went on. "You must have written letters after you left home. If I have to write anything, how do I fake your handwriting?"

"That's easy. Type it: except the signature."

"You think the signature's easy too?"

"Easier than you imagine." Larry repressed glee. "Now listen! Copy the signature on my passport. Copy it two hundred times a day, for a week. It'll surprise you. I mean that! Done it myself. Why, I've . . ." Larry paused and coughed "Er— it wasn't to cheat anybody, mind! Only to fool 'em."

"And did you?"

"Yes. Easy as shelling peas. So can you."

"Assuming I might do it with an ordinary letter," muttered Bill, "what about a check? I can't carry this cash about, even if they allowed you to keep dollars. It's got to go into a bank. And a bank is a little sharper than an acquaintance who gets a letter. How do I get round that?"

"You needn't. Deposit the money under your own name and signature. Dash it, don't you follow the simplicity even now?—Well, well! Didn't myself until George told me something tonight."

"Told you what?"

"Uncle Gay, the little swine, now thinks he's a semi-invalid. Never leaves his flat, except once a week to go to his club. Now you. If you meet any of your own friends, you're William Dawson, Esq. Got it now? Except in the furnished flat that's been booked for me, *you don't have to impersonate me in front of anybody but Gay.*"

Bill saw solid reality emerge out of mist.

"Has that fetched you?" inquired Larry.

"Yes. If you demonstrate just how the devil I can use your passport, I'm your man. Can't grow a mustache overnight . . ."

"Don't have to. Didn't wear one myself when I had this passport photo taken." Larry swung round. "Joy, my pet. Got that electric torch? Let's have it."

Joy twitched round. Her left hand gripped the open cigarette pack. Over her right arm, her handbag hung. Without a word she took a small flashlight from the bag and gave it to Larry.

"Ah," said Larry, not looking at her. "George," he added to Bill, "asked you for identification. Meant your passport, eh? Let's see it."

Bill put the brief case beside the radiator under the window. Opening the jacket of his suit—an American suit, loosely tailored—Larry switched on the torch and tugged at the paper-jammed inside pocket. His passport flew out. So did the card of a printer, a large and very old snapshot of a youth and an older man, and a small new snapshot of Joy in the nude. Joy did not see it.

"Hem!" said Larry hastily. But he did not trouble to pick up the card and the photographs. Instead he opened his passport, as well as Bill's. Holding them flat together in one hand, he slowly ran the beam of the torch back and forth over both.

"It'll do!" Larry said after a pause. "See for yourself."

What did the trick was the wrong lighting combined with

the strange expressions. While Bill looked like an unshaven tough with hollow eyes, after a night in the cells, Larry resembled an ascetic scorning the fleshpots.

"Yes, they'll do!" Bill said fervently. Now his dreams dazzled him. "The bargain is hereby sealed. Shake hands on it?"

"Rather!" agreed Larry, with relief.

And solemnly they shook hands, Larry dropping the passports to do so. The passports whacked the floor with a faint, ugly echo.

Joy had turned away again, facing across the broad corridor to a flattish tin receptacle for discarded paper; it was fastened to the wall. Some crumpled silver paper thrust up at the open edge of the cigarette pack. Tearing off a little, Joy rolled it into a pellet. With thumb and second finger, viciously, she flicked it across the corridor. It struck the wall just above the litter bin, and fell inside.

"Now, then," pursued the excited Bill, "what do you want me to do next? What are *you* going to do?"

"Me, old boy?"

"Just ask yourself the questions you asked me. What about your friends here in New York? If you're supposed to be in England—"

"Don't live in New York," Larry assured him, switching the torch on and off. "Hardly know the town, or anybody in it. Been out on the Coast for three years. Beverly Hills. Joy and I got here by plane."

"Yes," observed Joy. "Larry was keen to be here early. But we were grounded for three days, and only arrived this afternoon. It's a good thing our trunks were sent long ago by train."

"Trunks!" exclaimed Larry. "Glad you remembered that, old girl." He flashed the light in Bill's face, then away again. "As for me, I lie doggo for six months, with your name and passport. Joy stays with me. Today we put up at the Waldorf . . . er . . . separate rooms, of course. . . ."

"Naturally!" said Joy, in her tone of wide-eyed ingenuousness "Why mention that?"

Again the light went into Bill's face. "Want to know when your impersonation begins, Dawson? It begins tonight."

Bill felt as though scissors were poised to snap the last thread. He was not sure he liked it.

"Tonight?" he repeated.

"Yes. Joy will clear her belongings out of her room. But mine—a trunk and two suitcases full of clothes—mine'll stay. They're yours now. I can get a complete new outfit tomorrow, wherever Joy and I go tonight. You'll sleep tonight in my room at the Waldorf. From that time you're on your own."

"Steady your imagination," said Bill. "It's all right so far,

18

but don't make it too crazy. Won't the hotel people know I'm not you?"

"In a damn great hothouse like that? You're a key and a name and a bill, that's all.—Joy, my pet! Took those plane tickets from George, didn't you? Hand 'em over."

"But . . . !"

"Tickets, old girl."

Taking two long, very thin and light-blue booklets from Joy, Larry again studied Bill.

"My clothes," he said. "All marked. Complete transformation, eh? Shirts, socks, underwear, even shoes: all fit you perfectly. The suits . . . h'm."

Larry cocked his head on one side and squinted at Bill down the beam of light.

"Jacket and waistcoat," he went on, "fit you perfectly too. Lot of my height, see, is in my legs; I'm at least two inches taller. Trousers not so good. Won't matter, though. Before you get 'em altered, hitch your braces as high as they'll go; waistcoat'll hide the difference in trouser length. May catch you badly in the crotch."

Bill chuckled softly.

"Don't joke," snapped Larry. "I may not have a sense of humor, by George! But I know when something's serious."

"Serious?" said Joy, flinging the cigarettes into her handbag. "Call it off, Larry! For heaven's sake call it off! Do you know what you are? Both of you?"

"Swear, old girl. Do you good. But it won't change anything."

"I had no intention of swearing, Larry.—You two are nothing but a couple of school boys, excited about a new game. Playing pirates! Medieval knights! Oh, dear, why are all men so silly?"

"Pet of my pets, shut up."

"But, please, darling, give it up! Something horrible will happen. If Mr. Dawson makes a mistake, they'll put him in jail. . . ."

"Quite probably," admitted Bill.

Joy had hurried over and seized Larry's arm. She turned toward Bill, shaking back her hair. Against her moon-whitened face, a little cruel smile curled her mouth. "You can't expect me to be terribly cut up, Mr. Dawson, at the prospect of your going to jail. If Larry had never seen you, he'd never have thought of this. But he'll try to help you. And then *he'll* be put in jail."

"Nonsense, old girl!"

"Oh, yes, you will, darling. But even suppose this succeeds. You'll have to meet your uncle one day, won't you? And do

19

you think he'll ever forgive you for it? No, no, no! You'll never touch a penny of that inheritance."

"So!" said Larry. "That's what hurts you. Eh?"

"Of course it does. I keep telling you, darling, that someone must be practical. And I should do anything . . . to stop this!" Joy's voice shrilled up. "Don't you touch me! Don't dare!"

Larry pushed her aside and ignored her.

"Now, old boy," snapped Larry. "This is the last step. This is where we change passports, papers, and clothes." Dropping the torch into his pocket, together with the air-liner tickets, he whipped off his coat. "Get cracking, old boy: strip!"

Bill, embarrassed, glanced at Joy. Her eyes met his with a kind of demure mockery. Larry, unslinging his braces, saw that glance.

"Er—wait!" he ordered. Back went braces, waistcoat, and jacket. "No need to change clothes tonight. Look like the devil in your shorter trousers. But the papers, everything except money . . ."

"Just a moment," interposed Bill, dragging his gaze away from Joy. "You haven't said a word about what your Uncle Gay plans to do."

Every mention of that old goblin seemed to crumple Larry. He pulled his hat further down, and fumbled at his chin.

"No time now!" he protested. "George Amberley'll be down in a moment. Got to get to a bar. . . . oh, very well."

Catching sight of Bill's stony expression, Larry went on in a strained but level voice.

"What would you think," he asked, "of a grown man who devoted his life to frightening a kid?"

Again silence thickened. "I was kept constantly scared from four years old till I ran away to sea at sixteen. Gay was always there. Always creeping. Always with something new to give you the horrors. Gay said they were jokes.

"For instance. Imagine you're five or six. You find yourself, all alone, in a big room at a country house. Your parents aren't there. You think they're gone forever. In comes Gay, with the light on his thick spectacles. Carrying a big fruit jar, glass, with a screw top. 'Ah, old chap,' he says. 'See what the greengrocer found in a bunch of bananas.'

"Inside the jar there's a big tarantula. Black and furry. You know now tarantulas aren't poisonous; but you didn't then. 'Don't be afraid,' says Gay in that sad voice as if you'd always be a rabbit. 'Watch!' says Gay.

"And he unscrews the top of the jar, and takes it off. You can't scream, poor little devil. You can't run; you're too scared. Gay takes a school ruler. Reaches down in the jar, and prods the thing. Like a flash it runs up the ruler. Somehow it's out of the jar and running up your arm.

"Well . . . you fall on the floor. And then you hear Gay saying, 'Poor old chap,' he says, 'you're not afraid of a toy tarantula, I hope. Can't you hear the clockwork. Come, we must make a man of you.'

"But you can't tell your father and mother! I mean: you do tell, or try to. But they don't believe you. Your mother says: 'Now, dear, *I* know you're not telling lies. But you only imagine all this, don't you? You know Uncle Gay couldn't have done that, don't you?'

"Yes. Your mother's . . . what's the word? . . . she's enlightened. While they're telling you off, in slips Gay. Your mother begins to weep a bit. 'I don't mind what the boy tells; do I, old chap?' says Gay. 'But, Herbert'—Herbert was my father's name—'we can't have him grow up both a liar *and* a coward.' He'd look at you out of those pale bluish eyes. You'd know his next joke would be a dozen times worse.

"God help a kid like that! And this goes on for years and years. . . ."

Larry's voice trailed off. Bill and Joy looked at the floor. But doggedly Larry moistened his lips.

"Coward! Funk! Rabbit! That was the game. I think that's why I first took up sports. To show I wasn't. —I see what you're thinking. Why did Gay do this, eh? Is he scatty? Oh, no. Tell you what it is.

"He hates my guts. Always has. And I've hated him. Gay hated my father. Funny, too. Gay was the elder brother. Got the money. Dad was . . . not much, maybe, until the fourteen-eighteen war. After he'd got the D.S.O. and a lot more decorations, they hoicked him back to the War Office.

"They gave him a knighthood in '19. Potty little knighthood; died with him. But it nearly killed Gay. Gay'd have given his soul to stick 'Sir' in front of his name. Gay didn't dare try any games on Dad. But I was born in '17. What would you think of a grown man who devoted his life to frightening a kid?"

Snatching the flashlight out of his pocket with unsteady fingers, Larry directed its beam to the floor. It missed the photograph of Joy. But it rested on the old photograph of a man and a boy.

"You s-see?" demanded Larry, picking up the photograph and turning the light on it.

Two figures faced the camera. On the right stood a boy in blazer and school cap, Larry Hurst. He had begun to show gawky traces of muscular power. But his eyes were sunken in fright, as though he thought the camera might explode.

21

The man on the left . . .

Small and plump, Gaylord Hurst had hair of an untidy dark gray, like dirty sheep's wool. His long, thin face bore a strong resemblance to his nephew's. He had removed his thick spectacles, and held them primly. His washed-out eyes exuded virtue.

"You're not a child now," Joy pleaded, her hands clenched. "Darling, go back and hit him! I don't mean hit him literally. But don't you want revenge? Don't you want to get a bit of your own back?"

Larry's indrawn breath was like a prayer. But his shoulders slackened.

"Darling, I insist. Why—"

"Can't face him," said Larry, and abruptly turned away. "He did too much damage when I was still a kid."

There was a pause. The humiliation in Larry's voice was deep. "And now he's at it again. Why does he offer to make me his heir? Because he knows I've nearly run through my mother's fortune. How could he learn that? George Amberley's his solicitor. George is mine too; known him since I first ran away. George is straight as a die! Never tell old Gay. But there could be someone at the office . . ."

"Such as the missing Miss Ventnor?" suggested Bill.

"How should I know? Gay wants me back. This time to finish me."

"But he can't use any of those tricks now!" muttered Bill. "Have you any notion how he means to deal with . . . me, in your place?"

"Not the foggiest! As soon as you get to the furnished flat he's rented for me, you're to phone him at his flat. Then he'll want to see you. Then . . . *What's that?*"

The noise, in this shell of echoes, made both Larry and Bill jump. It was a high, thin hum from nine floors below, as an elevator began to rise.

"George," said Larry, "must have pressed the button upstairs. He'll ask Joe if we've left the building. We'll take to the stairs, and Joe won't hear us go. Mustn't make George suspicious!"

"Darling," said Joy, "do you think he isn't already? After your odd conduct tonight?"

"Nonsense! Here's my passport, Dawson; I'll keep yours. We'll change our pockets on the way down. Then we can get a taxi and hare off to a bar. Hurry!"

Bill snatched up the brief case.

4 THE FLASHING LIGHTS OF MURDER

THE taxi swept uptown. Joy sat between Bill and Larry. Not a word had been spoken since Larry gave (as Bill heard it) inaudible orders to the driver.

Bill, the brief case in his lap, now carried all Larry's personal effects: except the photograph of Joy. Bill suspected that in the confusion it had vanished at Joy's own hand, and that she hated him the more because he had seen it.

"Well," muttered Larry, without looking up, "you've seen I'm a ruddy weakling. There it is."

"You?" Joy spoke incredulously. "No, Larry. I knew a tremendous lot of it, naturally." Joy pressed closer to Larry, sliding her hand inside his coat and up toward the shoulder. "But, Larry, if you'd only confided in me! Told me everything!"

"Never confided in a woman," said Larry out of the side of his mouth. "If she lo—likes you, she'll never give you away. But she'll do some tomfool thing trying to help. Then you're' for it. And that reminds me. Dawson!"

"Yes?"

"This girl of yours! This Marjorie What's-her-name?"

"Marjorie Blair," answered Bill. "But—"

"Indeed?" observed Joy in a bright voice. Still softly moving her hand up and down Larry's chest, she looked round at Bill. "But, my dear man! You said you hadn't got a girl in America. You said you'd known some of them, but it was 'only the usual thing.' Do tell me what you mean by the usual thing."

Bill managed to smile. He liked Joy. But there are certain memories at which you must not stab.

"It would be crude," smiled Bill, "to draw a diagram." He paused. "Besides, Marjorie's in England."

"Really?" Joy said in a higher voice. "Then with Marjorie there was never . . ."

"No. Never."

"This is serious. Be quiet, both of you!" Larry interrupted. "Now understand, Dawson. You're not only impersonating me. You're leading a double life as both of us. It's understood, eh, that you never breathe a word to anybody?"

"Certainly it's understood!"

"And particularly to this Marjorie. After all, you're bound to meet her in your own character."

"No, I'm not likely to meet her," said Bill. "You see . . ."

He broke off. The taxi clattered into Sheridan Square, in

the Village. Swinging left into Bleecker Street, their taxi fled to the left, and presently into a dark little street Bill could not identify.

"Here!" called Larry, and rapped on the glass partition.

Then they were on the pavement outside a bar. It had no areaway; it was set flush with the street. Its plate-glass window was either so opaque or so begrimed that a glimmer inside touched only figures like ghosts on bar stools. Above, in red neon writing, shone the single word *Dingala's.*

Bill, who had tried to pay the taxi driver and was shoved aside by Larry, swayed as he gripped the handle of the brief case. Joy survey Dingala's and made a grimace.

"Darling," she suggested, "couldn't you possibly find a better place than this? Or is it a favorite haunt of yours?"

Another yellow taxi abruptly pulled up to the curb and its lights went off. Larry watched it. Then he seemed to wake up.

"Haunt of mine?" he jeered. "Only been in the place once before. But it is the only bar with a name I can remember. Once had a Swahili gunbearer named Dingala. Saved my life. In you go, now."

Dingala's Bar, seen from inside, was larger—in the sense of being deeper—than it seemed. The warm damp walls breathed out stale whisky and beer. The only illumination showed in a dim little yellow line of light under the upper edge of the long mirror.

The bar counter, against the left-hand wall, was deserted for more than halfway down. At the far end, all but in darkness, two or three men sat over their drinks. At the far end stood a jukebox: as incongruous here as it would have seemed in a church. Instinctively the newcomers walked softly, and spoke in low voices.

"Larry, I'm going to ask you for the last time," Joy whispered. "You haven't seen this uncle of yours in all those years. If you saw him again, you could laugh at him. I *know* you could. For the last time, will you?"

"No. But why for the last time?"

"Because I shan't bother you again, dear."

Snorting, Larry went over to the bar at the side toward the window, and hauled himself up on the end stool. Bill climbed up on a seat beside him, to Larry's right as they faced the blurry mirror.

"Damn you," Joy whispered through the dimness. Then she strolled across to a stool four seats away from Bill on his right. There was a rattle as she moved the stool and climbed up.

That sharp noise drew a faint response from the figures at the other end of the bar. Every man partly turned, without much interest, took in Joy's beauty, her figure, her trim and

24

fashionable clothes. They turned back to brood. Leaning against the heavy woodwork was a fat bartender with a round, pale, unsmiling face, eyes closed.

Now the bartender opened his eyes. He drifted indifferently toward the newcomers, a little less so when he saw Joy.

"Gin and ginger ale," said the girl. "Lots of ice, please."

"Yes, ma'am."

Clearly the bartender wondered whether she was with the other two newcomers, since she sat at some distance from them, and he decided she wasn't. He surveyed Larry and Bill completely without interest, not even seeing them.

"What'll it be?"

Bill knew that even one drink would whack him under the ear like a fist.

"Scotch and soda," he said. "No ice."

"And for me," announced Larry, loudly and in broad fake-American, "a plain ginger ale with a little ice."

'Now why hadn't I the sense to say that?' thought Bill. 'Too late now, though,' The bartender had moved away.

"Just before the taxi stopped here," Larry was muttering, "you said something about this Marjorie. You said you weren't likely to meet her in England. Why?"

"She married somebody else. They sent me an invitation to the wedding."

"Oh." Larry seemed about to add, "We-el! There are ways round that," when he caught sight of Bill's expression, and stopped. But his sympathy and concern were obvious. Larry fidgeted, pouring concern yet tongue-tied. "Er—what happened? Have a row, or something?"

Bill considered this.

"Yes. When a person's got it as badly as I had, he isn't reasonable. He must be forever wondering if she can possibly . . . care as much for him as he does for her. He torments her to tears without meaning it. Since he can read coldness of manner when she makes a remark about the weather, he's suspicious if she as much as mentions another man. He's an ass; she's best rid of him."

"Wrong approach, old boy. Treat 'em like dirt."

"And yet everything was magnificent until the end of '46. To be exact, until New Year's Eve of '47. Marjorie's parents gave a New Year's party; they lived at Highgate then. . . ."

Bill paused.

He could have sworn it was no freak of imagination. In a wink he was thumped down into the past, under a night of tiny stars. He breathed cold air, and felt the rime of frost under his shoes, in a long back garden. Behind him were three French windows, curtains not quite drawn,

Inside he heard voices. Bill's friend Ronald Wentworth—
who worked at the Marylebone Library—tuned a violin. When
the radio brought the clang of Big Ben, they would greet the
New Year.

Bill stood in the frosty garden, gripping Marjorie's arms and
looking down into Marjorie's eyes.

Marjorie, rather tall and soft of body, who never concealed
her feelings because she could not. Marjorie, of the fleecy
dark-blond hair and clear gray eyes and dark eyelashes. Neither had put on a coat, since neither felt in the least cold. They
stood uncertain, quick-breathing, while Marjorie's eyes searched his face.

The lighted room had grown silent. Then, through an immense hush, the reverberating note of Big Ben clanged. . . .

By this time he held Marjorie in his arms. Though her cheek
was cold, her mouth was very warm when he kissed her as
though he could never stop. Marjorie's arms tightened round
his neck, with spasmodic pressure; her body was warm too.
Neither of them heard the midnight note tremble away. But
piano and violin rose in those old strains.

> Should auld acquaintance be forgot,
> And never brought to mind . . . ?

Marjorie and Bill were locked together, only moving their
heads to mumble, with breathless incoherence, that they loved
each other, had never loved anyone else, would never part, and
wouldn't ever behave like foolish ordinary people.

Only an hour later their Arcadia ended in grotesque anti-
climax. Bill never suspected that in her softer way, Marjorie
was as jealous as he. She said that she didn't mind *his* jealousy;
but why must he spend twenty minutes alone in the library
with Ann Heston? Bill, amazed, replied that they had been
talking about Marjorie. But Marjorie asked whether he was
in the habit of discussing her with her friends. Bill ventured
on mild recriminations concerning Marjorie and Harry Trevor.
One thing led to another. Marjorie was in tears when he stalked
from the house.

Marjorie's father and Ronald Wentworth began to sing
lustily but with feeling. Just before Bill slammed the outer
door, he heard them.

> For auld lang syne, my dears,
> For auld lang syne . . .

"Marjorie!" Bill said aloud.

Then it was as though a bright wave had risen and dragged

26

him from the past and thumped him down again in a Greenwich Village bar with meager yellow light above gaudy bottles.

"Anything wrong, old boy? Steady!"

Then it must have been imagination after all.

"Nothing wrong," said Bill. "I was only thinking about you-can-guess-what. But it was a devil of a vivid hallucination."

"What about the swine who married your girl? Who's he?" growled Larry, implying that a little shooting would have been in order.

"I never met him. But he's a very good sort, everybody says."

"Ever see the girl again?"

"No."

"Hard luck! What I mean: rotten luck. I mean . . ."

With separate clinks, glasses slid along the bar. Joy's gin and ginger ale was palish, Larry's ginger ale a light brown. In front of Bill the bartender set an empty glass, stirring rod, whisky, and soda.

"Well, here's luck!" said Larry, with relief that an uncomfortable subject could be dropped. "Cheero," he added, and gulped down more than a third of the ginger ale.

"Cheero," Bill said without enthusiasm. Pouring the whisky, he added a fair measure of soda. For imported Scotch, it seemed raw and harsh.

Forgetting he had been dreaming, wondering how much Joy had heard, Bill glanced to his right. Joy seemed oblivious. Sitting some distance away, she regarded her drink with a hard fixity. To make sure he had dispelled all illusion, Bill glanced toward the rear of the room.

Used to semi-darkness now, he saw a telephone booth with its door pressed back inside. At the back were three or four little tables. At one sat a slender woman in a gray frock; she had her back turned, and an empty Martini glass was pushed to one side.

At the farthest table, a beer beside him, sat a shabby little man with a newspaper held up in front of his face. But the little man couldn't possibly read in that light! He . . .

As though in response to telepathy, the little man lowered the newspaper and his head appeared. Bill saw, or thought he saw, untidy gray hair like dirty wool. The face was long and sad. His thick-lensed bifocal spectacles turned toward the front like a glassy mask.

Then the newspaper went up.

"No!" Bill said to him. 'These hallucinations have got to stop. At this rate, the woman in gray ought to be Miss Ventnor, Amberley's secretary. That man can't possibly be . . .'

"Gaylord Hurst!" Bill whispered aloud.

"What's that, old boy?"

"Nothing. Forget my private life," said Bill, concentrating on that newspaper, "and let's get on to the job I've got to do."

That was the point at which Joy acted. After groping in her purse for coins, she slid down from the stool, and strolled toward the rear of the room. For a second Bill had the notion that she had seen the phantom face, and would tear the newspaper from in front of it. But Joy went to the dark jukebox against the far end of the bar.

Coins rattled. There was a click, and the upper part of the jukebox sprang into a brilliance of varicolored lights. That glow touched the upheld newspaper, bringing out the black letters *Herald Tribune*. The jukebox whirred, and a blast of alleged music smote the air.

The drinkers resented this and craned round. Somebody swore. Only the *Herald Tribune* remained motionless.

"What in the name of . . . !" Larry began.

Though he and Bill were looking at Joy as she returned. Joy pretended elaborate ignorance. But her steadiness seemed not crack-proof. As she put one foot on the brass rail, and pulled herself up to the same seat, Joy's eyes wandered to the left. She stumbled, and almost fell. Immediately she recovered, and sat staring down at her glass with her black hair falling forward to hide her face.

Larry, quickly following her glance as Bill did, saw somebody standing outside the window: a figure in silhouette, pressed against the glass.

No doubt it was only a vagrant, licking his lips at the paradise inside. But Bill felt as though they were now surrounded by a ring of enemies, slowly closing in.

Larry wrenched his attention from the window.

"What were you asking me, old boy?"

"About your uncle. You said you weren't sure how he would attack. But you seemed to have some notion."

"We-el. Been thinking about it since." Now Larry was the nervous one; Bill the more calm. "In the old days, all his little jokes didn't hurt you. They only scared you witless. This is only a guess. I said he couldn't use child's tricks. He could, though. And the tricks would be loaded."

"Loaded? As for instance?"

"Remember one beauty." Larry slapped the sides of his hatbrim over his ears. "Damn that filthy row!"

Half deafening, the record in the jukebox bawled and brawled.

"But it's no bad cover for a conversation," Bill pointed out. "You remember?"

"Eh? Oh! Gay's place in the country. Always had to sleep

28

alone in a big old room with bogy-furniture. 'Make a man of him,' says Gay. That was from eight until I was eleven. Couldn't sleep there; saw things opening cupboards until dawn."

"Go on."

"One night—moonlight, like tonight—I was broad awake. I didn't see Gay come in. But he had a razor, open, in his hand. Didn't say anything. Just dived at me under the shadow of the canopy, and drew the razor across my throat."

Whree! screamed the music.

"Tell you, I could *feel* the blood down my chest. Only what he drew across my throat was the edge of a feather. Found it on the bed when I woke up from a faint, and Gay was gone. Didn't dare tell anybody next day. Gay would have said—he'd said it before—I ought to be put in an institution. Not telling you this for the effect. It's got a moral. See the moral?"

"Yes. You mean," said Bill, "that for a grown-up Larry Hurst the feather might be a razor? And the tarantula a real tarantula?"

Larry nodded. The right side of his hatbrim was pulled down and he kept his face averted, as usual.

"Drink up!" he said, with the usual trick of hardly opening his mouth even when he shouted.

Bill stirred the whisky and soda. "By the way," he said, "are you a teetotaler? I rather gathered . . ."

"Teetotaler? Lord, no! Oh, the soft drink? Wanted my head clear tonight, that's all."

"Then there's all the more reason," Bill gulped, "for me to have a clear head. Mind if I don't drink this?—Just change glasses, will you?"

Whang! clashed the cymbals on a new record, after a brief healing pause. The new tune was loud and fast. Bill glanced sideways at Joy, four seats away, but she had turned her back.

"Glad to change glasses, old boy." Larry deftly made the switch. "Need a drink when I talk about Gay." He lifted the whisky and soda, but set it down again. "And that," he added, "reminds me of something else!"

"Of what?"

"George Amberley had a set of instructions for me, typed on a card. It's among those papers I gave you. Know where it is?"

"Yes, I think so."

"Then get it out, quick! I've got to brief you on this. Hurry; it's getting late!"

Larry's heavy platinum watch was now strapped to Bill's wrist. Bill saw that the time was ten minutes to midnight. In his pockets were Larry's silver cigarette lighter, a pack of Pall Malls, a ring of keys whose uses Larry had explained, and the key to room 932 at the Waldorf-Astoria.

The music jigged with loud merriment. The wad of Larry's papers was in Bill's inside breast pocket. He found the large typed card, and Larry snatched it from him.

"Now look here," he said. " *'Re: Laurence Herbert Hurst.'* See the instructions." And he ran his finger down the card. " 'On arriving at Heath Row airport,' " he read, " 'go to furnished apartment (C-14) at Albert Court, Albert Street, W.8 (opp. South Kensington Underground Station). Hall porter will have instructions. Rent paid.'

" 'Second!' " Larry continued. " 'Do not communicate the reason for your arrival to anyone. Telephone your uncle at number 68 St. James's Place. St. James's Street, S.W.1. (Tel. Regent 0088).' " Larry hesitated. "Now we've got it. *'Hatto is still with him.'* "

"Hatto? Who's Hatto?"

"Manservant. English. Been with Gay for a donkey's years. The complete picture of a gentleman's gentleman: grave, correct, impessive, all that. Only thiry when I saw him last. . . ."

"But what about him?"

The second record died. There was another click and whir as the third and last record began.

"Done much in the way of sport or games?" insisted Larry. He eyed Bill's heavy shoulders. "Yes, see you have. Haven't you?"

"Yes. But what has this to do with the grave and correct Hatto?"

Picking up the whisky and soda, Larry drained the glass. Putting down the glass, he handed back the card of instructions.

"Hatto's worse than Gay," he said.

"What?"

"Or maybe in a different way. Equally bad, anyhow. Maybe you've got the strength to handle Hatto when he . . . when he . . ."

Then it happened.

"God!" said Larry Hurst: not loudly, but with compressed bewilderment and terror.

Bill swung back on the bar stool. Larry, standing rigid on the rung of the seat, moved his jaws convulsively. He stumbled; he might have fallen if Bill had not eased him down to his feet.

Larry stood up straight again. His eyes, bloodshot and protruding, tried to fasten on Bill. His countenance was becoming putty-colored. When he tried to cough, there reeked from his

30

throat an acrid odor which had been hidden by raw whisky. A moan wrenched out of his shaking jaws.

"Clear out," he said, thinly but distinctly. "G-go on! Must have been two and a half gr—"

"What do you take me for?" Bill almost yelled. "There must be a hospital near here. We can—"

Wildly Bill whirled round. Joy was gone. On the bar counter beside her glass, lay a one-dollar bill.

Bill turned back to Larry, and felt a constriction at his heart. Larry, for all that swagger, looked at him now with the expression of a hurt child: the boy, Bill thought, whom they had tried to frighten to death, the boy who had run away, the boy who had beaten them all—until now.

"Don't let me down," begged Larry. His mouth worked. "Settle with Gay. Settle with G-Gay. . . ."

A spasm of agony caught him. Tearing away from Bill he ran blindly toward the back of the room. The patient tipplers woke up and shouted. The lights of the jukebox illuminated the telephone booth, and the *Herald Tribune* still held before the face of somebody.

For an instant Bill thought Larry would smash straight into that newspaper. But Larry swerved, staggered, and fell face down, with a broken thud, his head and shoulders in the telephone booth.

As though drums talked along the street, dark figures came hurrying into the bar. They gathered with the others, never noticing Bill by the window, round that sprawled figure on the floor. They talked and talked. Then a man's voice pierced through, in stunned incredulity.

"Jesus! The guy's dead!"

The jukebox clicked and went dark. For perhaps twenty seconds there was complete silence.

Bill, gripping the handle of the brief case, backed softly out into the street. Pity for a stranger, a foolish-honest man like himself, pity for Larry Hurst lying motionless and alone in the dark he had feared, rose in Bill's throat.

"*I'll settle with him, Larry,*" Bill said aloud. "*So help me, I'll settle with him.*"

He turned and strode away. The hands of his new wrist watch pointed at three minutes to twelve.

5 FLIGHT 505—NEW YORK TO LONDON

AT three minutes to twelve on the following night, the *Monarch,* crack liner of the British Overseas Airways Corporation, swept sixteen thousand feet above a dark Atlantic. Three minutes to midnight, of course, was New York time. By London time it would be three minutes to five in the morning.

The giant aircraft was nearly dark. Forward, two high lines of berths stretched away on either side of the carpeted aisle. Their occupants had been long asleep.

Aft, ran two lines of double seats on either side of the aisle, back to ghostly pantry and kitchen. Except for one or two reading lamps, directed to shine slantways down on seats and nowhere else, the after part of the cabin held an eerier gloom. Again most passengers, pillows behind heads, were hunched up asleep in deep comfortable seats. A snore gurgled up out of the dark. Someone coughed faintly.

Bill Dawson, whose experience had been only with wartime aircraft, remained surprised at the luxury and power. Only as a presence were you conscious of four great engines pounding against the night; you could not hear them. The *Monarch* made no stops between New York and London, unless bad weather forced it down for breakfast in Ireland.

Midway aft, Bill sat beside one of the little windows on the port side. The beam of the reading light was hardly visible except on the book in his lap. The seat beside him was empty.

Bill, full of food, brain alert, emotions and nerves stilled, nevertheless could not sleep. He ought to; it was a vital necessity, but he couldn't.

'Last night,' he thought, 'I wasn't up to scratch and made a fool of myself. Let's face it, Dawson: much as you hate it, you very nearly had tears in your eyes when—'

Emotions and nerves stilled? Not quite. Since last night, Bill could not force himself to wear Larry Hurst's wrist watch. It ticked in his pocket now. 'Furthermore,' his thoughts did continue, 'a man in that state can easily have hallucinations. I did not see Gaylord Hurst. I saw a shabby little man with a newspaper and a beer. It seemed real; but than I could have taken my oath I was with Marjorie. Gaylord Hurst is waiting for Larry in London. He could not possibly have been in that bar last night. Unless he's aboard now.'

Despite the cold outside, it was stuffy in the cabin. Bill reached up and twisted the little ventilator, which sent down a shaft of cool air into his face.

'Even now,' his thinking went on, 'sensible people would say I am behaving like a fool. Larry Hurst is dead. The question of his inheritance no longer arises. But I made a promise to settle with the person who had hounded and terrorized a child. Even in the cold reality of next day, no man with any decency could forget the promise. Larry wasn't the sort to take his own life. He was murdered.' [2]

A touch of drowsiness weighted him. He remembered the work he ought to be doing. But he leaned back, eyes half closed, and lost himself in going over the past twenty-four hours.

That red neon sign over Dingala's! The policeman, escorted into the bar by a fat woman speaking broken English and cursing foreigners. When Bill hurried away, his first thought was to get something to eat. He didn't want it. But he must. Yet at any moment the policeman might be after him—Bill ran.

Many streets away he found a dog-wagon. Ordering bacon and eggs, pie, and coffee, he held the brief case on his knees and felt it as transparent cellophane which showed bundles of money. As a result he bolted the food, and just missed being sick in public. Two brandies, snatched in a bar still farther away, eased out digestive wrinkles. Twenty minutes later, a taxi set him down at the Waldorf.

The doorman saluated him without suspicion. Once inside, he hesitated. Discreet signs, of illuminated glass, pointed everywhere except to the place you wanted to go.

But, with the key to Larry's room in his pocket, he need not even approach the reception desk. In the crowded elevator, where he conspicuously displayed the key, nobody even looked at him when he got out at the ninth floor. Sweating with relief, he hurried through hushed corridors to room 932.

To come straight to the Waldorf, with Larry dead, might have seemed sheer lunacy. But, Bill argued, in Larry's pockets, the police would find the passport of one William Dawson—his quota card and union card stuck in—together with letters addressed to him in upstate New York.

Nobody would look for William Dawson, mechanic, at the Waldorf-Astoria. By the time the police picked up his trail, he would have gone. It was unlikely that an insignificant death in a dingy bar would make much copy for the American newspapers, let alone the British. Meanwhile this was the safest place in New York.

[2] The justly suspicious reader may have thought that Larry Hurst had staged only a fake suicide, and had not been poisoned even by his own hand. This is wrong. He really had been poisoned with two and a half grains of potassium cyanide; not by himself, but by somebody—seen or unseen—who was in Dingala's Bar at the time. Discard solution number two.

And there was another reason too.

He had to see Joy Tennent! He had to straighten out some of this tangle! Wherever Joy was now, she must eventually return.

Finding number 930, Bill hesitated again, glanced left and right. Number 930, was an adjoining room; the odds favored its being Joy's.

True, it would not be pleasant to find Joy waiting for him, with her catlike soft-stroking mockery. With Larry gone, she alone knew that Bill had come honestly by that money in the brief case. If she meant to accuse him of theft and murder . . .

But she wouldn't get away with it! Ten thousand dollars meant a return to his studies; repayment to aging parents in Sussex; weapons in vengeance against Gaylord Hurst. It meant everything—except Marjorie.

Besides, it wasn't likely that Joy would try. If what he half suspected about her were true, she wouldn't dare. Anyhow, he had to see her! Fitting the key into the lock of Larry's room, he quietly opened the door.

And Joy was not there.

Gentle lights softened the sheen of luxury in a spacious bedroom. Larry Hurst's trunk, still locked because Larry had been allowed no time to unpack, stood beside two suitcases and a portable typewriter.

One door stood open on a sybaritic bathroom. Another door, in the right-hand wall, must communicate with 930. The bolt was unfastened on this side.

Bill rapped. There was no reply. Turning the knob, he found the bolt also unfastened on the far side. The door opened into a dark room.

Bill switched on a lamp. This room was empty too. But an open trunk, painted with initials J.T., dominated six suitcases and a leather hatbox. There was a broad low bed discreetly veiled in blue and silver. A modish hat lay on the dressing table. He switched off the lamp.

Returning to Larry's room, he prowled back to the bed, and sat down.

"She's bound to return sometime," he declared aloud. "And tonight, however late."

Taking a cigarette, he spun the wheel of a silver lighter; realized to whom it had belonged, blew out the flame, and threw it from him. Becoming conscious of the wrist watch, he tore this off too. He lighted the cigarette with a match, but put it out.

So he stretched out on the bed, hands behind his head, merely to stare at the ceiling and reflect.

Look out! Look out!

There was no noise. But Bill sprang up, in clothes badly rumpled and with daylight outside the windows. Though refreshed, he was still dazed until he saw the unbolted door to 930.

Bill ran and threw it open. The bed had not been slept in. Joy's trunk, the suitcases, and the hatbox had all disappeared. Joy had been here and gone.

Joy must be far more afraid of him than he was of her. Certainly she had not given him away to the hotel authorities: his phone would have rung, or there would have been a knock.

At the same time . . .

Bill turned toward the black, almost new brief case, with the initials L.H., which lay on the bed. He tore open its fastener. Except for what remained of three bills in his own pockets, the money had not been touched. The loud-ticking watch said half past eight.

Another thought, fanged with danger, straightened Bill up. He had promised to call at Amberley's office, at half past nine, to receive a check for old Gran's legacy. But Amberley knew him as Bill Dawson, knew his true appearance. If the papers had published any story about the death of William Dawson, and if Amberley had seen it, Bill was finished at the start.

On the other hand, it was vital to keep the appointment. If a near-penniless man did not appear to claim a legacy, Amberley would make inquiries—and find the body of Laurence Hurst.

"It would appear," said Bill, "that they have me checkmated. Still, let us see if we can't find some means of . . ."

His gaze, wandering round the room, met the outer door. An envelope had been pushed under the sill.

Bill picked it up. It was sealed, of Waldorf stationery. He tore it open. Inside was a press clipping. The head was small: an unimportant story.

UNKNOWN POISONS SELF
POLICE SEEK CAT GIRL

New York, June 15th—An unidentified man, robbed of everything, died of cyanide poisoning at midnight last night in Dingala's Bar, 18 Arcadia Street, Grove Street, Village.

Police say unknown, about 35, well-dressed but in custom-made suit without name on label, was robbed when carried by several men, in crowd, to back room from the telephone booth in which he collapsed.

G. V. Aguinopopolos, bartender, 52, said deceased had

been drinking at the bar with another man, unidentified, but that this man left the bar too early to have poisoned the whisky at which deceased had been sipping for some time. . . .

"But that's not true!" Bill said aloud. "The barman gave me whisky, and Larry ginger ale. Larry hadn't been 'sipping' anything. I didn't leave until—"

Whereupon Bill realized what it means to be an honest witness trying to describe what he thinks he has seen or heard.

Attention is focused on a pretty brunette, unknown, 26, dressed in brown with costume jewellery shaped like a cat—

"It's a reasonable description of the diamond leopard," Bill told the news item. "But Joy was in a dark green suit."

—who police say is key-witness. Attractive brunette ran out of the bar just before deceased rushed in agony toward telephone booth. Bartender Aguinopopolos said cat girl was English, French, some foreigner; but was not in the company of deceased, American. James Brook, salesman, 22, Howard Fowler, artist, 24, and G. Vassilov, writer, 61, who said he had been studying human nature through a hole in a newspaper, all testified cat girl had never gone anywhere near deceased and could not have given poison. Lieutenant Michael T. McGinnis, Homicide, admitted . . .

"And that's true!" Bill announced. "Joy couldn't possibly have come near me without being seen, to say nothing of Larry. She didn't do it—but then neither did anyone else."

The story ended in a few lines. Assistant Medical Examiner Gortz said "no post-mortem could yet be done, but the odour of the death-glass indicated potassium cyanide." Lieutenant McGinnis believed it to be suicide, but thought the cat girl might have noticed the deceased swallowing poison, and asked her, and the other unidentified man, of whom they had no description, to assist the police.

'So!' thought Bill, with delight.

The police had been given just that mixture of truth and falsehood which so often led them astray. Larry, ordering drinks in broad fake-American, had dented the skull of G. V. Aguinopopolos with the belief that he *was* American. Joy, with her elaborate pretense of not being with her companions, had succeeded too. This cleared everybody, including Joy.

Since a sneak thief had taken Bill's passport as well as Larry's money from the body, it would be some time before anybody would connect Bill or Larry or Joy with Dingala's Bar. Bill could meet Amberley with safety.

Hastily he bathed and shaved. A fine set of shaving tackle had been put out. Despite his distaste for Larry's clothes, he would have liked a clean shirt. But it would be better to appear before the lawyer in his own rumpled attire, suggesting he had spent the night in a flophouse.

His luck was in. He couldn't make a mistake! Catching up the brief case containing the money, he hastened out to find Amberley.

Breakfastless, detained by a brief errand in Madison Avenue, he took the subway to Wall Street. They ushered him into the lawyer's office just ten minutes late.

"Ah, Mr. Dawson!" said George Amberley, rising. His countenance breathed out bay rum and cleanliness. Despite the pouches under his eyes, he looked fresh. He towered over Bill and extended his hand. "Glad to see you, Mr. Dawson! Glad to find you so prompt."

This was not sarcasm. Nobody in New York is late for a nine-thirty appointment unless he arrives at a quarter past ten. And yet Bill sensed suspicion behind the lawyer's affability; and he braced himself.

"Sit down, sit down!" beamed Mr. Amberley. Bill sat in a deep chair across the desk. Amberley also seated himself. "I have all the documents here. It won't keep you a moment." The lawyer picked up his fountain pen, and glanced at some papers on the big desk blotter.

"Now, then!" he said briskly. "May I trouble you for your passport once again?"

Bill's hand traveled toward his inside breast pocket, and stopped. Looking squarely into the bulbous blue eyes, he smiled.

"I'm afraid I forgot it," he said.

"Didn't . . . This is unfortunate. Very." The lawyer frowned. "Couldn't you go back to—er—wherever you spent the night," he looked at Bill's rumpled clothes, seeming reassured, "and bring it to the office?"

"My dear sir, you saw the passport last night. Surely you don't doubt I am the person I say?"

"No. Not at all. But this is serious. Extremely. Are you aware, young man, that I can withhold this legacy until you bring me your passport?"

Bill stood up, dusting his knees, and swung the brief case carelessly.

"Entirely," he said. "That is, until I show my passport to some lawyer who tries to intimidate his opponents rather than his clients. Good day, Mr. Amberley."

"Just a moment!" said the other, in a slightly different tone. "Will you be good enough, Mr. Dawson, to return and sit down?"

"Thank you." Bill complied.

"I have seen your passport; that's true. . . . Well," the lawyer said soothingly, "I suppose most of us do fall into the habit of treating people's rights as though they were great concessions. There's no harm in it; it impresses the client."

"I'm afraid I'm not im—"

"No; you English are peculiar. But you must admit you've put me in a spot. If only you could remember the number!"

"But I can. The number is 301984."

"Sure of that? Fine!" The fountain pen entered fine, small numbers. "Issued at . . . ?"

"London, 27th September, 1947."

Falling into deep concentration, George Amberley's eyes ran slowly down the first page. The pen nib followed the eyes. Even when he spoke, absently, he did not look up.

"Going back to England, you said?"

"I told you last night I wanted to stay here."

"Yes, of course. I forgot. Do you remember our young friends? Miss Tennent and Mr. Hurst?"

"Very well."

Amberley did not look up, while eyes and pen slowly moved down the page.

"They're flying back to England, by the five o'clock plane this afternoon," he remarked.

"So I understood last night."

Murmuring, "Careless!" Amberley corrected an error. He pushed the page aside and started down another. "I'm thinking of running out to Idlewild this afternoon and seeing them off."

Bill's heart jumped. But Amberley was not looking.

"Good idea," Bill said calmly. "Fine weather for it too."

"Yes, that's what I thought. . . . Wish they'd teach stenographers to spell! . . . Where did you go with our young friends last night?"

Bill felt a lump in the middle of his back.

"Go with . . . oh, you mean Miss Tennent and Mr. Hurst?" Bill sounded surprised. "I go with them? I left your office before they did." Bill attacked instead of standing at defense. "I hope they didn't keep you too late?"

"Not very. But I stayed on afterward. I had a letter to write. Since my secretary wasn't here, I had to type it myself."

"I hope Miss Ventnor wasn't really murdered," said Bill.

"Mur . . . Ah, you mean that little joke Miss Tennent made." Amberley turned over the last page, still speaking absent-mindedly, head down. "No. Miss Ventnor had phoned. I didn't get the message. The poor girl's laid up with summer flu. She'll be back in a week. Strange atmosphere last night: did you notice it?"

"Yes."

"Larry Hurst behaved rather queerly, didn't he?"

"How?"

"With his brief case, for instance. Ah, I forgot. You couldn't have seen it."

Finishing the third page, Amberley laid down his pen and looked up. Though his round jowly face wore a faint smile, his eyes were as cold as marbles.

"It's a curious coincidence," he said. "Larry's brief case looked like the one in your hand now."

6   THE FIVE STABS OF DANGER

TAKING a cigarette from his pocket, Bill leaned toward a glass match-holder on the desk.

"Er—you'll permit me?"

Mr. Amberley nodded.

Bill, still conscious of that lump against his back as he sat back, lighted the cigarette with a match and dropped the match into an ashtray. Amberley saw in front of him a medium-sized, heavy-shouldered young man with an honest face looking completely perplexed.

"This brief case?" Bill asked.

"Yes."

"I'm proud to say it looks fairly new. But I've got to keep my possessions in good shape. Here."

Lifting the brief case, he put it on the desk with its narrow end toward the lawyer. Amberley tilted it a little sideways. On the side shone the clear gilt letters W.D. on leather never stamped before. The lawyer pinched the sides together, and his expression altered a little.

"This is a little embarrassing," said Bill. "But please open it."

"Now, now! I couldn't think of . . ."

"Frankly, sir. I don't know what this is all about." Bill spoke earnestly. "But ever since I walked in here, you've been suspicious. It seems to concern a brief case. Please open it."

The lawyer drew back the fastener and peered inside.

"You see, it's empty." Bill hunched his shoulders as though

in embarrassment. "I carry it, you might say, to impress people. And you were quite right last night. I was nearly stony broke, but for some idiotic reason I couldn't accept your money."

Slowly Amberley closed the brief case and pushed it toward Bill. Rising, he inclined his head with that American courtesy which can so much resemble the chivalry of Spain.

"Mr. Dawson, I beg your pardon."

"Well . . . thanks. But for what?"

Amberley swept this away. He became all kindly bustle. Papers appeared before Bill, and a pen was pressed into his hand.

"Sign here, and here, please. You might initial the changes I've made."

Bill complied. Amberley wrote more words; a rubber-stamp machine banged and clicked.

"Here, Mr. Dawson, is our check in dollars for Lady Penrith's legacy. Less our fees; you won't find them heavy. You can cash the check at the Corn Exchange Bank Trust Company just around the corner. They'll insist on identification, I warn you."

A yellow slip was handed to Bill. All Amberley's stateliness dropped away.

"But look, young fellow. For Pete's sake don't be so touchy and so tough. Ever do any prize-fighting?"

Bill was genuinely startled. "I boxed for my University. But—"

"Well, just don't murder anybody."

"Mur . . . I beg your pardon?"

"Why, God damn it," said Amberley, coming round and slapping him on the back, "back there I thought you were going to murder *me*. Be careful; you might do it some day. Wait; did you give me your address? 'Mrs. Walker's boarding house, 26 Elm Street, Aphasia, N. Y.' They didn't type it in; never mind. Now good-by," he wrung Bill's hand, "good luck, and don't take any wooden nickels."

A minute later, and Bill was in the tile-paved corridor of the tenth floor. He went straight to the men's room. He leaned against the wall, upset and shaken. Bill thought:

'It was fortunate I remembered to buy another brief case at that Madison Avenue shop.'

Again he felt the flat lump against his back, not too well hidden by the coat. Reaching inside, where its narrow end stuck under the belt of his trousers, he drew out Larry's brief case with the bundles packed flat.

Bill thought to himself: 'Amberley was bound to be suspicious about Larry's conduct with the brief case last night. Amberley would instantly have spotted that bulge under my coat, if Amberley's eyes had not been riveted by a brief case in my hand. And the trick worked.'

But Bill didn't like this deception of Amberley, a very decent sort. But his check was no good now; Bill had no identification.

Wasn't he trying to be too clever? Too subtle? Then the real truth flashed over him:

'I deliberately did all that hocus-pocus as practice for the duel against Gaylord Hurst. On guard, you old swine!'

Now he had to get out. Swiftly transferring the money to the new brief case, he returned the old one to its place beneath his coat. Its shape was not visible. But, when Bill went downstairs and out into the sun, new dangers rose round him like heat waves.

If Amberley really went to Idlewild this afternoon, and saw the plane go . . .

But that had been only bluff. Amberley's suspicions had been cleared away. None the less, when a man who has been plagued with worries clears his mind, he will find another worry instead. Bill's doubts again fastened on Joy Tennent.

Only Joy could have slipped that press clipping under the door. She must have known she was in no danger from the police. Then why clear out, without a word to Bill? Of course, it might have the panic of sheer innocence—or guilt. And yet, Bill felt, Joy was not a girl to panic.

Thus Bill, attempting to pace up and down a fairly crowded pavement, was bumped into a cigar store.

The cigar store had one slanting side window, forming a little embrasure in front of the door. Bill stepped into the embrasure, and reached into his inside pocket, touching the papers, the passport, the large card of instructions—and two blue-bound tickets for the B.O.A.C. air liner that afternoon. Taking out the tickets, Bill weighed them in his hand.

Last night, when he had exchanged possessions with Larry, the latter had given very definite instructions.

"These tickets, old boy," Larry had said. "Keep both of 'em. One's in my name; that's yours. But hold Joy's too. Confirm her reservation; get her seat number. Until the last second, swear she'll be there. She won't be. Be with me. But nobody'll know she's not gone except the air line. And they've been paid."

Bill remembered his own reply: "But isn't your uncle expecting her?"

"Yes."

"And when she doesn't turn up?"

"Gay's bound to cut up rough. Know why, don't you? He'll want my fiancée to be there when I—you, that is—call on him each week. He'll want to torture me, humiliate me, while my fiancée looks on. He'll do it to you."

"Will he, now?" Bill had muttered between his teeth.

"I'd give anything, old boy, to provide a fake fiancée! A lady, mind, or Gay won't wear it. Don't suppose you know any girl here who . . . No, you don't. Too late anyway. There it is."

Bill, standing in the embrasure of the cigar-store window, juggled the plane tickets. Again inspiration came to him. But the taste of it was dry and bitter.

Suppose Joy intended to go with him in that plane?

It would explain her actions today. And she could do it. It would do no good to tear up her ticket. She could point to the paid reservation in her name, identify herself, and remain with him as the fiancée of "Larry Hurst." And Bill couldn't prevent it. If she dared not betray him, he dared not betray her.

No matter! For he wouldn't—he couldn't—be encumbered with a girl, however alluring, whom he didn't want and couldn't manage. Joy's jaw muscles were a trifle too firm, her dark-red lips too knowing. And he more than half suspected her of being the murderer. No!

On Bill's right, behind the window of the store, began a faint clicking of clockwork. Bill looked round. Six smallish kewpie dolls now circled round and round a large glass disk. Behind them a sign read, "Best Imported Pipes, 49c." To the left, facing out, was a very large French doll.

Except for black hair parted on one side, the doll bore no resemblance whatever to Joy. But Bill felt the need to clear his mind and arrange his thoughts.

To the doll he addressed imaginary questions, not even moving his lips, and in turn imagined what Joy would answer.

'You poisoned Larry, didn't you?' was his sharp imaginary query. 'You are the most logical suspect.'

Joy in the shape of a French doll opened her large eyes wide, and pouted reproachfully.

'Dear Mr. Dawson! Aren't you being rather unfair, and a bit silly too? Why on earth should I, of all people, want to kill Larry?'

'You didn't want to kill Larry, Miss Tennent. You wanted to kill *me*. It was my glass you poisoned. Larry and I changed glasses. But you couldn't have seen us change. You were sitting with your back to us, listening to the jukebox. You couldn't have known until Larry's first convulsion. Then you ran away.'

'Kill you, dear Bill? And what reason would I have to poison you?'

'Because you refuse to be beaten at anything you've set your heart on.'

'How thrilling I must be! Still . . .'

'You were determined Larry should go to England and get the inheritance. You were furious. Twice you said it was all my fault: if "dear Mr. Dawson" hadn't appeared, Larry would never have thought of the impersonation. *I* was the villain and the stumbling block. You have much intelligence, Miss Tennent. But no real understanding.'

'Of men? How laugh-making!'

'Of anybody. You couldn't understand, *couldn't*, how Larry could be such a wreck of nerves about his uncle. Your every remark was a jeer. You prodded him into signing that paper. You swore that he would be quite all right if only he went back and faced his uncle.'

'What an amazing memory, dear Bill!'

'A would-be historian has to remember facts. When we were outside Dingala's, you begged Larry not to go on with this, and said you were asking him "for the last time." With me out of the way, Larry would have to go to England. You tried to poison me, and killed Larry instead.'

'Dear Bill, how could I have poisoned your glass, or Larry's either?'

That was the stunner. That stopped him.

'I don't know!' his brain shouted. 'I don't know!'

'Those stories in the press,' continued Joy's image, 'were terribly accurate in some ways. Excepting myself and that girl in gray, who must have been awful, all the people in the bar were men. They didn't glance at you or Larry. But they watched *me*.

'Two young men watched me, thinking how nice it would be to . . . And the dear old gentleman, watching through a tear in a newspaper, thinking the same thing. Silly men, weren't they? But all of them say I never came within a long distance of you or Larry. Then how could I have . . . ?'

'I've admitted I don't know!'

'The police are nearly always right, aren't they?' innocently murmured Joy's doll self. 'Poor, dear Larry wasn't himself. That's why he put the poison in his own glass, you see. And poor me! What am I to do?'

'You're thinking of flying to England with me?'

'And if I am?'

'You'll be stopped. Somehow.'

'We'll see.'

'Right! Besides, why should you be interested in me? I'm not rich.'

'Darling! You mustn't think me mercenary. But you're the new Larry Hurst. And your dear Uncle Gay is . . . well! Of course, dear, it is such a pity! You do so love your women

43

dewy-eyed and clinging. Like Marjorie. You can't forget her, can you?'

'Marjorie Blair? She's married. I've got to forget her!'

'But, darling!' Radiance shone. 'That's wonderful! You don't find me repulsive, do you? I rather think you'd like me very much if I . . . some American terms are too vulgar; but they're awfully expressive . . . if I worked on you.'

'Satan's teeth!' Bill was reflecting. 'The image of Joy could have thought only what I was thinking. Have I been cherishing lecherous thoughts about the wench without knowing it? But she won't get aboard that plane. —Plenty of time. Let's have at least one hour of forgetfulness.'

Bill found a taxi. It carried him up to Fourth Avenue below 14th Street. In the secondhand bookshops he found peace. Since his field and his passion lay in history, Bill gathered up a large armful of books, including another history of the War Between the States, and a noble Lenotre called *France Under the Terror*.

But, when he returned to upper Park Avenue, he felt as refreshed as though he glowed from a Turkish bath amid dust and shelves. Joy's expression returned to Bill only when he reached his cool, subdued bedroom at the Waldorf.

Carefully he put aside the thought of Joy. Putting a book on Larry Hurst's passport, to hold it open at the identification page, he sat down and began copying the bold signature, "Laurence H. Hurst." For two hours Bill practiced forgery, with intense concentration, burning each sheet when he had covered it. Though Bill's first attempts seemed impossibly bad, they were growing a little better. The wrist watch, on the dressing table beside the silver lighter, ticked away. Sooner or later he must face the ordeal of meeting the hotel people.

Bill got up, shaking his crampd wrist, and went to the telephone. "Reception desk, please," he said, sitting on the bed. In a moment Bill was answered by a courteous, correct male voice.

"Is that the reception desk?" asked Bill, steadying himself. "This is Mr. Laurence Hurst, in 932."

"Yes, sir. I recognized your voice, Mr. Hurst."

"You rec . . . ?"

Bill held the telephone away and studied the mouthpiece. Larry's voice, so far as his remembrance went, had not sounded in the least like his own. Then the receiver chuttered at him.

"Sorry," he remarked. "I want to pay my bill. I'm flying to England, B.O.A.C., by the five o'clock plane today."

"Yes, sir. Er—Miss Joy Tennent, I believe, is taking the same plane?"

"So far as I know." Bill spoke casually. "And Miss Tennent's account . . .?"

"I'm afraid you want the cashier's office, sir. But, if you'll hold the wire for a moment, I can make inquiries."

There was a long silence. How to stop Joy? How to head her off, without a scene and without betrayal? How?

"Miss Tennent's account has been paid, sir," the well-bred voice assured him. "She seems to have checked out early, and taken her baggage. No message and no address. But I have no doubt she'll meet you."

"Neither have I. Since I can't take more than sixty-six pounds by plane, where do I go to have the rest of my luggage sent by ship?"

"Here in the hotel, sir. Shall I connect you?"

"No; I'm coming down myself, thanks. One final point: where is the B.O.A.C. terminus in New York?"

"Also here at the hotel, sir. On the 49th Street side. The limousine for the airport leaves there. If I may advise you, it's best to be there at a quarter to four, and weigh in your baggage. . . . Not at all; thank *you*."

Then time raced past in a blur of new danger. Bill went downstairs, paid his bill, arranged for shipment by sea of one trunk and one suitcase—to sign a form, made Larry's signature in that illegible scrawl we all make in hurried formalities —and was whisked upstairs without suspicion.

He opened everything and quickly packed a big suitcase with a large assortment of clothes. Larry had been right. The shirts fitted. The jackets fitted, since Larry's tailor allowed much shoulder room. But the trousers were even longer than Larry's estimate. Bill packed them, awaiting alteration in London. Everything was flung in, including Larry's shaving tackle, a new toothbrush Bill had bought, and all but one of the second-hand books.

This big suitcase, with the portable typewriter, he set aside for the plane. Putting on one of the shirts, with a conservative tie, he wore his old but well-cut suit.

"I hate to wear this stuff, Larry!" he said aloud to a ghost desperately unhappy yet praying to be even with Gaylord Hurst, which Bill had sensed near him all day. "But," Bill added, putting watch and lighter into his pocket, "we're moving to attack now."

Warm, laden with Larry's topcoat and hat, a brief case, a suitcase, a typewriter, and Lenotre's *France Under the Terror*, he entered the airways terminus at ten minutes to four. Joy was not there.

She was still absent when the "limousine," left the terminus. Bill was so absorbed in looking for her that he scarcely observed the other passengers. The bus was far from full; no doubt many passengers would go to Idlewild by taxi. But every minute of delay in seeing Joy increased the certainty of a worse scene when he did meet her. Bill put on Larry's hat; it was too small; he removed it.

The bus presently swung in at Idlewild, where more passengers joined their group. And again no Joy. They were herded through long corridors, and finally to the far end of a large waiting room.

There the passengers flowed toward a long counter. A blurred loud-speaker talked from a wall. Standing out of the crowd, Bill leaned against the counter and stared round for Joy.

"Will passengers for B-Oh-blu-bluh Flight Five-bluh-bluh," firmly said the loud-speaker, "who are not American citi-whoa, please go to the desk under number four, with their passports?"

Bill found that he was under a high card numbered four. He turned round, scenting danger again.

Behind the counter was a lean, bald man, with severe businessman's spectacles.

"May I see your passport, please?" he asked.

Bill produced Larry's passport. The brisk official studied the pages, but merely glanced at the photograph.

"Thank you, Mr. Hurst. Have you your re-entry permit, in case you want to return to America?"

"No. I'm afraid I . . ."

"That doesn't matter. Just let me see your income-tax certificate."

"I beg your pardon?"

"You must have a certificate that you have paid your income tax while in this country. You can't leave without it."

Here was real trouble.

"Didn't you know that, Mr. Hurst?" The eyes became sharp and keen.

"Yes, I knew it," lied Bill, with an air of mingled embarrassment and shame. "But my income . . . I haven't made . . ."

"Do you mean you haven't earned more than five hundred dollars a year in America?"

"I'd better be frank," Bill muttered rapidly. "I've been a failure here. My uncle has had to pay my fare back to England, with all conditions attached. Look at this!"

He brought out the card of instructions for Larry. With its "rent already paid," "Do not communicate," "Telephone your uncle," all the contemptuous peremptory orders showed an uncle who has at last relented toward the prodigal. But the official glanced at the prosperous-looking hat and topcoat.

"They're not mine," said Bill. "Had to borrow them from friends here. You see I've got just a dollar and ten cents. If I stay here, they'll only deport me. This is the land of opportunity, but it's too tough for me."

"Yes, it's not easy," said the bald-headed man, with a touch of complacency. "You'll have to show me an income-tax certificate," he said, with unexpected loudness and dominance, "or you can't leave the country. That's the law! —Oh? You *have* one?"

Here he leaned across the counter conspiratorially. "It's all right. Go on and catch your plane. But don't open your mouth about this, understand?"

"Thanks. I . . ."

"Yes, madam?" he smiled to the fuming woman behind Bill.

The girl behind the air-line counter gave Bill his seat number and the card which enabled him to leave the building for the plane. But, though English and soft-voiced, she was adamant about Joy.

"I'm awfully sorry. But I can't give the card to anyone except Miss Tennent herself. Your—er—friend must hurry now, you know."

"B.O.A.C., *The Monarch*, Flight 505 to London," announced the loud-speaker, "is now ready for departure. Will passengers please leave by gate number one, giving their cards to . . ."

And still Bill had seen neither Joy nor Amberley.

Shortly afterward, Bill was crossing a windy airfield toward the aircraft, silver against a light-blue sky. The cabin was hot and confused with people jostling. After he was seated, the wait seemed interminable. Joy might run across. . . . Even now the loud-speakers must be calling her name. But the plane door slammed. The steps were rolled away.

Softly, slowly, the engines began to growl. Fore and aft the signs flashed up: no smoking; fasten seat belts. *The Monarch* bumped gently forward, maneuvering for the runway. Joy Tennent appeared to be definitely missing.

At what had become fifteen minutes past midnight, New York time, and fifteen minutes past five A.M., London time, Bill sat back and ended his mental reconstruction of the past twenty-four hours.

All about his reading lamp, on the pages of *France Under the Terror*, stretched the eerie gloom of the air liner. Beside Bill, between the seat and the port bulkhead, his brief case was so wedged that he could touch it with his left knee. Pressing his cheek partway against the window, he peered out. He could see only a dark phantom of the giant port wing. Below lay dim unmoving cloud, or flying mist wreaths whipped behind.

47

Leaning back, he looked dully at the fold-down shelf attached to the seat in front. Work, work! He should be working, endlessly copying Larry Hurst's signature. Already they had given him a customs declaration to fill up before landing.

Yet, despite mental alertness, his body felt too tired to drive a pen with accuracy. After all, he must sleep. Tomorrow morning, today by Greenwich time, he would be in England. Within twenty-four hours, he would have finished his first battle with Gaylord Hurst. Gaylord Hurst, St. James's Place. England again . . .

And inevitably, England brought the thought of Marjorie Blair.

Now, Bill pictured Marjorie's hair and lips and eyes. Marjorie would now have been married for nearly four years to that worthy—damn him!—Eric Cheever, Assistant Controller of Programmes for the Drama Department of the British Broadcasting Corporation.

Marjorie might have changed. He, Bill, must not be afraid to think of her occasionally, or the pain he felt might become an obsession. There, now! That thought was over.

Smiling, he looked at the seat beside him, which Joy was to have occupied. Well, she had missed the plane and left him free. He need worry about Joy no longer.

'Now!' he said to himself, 'three more pages of Lenotre, and finish the chapter. Then turn out the light, curl up, and sleep.'

But those three pages seemed hard going. Somebody was snoring again. The figure of a woman, probably the stewardess, moved slowly and without any sound along the aisle, toward the forward cabin.

Bill forced his eyes on the book. He understood not a word. From the corner of his eye he believed he caught a shadow of the woman returning, but he had a sense of someone near him. . . .

"Hullo," said a female voice, not loudly. "You're Laurence Hurst, aren't you?"

Bill sat paralyzed.

It was not the words. It was the familiar voice. For fully twenty seconds he kept his eyes on the book. Then, slowly, he turned his head to the right and looked up.

In the aisle stood Marjorie Blair.

7 OF MARJORIE, AND LOVE IN AN AIR LINER

SHE stood there leaning a little forward, her left elbow on the back of the empty seat, arm and hand hanging down. Her right held some round boxlike affair painted gray.

Changed? Marjorie had changed not one bit since he saw her last. Perhaps her face was a little more mature, but this only heightened her beauty. Marjorie's fair complexion still needed little powder and no lipstick on the full pink mouth. Her nose was short. She wore a black silk blouse, with a short double rope of pearls, and a dove-gray skirt. Despite her slender figure, the clothes brought out a fullness at breast and hip.

She looked at him with interest, as someone not a stranger but not quite a friend.

Steady, now! Steady!

"Yes, I'm Larry Hurst," he managed to say.

"You don't seem certain," answered Marjorie, trying to smile and not managing it. "Of me, that is. I'll bet you can't remember where we met."

Bill risked a shot which had twenty to one in its favor.

"California, surely? Beverly Hills. Let's see: that would be . . . ?"

"A year ago. Then you do remember me!"

Bill put up a hand to his forehead. Not every night does a man wander amid fantasy, as he seemed to have done on two successive nights.

His face was clear in the reading light. He did not look like Larry Hurst. No person who knew both could possibly be deceived. Yet here was Marjorie, who could never conceal her feelings, regarding him with the image of Larry Hurst in her eyes.

Bill coughed. "Er . . . how did you know I was in the plane?" he asked.

"I saw your name on that list at the airport. Then I saw you at the counter. But you seemed to be . . . accompanied. By that girl who . . . I didn't want to intrude. But later I was sure you weren't accompanied. Finally I came up to say hello."

It was odd how long both had remained there, merely looking at each other, speaking only at intervals.

Bill got to his feet. "I—I seem to have lost my manners," he stammered. "Won't you sit down?"

"Well . . . it *is* very late."

"Late? No! Not in the least! Who the devil wants to sleep?— No, not in the empty seat. Sit here by the window."

He edged out into the aisle, and she edged in past him. Momentarily their arms touched; both flinched. But Bill, preoccupied, noticed only that he had flinched. Nor, while she stood in the aisle, had he seen the growing strain round her eyes, the nervous fingers of her left hand, and breathing as irregular as his own.

Now, as she occupied the inner place by the window and Bill was very close, he could think only of her physical presence. After that long absence, he knew now that he loved her more than ever; he was doomed, past hope. One bitter question he must ask, but he had to lead up to it.

"I think you told me," he said casually, "that you came to America because . . . ?"

Neither looked at the other.

"Oh, various reasons. But mainly secretarial work."

Bill cleared his throat.

"By the way," he asked, "how is your husband? Is he with you?"

"Husband?" Marjorie's soft voice grew blurred. "But surely I couldn't have told you anything about a husband. I'm not married."

"*Not married?* But I got an invi . . . that is, somebody told me!"

Marjorie showed her left hand. The third finger bore neither wedding nor engagement ring.

"But, good God! You never . . ."

"We weren't much more than acquaintances, Mr. Hurst. I'm sure I shouldn't have s-said anything about my—my private life. But I don't in the least mind telling you. If it wouldn't bore you."

"No. No, it wouldn't bore me."

"Well." Marjorie flinched. "Years ago, you see, I thought I was madly in love with a man named Dawson. Bill Dawson."

"No. Never heard of him," said Bill.

"His beastly jealousy . . . it was awful. I couldn't stick it!"

Marjorie would not turn round. On the arm of the seat she still gripped the object Bill had seen before: the round box, some three inches high, varnished gray with a painted design on the lid. Bill's dull gaze fastened on it.

Marjorie gulped. "We had a quarrel," she went on, "on New Year's Eve. He was beastly!" The front of Marjorie's black silk blouse, rising and falling heavily, slowed down a little. "No. That's not quite fair. I know now I was just as jealous as he was. All I knew than was it would be hopeless for us to get married, with that jealousy of his. I hoped and prayed he'd ring up or something. He didn't. He was as proud as Lucifer and as hard as flint."

50

"For God's sake! That's the third time in two days somebody has called me . . ."

"Wh-what?"

"Nothing! Go on."

"Well, you wanted to know about my 'marriage.' I very nearly did marry a man I met two months later. Eric Cheever. Oh, he was different from Bill Dawson. Eric was splendid! He still is."

('Lord, what wouldn't I give for boiling oil, and slowly lower into it the splendid Mr. Cheever!')

"I didn't love Eric Cheever—" said Marjorie.

"You didn't love . . . Stop, that's different!"

"It was only two days before the wedding when I realized I couldn't go on with it. Then . . ."

Bill, seeing a sudden hope, felt his throat become so dry that he could not prompt her. Marjorie's fingers tightened on the little box.

"It was late August," she said. "The day before the wedding I was sitting in my room. My father knocked at the door. He coughed and fidgeted. Finally he said, 'Not good enough, is it?' I only said, 'No.' He said: 'Then don't do it, my dolly. Leave this to me.'

"And," Marjorie added in a voice of awe, "he called off the wedding, and had the presents sent back. Poor mother was in a flat spin. But Eric was wonderful. He simply said he couldn't understand, but he wouldn't ask question. He said he would wait for me forever, in case I changed my mind."

Bill tried to clear his throat.

"If you couldn't go on with it," he said, "was it because you were still in love with this—what's his name—Benson? Dawson?"

"Good heavens, no! Certainly not!"

"Oh."

"I hate him!" whispered Marjorie. The dark-gold curls trembled at the nape of her neck. "I hate him! You see, I sent him an invitation to the wedding. But not out of spite or meanness. I swear it wasn't! Even all those years ago," she whispered, feeling the great age and cynicism of twenty-five, "I was never romantic. Not a bit. But I thought Bill might be practical. I thought he might—well, prop a ladder up against my window, and hoick me down in my nightdress, and carry me away . . .

"But he didn't," she added. "A few months later he'd gone off to the States and forgotten. He'd only been pretending. I hate him!"

Steadying herself, she attempted to be fair.

"No; that's not quite true. I don't hate him. By this time I'm simply indifferent to him. I haven't kept one single sou-

51

venir, not one. If I ever meet him, of course, I shall be perfectly polite. But he doesn't mean anything to me."

"I see," said Bill. Well, that was that. He had been given his chance, and failed. Nobody could blame Marjorie.

Bill once more became conscious of the metal box.

"Er—by the way. What's that in your right hand?"

"What?" Her head flashed round.

"That round gray box."

"That? It's only a powder compact! I've carried it for years."

"It's a big compact. May I see it?"

"It's only a compact, I tell you!" Marjorie grew tense, alarm in the gray eyes. She opened the shallow lid, displaying powder, a large powder puff, a mirror; then she closed the lid with a click. "Why on earth should you want to see it?"

"It's a combination powder box and music box. Underneath there's a little spindle with a key. If you keep it on a table, or hold it underneath, it won't play. But, if you take the pressure away . . . Here, let me show you!"

"Really, Mr. Hurst! This is not at all funny! Please let go the box . . . Oh!"

At what Bill believed was a gentle pressure, the box flew out of Marjorie's hand and landed on the floor at Bill's feet, rolled over once, and stopped on its side. There was a click. Then, in the half darkness, the music box softly tinkled out an unforgotten tune.

Should auld acquaintance be forgot,
And never brought to mind?

Very calm now, Bill leaned down and set the music box upright, so that the tinkle was stilled. He sat up. Marjorie was looking out of the window again; but he saw by reflection that her eyes had brimmed over.

"Marjorie," he said quietly, "you know who I am. You've known all the time. Turn round."

"I . . ."

"Marjorie, turn round."

As though in one flash she had whipped toward him; he was holding the slender body so fiercely as to hurt her against the arm rest; she was sobbing, and the taste of salt tears mingled with frantic kisses.

Vaguely, remembering possible passers-by, Bill reached up and switched off the reading lamp.

"Marjorie, do you really love me?"

"You know I do! You know I do!"

"But I thought you didn't. Especially tonight."

"And I thought *you* didn't, especially tonight. *Do* you love me?"

Now this sort of conversation, good for at least an hour and utterly absorbing to those who say the same words over and over, is apt to seem repetitive in print. But these two were human, and they had walked a weary road to meet above the Atlantic this night. In that dark little cubicle, formed by the seats, they were incoherently happy.

"Marjorie," Bill said at length, "tell me something. Were you really acquainted with Larry Hurst on the Coast? And all the rest of it?"

"Yes! Yes!" Marjorie's eager whisper hesitated, and became elaborately unconcerned. "There was a woman named Joy Tennent. . . ."

Bill swept this aside.

"Listen, my sweet. Why all that pretending? I didn't even know you could pretend."

"I can't," admitted Marjorie. "But you were so upset you didn't notice it."

"What I mean is: why pretend to think I was Larry?"

Marjorie, her face on his shoulder, tightened her arms round him. Her voice sounded muffled, penitent. "Bill . . . I'm not trying to evade your question. But I couldn't—positively couldn't—talk about *us* like that, unless I pretended I was talking to somebody else. Do you see?"

"Marjorie, I'm sorry!"

"No! Don't say that. And another thing. I—I wanted to find out whether you cared a little about me; so, of course, I had to tell you I hated you to see if you would say you loved me. I haven't any pride. I'm absolutely shameless. I wasn't following you. This plane was pure coincidence. But I did see Mr. Hurst's name on the passenger list. I heard you telling the girl at the counter you were Laurence Hurst, and making a frightful row because she wouldn't give you an exit card for this Joy Tennent . . ."

"Marjorie!" he said abruptly.

"Yes, dear?"

"This isn't any more jealousy, is it? We can't have it! I swear I'll never be jealous. Will you?"

"Yes!" sobbed Marjorie. "Never again. I couldn't bear it. I didn't mean that! You didn't hear my last question."

"What was the question, then?"

"Bill. You're going to England to impersonate Larry Hurst, aren't you?"

"I'm going to England *as* Larry Hurst," he smiled. "I can't very well deny that."

"You're on guard," said Marjorie. "I can feel it. I always

can, with you. Darling, please don't. You've got . . . a mission of some kind. What is it?"

Thus he faced what sooner or later he must face.

"I can't tell you, Marjorie. I've made a promise. You couldn't expect me to break that promise, could you?"

What he dreaded was the probable statement: 'You could if you loved me.' But Bill remembered something else. Marjorie wasn't like that; she was too good a sport. No; she would never use that hurt, reproachful: 'You could tell me if you loved me.' And she didn't.

"Bill." Her whisper was agitated. "To whom did you make this promise? To the Tennent woman? —It's not jealousy! It's not! —Did you make the promise to her?"

"No."

"Then who?"

"To Larry Hurst himself. He's dea . . . that is, he's still in America. There are vital reasons why he couldn't come himself."

"Is there danger for you?"

Bill laughed. "Certainly not," he lied.

"Bill," she said after a long pause, "I'm livid with curiosity. But I won't ask questions. I won't!" This last seemed to be to herself.

"Marjorie, I knew—!"

"And I think there *is* danger. I wish you wouldn't tell me fibs. If you think somebody's not fair, or is hurting someone weaker than himself, you go in with your head down. You once said those were the only two sins."

"So they are."

"When you got your first decoration in the Raf, I was still a girl in school. I read about it in the newspaper . . . I loved you for it. But I was sick. I kept saying to myself, 'If only I could have been there, and helped him!' "

Bill stared into the near darkness, gripped by a new idea.

"Hold on, Marjorie! Let me think!"

Larry Hurst would not let Joy Tennent go on this mission, while Gaylord expected her. *'Gay's bound to cut up rough. . . . He'll want to torture me, humiliate me, while my fiancée looks on. I'd give anything, old boy, to provide you with a fake fiancée! A lady, mind, or Gay won't wear it.'*

What if Marjorie were to play the part of Joy Tennent as he played the part of Larry Hurst? She at least would be in no danger. Bill could keep her near him. And furthermore: 'Humiliate me, eh?' he thought grimly. If Marjorie were there to watch, then he would guarantee to outwit the devil himself.

"Listen, my dear," he said aloud. "It's damnable that we should have to separate for six months. . . ."

"Six months?" Marjorie started.

". . . when we've just found each other. And all this secrecy making you unhappy. But there is a way out."

"What is it?"

Briefly, guardedly, he explained.

"Then you want me," Marjorie said, "to play the part of Joy Tennent?"

"That's it. Do you think you could do it?"

Marjorie's romantic soul took fire.

"Of course I could," she whispered eagerly. "I knew Joy very well. Far better than Mr. Hurst: he was always away fishing, or something. She told me so much of her private life, and his, that I could . . . well!" Marjorie paused. "And if I do this, we could be together?"

"Yes! That's just it!"

"I mean, we can be closer together, even than we are now? Oh, I told you I'm shameless. But I mean . . ."

There ensued another turbulent interval, after which Marjorie pushed him abruptly away.

"Bill, this must stop! Only for now," she added quickly. "But I mean . . ."

"Yes, I know. It must. —Damn this arm rest between us! It's like the wall between Pyramus and Thisbe."

He slipped the arm up and back, making one seat.

"Bill, please! I'm—"

"It's all right," he assured her gently. "Sit closer to the window, and put your head on my shoulder. That's it."

"Then, if I pretend to be that woman, I can help you? Really help?"

"Yes. I don't have to break my promise by telling you anything; you'll see it for yourself. At the same time, we can manage exactly what Larry wanted. By the way, your own double life will be only once a week: when we call on Larry's uncle. Gaylord Hurst."

Marjorie gave a slight start.

"Gaylord Hurst?" she repeated. "*Gaylord* Hurst?"

"Yes. Do you know him?"

"No. But everyone in London has heard of him. He's an institution now. When that woman spoke about Larry's uncle, I never connected him with the English Hurst. My father says—" Marjorie stopped.

"What does your father say?"

"Mr. Hurst really is a great philanthropist and all that. But in business, I've heard, he's as hard as Scrooge."

"You don't surprise me, pet."

"Oh, let's not talk about it! It's not important." Marjorie's voice quickened. "I know Joy Tennent's life history, Bill. But do you know everything about Laurence Hurst?"

"No. As you said about something else, I rushed in blindly. It'll want cheek to manage this."

"But suppose I told you everything that woman told me? Would that help you?"

"Help? It'd be a godsend!"

Marjorie sighed with pleasure. Her head on his shoulder, she talked on and on and on, with pauses only for recollection, while Bill's immense memory took in every detail. This was real briefing, every bit usable! But presently Marjorie faltered drowsily; Bill's head grew heavy.

"I *won't* sleep," persisted Marjorie. "I won't even doze. I'm afraid to wake up and find you're not here."

But she pressed closer, drowsily, and her body relaxed. Bill, looking down at her hair, felt so fierce a sense of protectiveness that a lump came into his throat. He held her lightly, so as not to disturb her. His own eyelids drooped.

From somewhere far away, now, but growing closer, there was a whisper of "Bill!"

Bill, shocked awake, at first could not remember where he was. Then he remembered: his arms, legs and neck were cramped. The cabin felt cold.

"Awake?" asked Marjorie.

She was smiling at him, sitting up straight. Marjorie could look as pretty at daylight as at any other time; her dark-gold hair was not at all rumpled, and a fresh fragrance surrounded her.

"Oh, I've been down to tidy up," she smiled. "But who put this blanket round us? Did you?"

Bill shook his head.

"There are two stewards and one stewardess. Probably one of them. —Look there!"

The sky was a transparent pink: unearthly. A pink tinge, edged with gold and threads of purple, painted the inside of the cabin.

Bill gave it only a glance. With one impulse, they made sure of each other's presence. It had become a tableau when there was a discreet cough in the aisle.

"Cup of tea, madam? Cup of tea, sir?"

"Real tea?" demanded Bill. "Admirable, admirable!"

Sliding the tray across their laps, the steward permitted himself a smile.

"Breakfast in twenty minutes, sir."

"Good! Where are we now?"

"Just over Ireland, sir. The weather's fair in the London area; we should be at Heath Row on time."

He melted away. The tea was hot and black, with just the proper amount of milk.

"And today," said Marjorie, "the great plot begins. Oh, Bill! Hadn't we better get our plans in order?"

Her companion slopped tea into the saucer. His romantic notion of last night, which had seemed brilliant, now made him apprehensive: Marjorie was a poor actress. But he had promised.

"First of all," said the eager Marjorie, "where are you staying? With your parents in Sussex?"

"No, no! At a furnished flat in Kensington close to the Chelsea side." Putting down the cup, Bill tore a slip from the many papers he carried, and handed it to Marjorie with a pencil. "Here you are. 'Flat C-14, Albert Court, Albert Street.' That's opposite the South Kensington Underground Station. I haven't got the phone number, but it'll be easy to find."

Bill paused. He was startled by the apprehension that Marjorie might be lost to him—if he could not reach out and touch her.

"Marjorie. Could you come to the flat with me straightaway?" Marjorie swiftly looked up with a "yes" as plainly as eyes could shine. But she caught herself up, and he thought he knew why.

"No, that's no good," he admitted. "You must go to Highgate first."

"We—we don't live at Highgate now." Marjorie handed back the pencil. "But the trouble is . . . my father and mother are meeting the plane. And, of course, Eric too."

There was a pause.

"I particularly appreciate," said Bill, "those frank words 'of course.' Eric, or Little by Little. Mr. Eric Cheever, pride and joy of the B.B.C."

"You're jealous," Marjorie moaned. "That's all it is. Darling, you mustn't be."

"I am not in the least jealous. I merely wonder. Or do you still encourage him?"

"No, no! I don't want him there. But what can one do? He's been a perfect ba . . . I mean gentleman."

"Then give him wings. Give him a bloody great halo. But get rid of him; or I will."

"Anyway, darling, why should you sneer at the B.B.C.?"

"On the contrary," retorted Bill, "I don't. At Rothwell House, during the war, I met most of the group in Features and Drama. When Howard McHavern was doing those shows about the Raf, I was glad to go in and give technical advice. Every person there was first-rate, doing brilliant programs twelve hours a day for tenth-rate salaries."

Marjorie spoke with patience.

"*I* could have been jealous, you know," she said. "But I've grown up, I hope. I wasn't in the least jealous, as you saw."

"You could have been jealous of whom?"

"Well, I like that," said Marjorie. "You weren't coming to England with that horrible Tennent woman, were you? Oh, no! She was Larry's mistress once. She isn't yours now, I daresay. Oh, no!"

"Never heard such nonsense in my life."

"I hate you!" said Marjorie, her color coming up and her eyes filmed. "You haven't changed. You're as beastly as you ever were. I hate you! I—"

She stopped, appalled, and put one hand over her mouth. The same consternation appeared on both faces.

"Bill . . . I'm sorry. I didn't mean it. I didn't!"

"No; it was my fault!" he groaned. "I shouldn't have mentioned Eric Cheesecake. We must swear never to do this again? Swear?"

"Oh, Bill, yes! Never again in our lives."

Marjorie and Bill sedately finished their tea.

"I suppose," he frowned, "you can meet me early this evening? Gay is almost bound to ask us to dinner."

"My dear, I can meet you anywhere and at any time you like! Bill, why are you looking so black?"

"It's this infernal game we're playing. Marjorie, I have a premonition. . . ."

"Yes?"

"When we meet Gay, we're going to get a new jolt from a direction we don't expect; and it'll turn the whole business upside down again."

8 LIGHT POINTS IN A WINDOW

ON the desk of the new furnished flat at Albert Court, the card of instructions lay beside the telephone.

Bill Dawson's palms were sweating a little at the prospect of the first brush with the enemy. 'Telephone your uncle at number 68 St. James's Place, St. James's Street, S.W.1. Tel . . .'

Picking up the phone, Bill drew a deep breath.

"Regent double O, double eight," he said.

"Very good, sir."

That was the hall porter. Bill heard a pencil slowly dialing the number.

It was five o'clock in the afternoon. There was soft sunlight. Bill's phone call came very late. Though he had gone through the passport office without delay, and through the customs in the same way despite a forged signature on his declaration, Bill had been detained afterward.

Now he heard the ringing-tone, far away in his so-called uncle's flat. Who would answer him? Old Gaylord, or . . . or Hatto, the ideal gentleman's gentleman?

The ringing-tone stopped. Somebody answered.

"Regent double O, double eight?" asked Bill not without nerves. "Is that Mr. Gaylord Hurst's flat?"

The other voice was so very correct, so almost godlike, that it could belong to nobody but an ideal gentleman's gentleman.

"Laurence Hurst here," said Bill, and chuckled. "How are you, Hatto?"

"Mr. Laurence!" Hatto conveyed just the proper shade of respect with a suggestion that he was an old retainer speaking tolerantly to a boy. "It is a pleasure, sir."

"Thought I recognized your voice, Hatto. Is Uncle Gay at home?"

"Mr. Hurst is at home, sir. But I am instructed to say . . ."

Bill could hear another voice in the background. This voice, he decided, belonged to his alleged uncle, Gaylord Hurst, who hated telephones—as Bill was to learn—would not give himself the trouble of speaking to anyone like this, least of all to his nephew. The voice in the background was soft, melancholy, cultured, and even more godlike than Hatto's.

"Yes?" prompted Bill.

"Mr. Hurst, sir, is not altogether pleased with your conduct. You were told to telephone as soon as you reached your flat. You will find it less pleasant, Mr. Laurence, if you have not learned discipline. Mr. Hurst is in the habit of having his orders obeyed."

The blood rushed to Bill's head.

"Are you there, Mr. Laurence?"

"Yes, Hatto," Bill said easily. "Convey my apologies to my dear uncle, and tell him I was unavoidably detained."

"If you wish it, sir. I must now give distinct orders. You and Miss Tennent—"

"By the way," interposed Bill, "how did Uncle Gay like that photograph of my fiancée? The one Mr. Amberley sent him?"

Hatto turned away and asked the question. The reply had a snap in it.

"We have received no photograph, Mr. Laurence," said Hatto. "Mr. Hurst begs to state that your duty is to answer questions; not ask them."

"Forgive me," requested Bill. Then they didn't know what Joy looked like! And Marjorie could . . .

"Mr. Hurst, sir, has been kind enough to invite you and your fiancée to dinner," Hatto proceeded. "You will arrive at precisely eight o'clock. Mr. Hurst is not in the habit of permitting unpunctuality."

Now Bill couldn't control himself.

"Indeed?" he said softly. " 'I have been almost obliged to wait.' "

"I beg your pardon, Mr. Laurence?"

"Inform my dear uncle that this statement, one of the most insufferable in history, is attributed to Louis the Fourteenth. —However, we shall be there."

"Naturally, sir. And white tie is imperative. Good day."

There was a soft, serene click as Hatto put down the phone. Bill, resisting a different impulse, replaced his phone with smiling carefulness.

Now they were off to a fighting start. After his premonition that morning, Bill had cast about for some new jolt, from a direction he would not expect, when he met Gaylord Hurst and Hatto. Bill could imagine only one sort of surprise: that this evil-sounding pair might prove to be kindly, at least half-innocuous men, distorted by Larry's imagination into the semblance of devils.[3]

But it must be something else. The very atmosphere over that phone had brushed the cheek with a spider web.

And what about the curious Hatto?

'Hatto's worse than Gay. Or maybe in a different way. . . . Maybe you can handle him when he . . .'

When Hatto did what? Got drunk? Took drugs? But the vision of that stately Hatto, whom he pictured as like a bishop, became fantastic if you saw Hatto swinging his fists in a frenzy of whisky or cocaine through the flat of an art collector such as Gay.

True, Larry had looked at Bill and told him he must be an athlete, before making the remark about "handling" Hatto. Bill, though an amateur welterweight, did not relish the prospect. And he didn't believe it. If Hatto were erratic in any sense, he would not have remained in Gaylord Hurst's service. Besides . . .

At Bill's elbow the telephone began stridently to ring.

As though a rattlesnake had whirred beside him, Bill scraped back his chair. He reached for the phone, and hesitated.

When he had first arrived at the Albert Arms by taxi, he had already completed a plan for his double life. Marjorie knew it too. Going into the big red-brick block of flats, he had

[3] The experienced reader may perhaps have come to share this belief too. Let him be assured that it is wrong. One of the pair, at least, meant murder. And Bill Dawson never guessed the direction from which the blow was coming; at least, not until after the dinner in Gaylord's flat. Discard answer number three.

60

met an affable hall porter—short and bulky, like a sergeant major—whose suspiciously bright-red complexion was belied by clear twinkling eyes behind shell-rimmed glasses. To Tuffrey, the porter, Bill had presented his credentials as Laurence Hurst.

"By the way," he had added, nodding toward the switchboard. "Are you always here?"

"Can't be, sir." Tuffrey intimated a weight of work beyond human effort.

"There's a friend of mine," Bill had continued, "who will drop in occasionally to sleep on the sofa, or perhaps even in the daytime. Mr. William Dawson. If you don't see him, it doesn't matter. If you do, he'll prove his identity. I can guarantee him as absolutely honest. But—"

"Oh, ah, sir?" All servants are suspicious.

"But he has a genius for picking the wrong horse. He doesn't want to meet bookies just at the moment."

"Ah!" Tuffrey's face grew redder with sympathy. "Wrong horse, sir? Yes, sir. Know what it means meself. But what about phone calls?"

"I was coming to that. If there's a call for me—Mr. Hurst —put it through without asking questions. If there's a call for Mr. Dawson, and I'm not in, tell 'em he's out. If there's a call for him and I *am* here, find out who's speaking and put the call through to me. I can keep away undesirables from Mr. Dawson."

Tuffrey beamed.

"Leave it to me, sir. I'll take care of you. And tell the night porter too."

A banknote changed hands. Tuffrey swelled with gratification. The plan, Bill decided as he was carried up in an openwork lift, was far from foolproof, but it would do for the moment. And now . . .

Tr-r-ring, screamed the telephone bell. Bill picked up the phone.

"Yes?"

Tuffrey spoke guardedly.

"Call for Mr. William Dawson, sir."

"Who is it?"

You could almost see offended dignity.

"Can't rightly say, sir. Some gentleman's lady secretary."

"Never mind. Let me speak to her boss."

Bill stared at the lace curtains on the window toward his left. Who could have given his real name away so soon? Marjorie wouldn't do it!

"Hello?" said a comfortable male voice. "May I speak to Mr. William Dawson?"

"Who is speaking, please?"

"Didn't they tell you? Eric Cheever here!" sang the voice. "B.B.C., you know."

"No," said Bill. "I didn't know. Dawson speaking."

Eric, eh? The splendid Mr. Cheever—forever blackmailing Marjorie with his noble conduct after she had turned him down.

"Oh, *you're* Mr. Dawson." Though Cheever might be a shade less cordial, he retained all the reserved heartiness of a fine character. "We have a mutual friend, I believe."

"What mutual friend?"

"Oh, come! I'm sure you can guess it. She . . . our mutual friend, that is, told me where to find you."

Bill's eyes wandered over toward the window curtains on his left. Against the curtain two flashes, like tiny arrows, seemed to flicker and vanish. Marjorie had given him away to Cheever!

"To be exact," said Cheever, "our mutual friend told me you'd arrived in England several days ago, and were staying temporarily with a friend named Harper? Hurst? I've forgotten."

Good old Marjorie! He had been an ass to doubt her!

Cheever's efficient voice suddenly became sharp, with a hint of ominousness. "To be frank, Mr. Dawson," he said, "I think we should have a little talk about a certain problem, regarding our mutual friend, which also concerns us. I think it should be as soon as possible."

"By God, so do I!" said Bill.

"Excellent!" Cheever ignored Bill's tone. "Aside from the pleasure of meeting you this excuses my unpardonable rush. Could you possibly have dinner with me tonight?"

"I'm sorry," said Bill, with real regret, "but I've got a dinner engagement."

"My dear fellow! I quite understand. Let me see, now."

When Marjorie had hurried away from him on their arrival at the airport, so that her parents should not find Bill posing as somebody else before passport and customs authorities, he had caught only a distant glimpse of Cheever, a tall, fair-haired, self-confident blur.

"I've got it!" announced Cheever, with modest pride. "You're an expert on American history, aren't you?"

"No. Far from an expert. But I've studied it. Er—did our mutual friend tell you that?"

"To be frank, yes." Cheever grew less modest. "Tonight," he declared like a B.B.C. announcer, "we present a special program. It's a baby of mine, to be frank. A factual program called *Fateful Lightning*, the story of the American War Between the States. Transmission time is ten-thirty to eleven-thirty."

"But I don't see——"

"I am happy to say, Mr. Dawson, that many of your friends at Rothwell during the war still remember you. Walter Kuhn (remember Walter?) is producing *Fateful Lightning*. He's not very happy about one part of the script. Now if your engagement happened to be over, say, by ten o'clock . . ."

"I see," observed Bill, bile rising in his soul. "Where are you doing the show?"

"Here at Broadcasting House; studio 8-A, top-floor. If you could be there twenty minutes before ten-thirty, you could vet that one part of the script. Afterward, if you are willing, we can go to my office and discuss a problem concerning our mutual friend. Of course, if you can't be there . . . ?"

"Don't worry. I can be there."

"I may be able to convince you I am right. In any case, I promise you something you don't expect."

"And I promise you," snapped Bill, loosening his shoulders under his coat, "something *you* don't expect."

"Agreed, then?"

"Agreed!"

Both phones slammed down at once.

Bill sat back and folded his arms. If Marjorie didn't get rid of the blighter, he would!

Idly his gaze wandered to the left-hand window. Again he saw two tiny crumbs of light stab the curtain, swerve, and twitch away. What caused those shiny points? The sunlight, in addition to being low, lay southwestward on the other side of Albert Street; the windows on this side of the Albert Arms were not touched.

Never mind. It didn't matter.

For, as Bill considered his problems, his sardonic humor compelled him first to grin and then to laugh.

For "getting rid of" Eric Cheever, in actuality, was as grotesque as "handling" Hatto. How did you get rid of a tenacious rival? If life moved amid the hashish fumes of a cheap novel or film, the matter was simple. You beat him up. But the ordinary grown-up person never thought of it: if only because he had never boxed.

Bill, more than a tolerable welterweight, had liked boxing as an easygoing sport. He had been pitched into it, from early boyhood, by an admirer of his clergyman father, Al Warringer, the old American pug who for eleven years had held the middleweight championship of the world.

Al, sneering at payment, had made a life work of training

63

the parson's son. One night at Harringgay, in '44, saw Bill out-point the welterweight champion of the Royal Navy; and Al had groaned aloud.

"Look, kid," had been Al's final wail, "they can't lay a glove on ya. But this Fancy Dan stuff's no good. Ya don' wanna win on points. Ya gotta have a *punch!*"

"Now steady, Al! This is a sport."

"I'm tellin' ya; that's all. Ya can't get *mad*. And ya pull ya punches, kid, even when you don' wanna. Ya just can't bear to hurt anybody."

For some time, especially in early days, this had worried Bill. Were you weak because you disliked cruelty? The war had taught a different, true lesson. Yet how many good men, drugged with nonsense, thought themselves weak because they were not "killers."

That was why Bill laughed.

'Now why,' he thought, as he sat at the desk by the tele-phone, 'should I hate Eric Cheever? He's probably a very decent fellow.' If I hate anybody, it's a poison snake puffed out with conceit. Gay is in the habit of having his orders obeyed, eh? I must learn the meaning of discipline, eh? I must—'

The telephone rang again.

"What the devil is it now?" he demanded.

Evidently this call had been put through to "Larry Hurst," since he did not hear the hall porter.

"Oh!" said Marjorie's soft voice. "Bi—I mean: Larry. Is anything wrong?"

"Venus! Eve! Astarte!" said Bill. "There's nothing wrong, no. But you haven't run away? You haven't been kidnapped? You haven't decided to fall for Cheever?"

"Good heavens, *no!* What made you think that?"

"I didn't, actually. But I've just had a phone call from Mr. Cheever. He said—"

"What?" Marjorie asked too quickly.

Here Bill raised his eyes. Against the lace curtains again appeared those two small light points.

"Marjorie!" said Bill, in a whisper. "Will you hold the line a moment? Something's been happening here . . . no, noth-ing important . . . but I've just guessed what it means. Wait, now!"

The light arrows whisked away, but returned immediately. Bill's desk stood between the two windows. Edging against the wall, Bill moved toward the left-hand window. On either side of its curtains hung a strip of velvet. Easing his head inside the velvet and one side of the curtains, Bill kept his head shadowed and peered out.

9 SHE LOVES ME; SHE LOVES ME NOT

JUST opposite him in Albert Street rose up another large block of new flats, dull yellow instead of red, the two hives looking so alike that they might have been built by the same firm. Over each of the three entries, gold lettering proclaimed the Victoria Arms.

Then Bill caught the two flashes—same entry, same floor—from a window just opposite in the Victoria Arms.

They were sharp reflections from the lenses of big field glasses. Somebody across the street was following every move Bill made.

Sliding his head out from under the velvet, Bill looked round the sitting room. Cream-colored walls, good but aged carpet, furniture bought second-hand, all had the flat unlived-in look of such places, except for one incongruity. Over the mantelpiece hung the mounted head of a tiger. Two tiny light arrows again struck the curtains, and seemed to glimmer in the tiger's eyes.

Bill went back to the phone.

"Marjorie, something turned up. . . . No, no! It's not important. But I must do a bit of tracking down before I'm tracked down myself. Where are you now?"

"In a public call box."

"Will you stay where you are, and ring me in ten minutes?"

"Of course I will! What's happened? What were you saying about Eric Cheever?"

"Later, my pet," Bill replaced the phone, waited, and spoke to the hall porter.

"Tuffrey," he said, "about the Victoria Arms. Is that building just like ours? Arrangements of rooms; all that?"

"Sir?" blankly. "Oh, ah! The Victoria. Yes, sir; exactly like. The porter in the first entry's a pal of mine."

"Then the flat on the third floor, to the left of the first entry, would be the same as mine? C-14?"

"C-*16*, sir. It's turned round."

"Now listen. Could you find out from your friend who lives in C-16 over there? It's very important."

"I'm sure you won't mind this, sir. There's no 'anky-panky about it, is there?"

"No! Certainly not! If you wonder who I am . . ."

Tuffrey's chuckle removed all doubt. "I know your flat was booked by your uncle, Mr. Gaylord Hurst, and everybody knows what a fine gentleman *he* is."

"Yes. Then will you nip across the road and find out?"

"When, sir?"

"Immediately! Now!"

"I'm not supposed to leave here, sir. Still . . . I might put young Thomas at the switchboard." Tuffrey could be heard bellowing for Thomas like a sergeant major. "Back in half a tick, sir," he told Bill, and rang off.

Bill got up restlessly and looked out of the right-hand window behind its curtains, in time to see Tuffrey march toward the Victoria Arms.

Bill surveyed the little shopping center. Since this was late afternoon, the shops were closed. There was the branch of the Midland Bank, where Bill had turned over his money and had received a checkbook and a passbook inscribed with the sum of just under three thousand four hundred pounds.

There was the little tailoring shop, where he had persuaded them to cut a number of inches off two pairs of Larry's trousers, one pair dress trousers. Far up was the restaurant at which he had eaten a vile lunch.

And yet, despite bad food . . . This was Festival Year, the year of floodlighting, of exhibitions galore: the South Bank exhibition, the fun fair at Battersea, even (what most interested Bill) the Sherlock Holmes exhibition in Baker Street. He had seen, during his drive through Chiswick and Hammersmith, houses freshened with a lick of paint. There were—

Here Bill whipped round. On the door of his flat, somebody gave a quiet, but peremptory knock.

Hurrying into the foyer, Bill opened the door. It was only Tuffrey. The deeper red of his face, the reproachful look, all shouted bad news.

Bill beckoned him in.

"Yes?" he asked in an easy tone. "Did you discover who lives in C-16?"

"Yes, sir," replied the hall porter, avoiding Bill's eye. "I said to my friend Bob Lewis, the hall porter: 'Mr. Lewis, I hear you've got a big pot in C-16.' "

"Well?" demanded Bill. "Who's the occupant?"

"Mr. Lewis kept saying *Mr.* Partridge, sir, until all of a sudden I connected it with the gentleman." Then reproachfulness beat across from Tuffrey's eyes. "*Mr.* Partridge is Chief Inspector Partridge. C.I.D. Scotland Yard, sir."

Bill, turning away to hide his expression, found himself looking at the mounted tiger's malevolent eyes.

Trr-ring trr-ring squalled the telephone bell. Bill turned back again.

"Good! Thanks very much."

"Good, sir?"

"I thought I saw old Partridge over there. But you can't be sure at a distance. Keep a secret, old man?"

"Yes, sir!"

"I worked with him when I was in the Special Branch, during the war. I mean to go over and surprise him."

Tuffrey exhaled a gasp of relief. "Er—your phone's ringing, sir."

"Ah, yes. So it is." Bill chuckled. "Putting Partridge across from me might be some of my Uncle Gay's work. I shouldn't be surprised if my uncle had a large share in the property. But he wouldn't like his name mentioned; or mine."

"No, sir."

The telephone now seemed to be having hysterics.

"By the way, how long has Partridge been in that flat? Did you ask?"

"Yes, sir. He only moved in early this morning. And now, if I may go—?"

Uncle Gay again? No way of telling. If he had brought in the police . . .

Waiting until he heard Tuffrey close the door, Bill caught the telephone just before its final ring.

"Bill?" spoke Marjorie's anxious voice.

"You have confused your men, angel face. This is Larry Hurst. Definitely Larry Hurst."

"Yes; I know. But the phone rang and rang until I thought you'd gone out. You said something had turned up. Is it all right?"

"All right," he lied cheerfully.

"But, Bill! Larry, I mean. You were telling me about a phone call from Eric. Darling, what *did* he say about me?"

Bill had decided long ago not to tell her of that last challenge flung down by both of them; it would only alarm Marjorie.

"Very little, my pet. Cheever referred to you under the delicate Dickensian title of Our Mutual Friend. He seemed to intimate that he had some sort of claim on you. He hasn't, has he?"

Did he only imagine a very slight pause?

"No!" she said. "Of course not! You don't believe that, do you?"

"No, I don't believe it." (Or did he?)

"Well, then, the real reason why I rang was to find out what happens tonight. Do we go to your uncle's for dinner? And how are the indications?"

"Bad. East wind blowing. You see, I didn't ring up until five o'clock. . . ."

"Not until five?"

"Hang it, I had errands to do. Then—you wouldn't believe

67

it, but I'm a bit absent-minded. I sat down at the typewriter, and banged away most of the afternoon."

"But what for?"

Bill glanced at the portable, with the stack of sheets beside it. Another puzzle concerned that very typewriter. But he put it aside.

"Tell you later," he said. "Meanwhile, here are the orders. We arrive at his flat punctually at eight o'clock. It's formal; wear an evening gown. I am to be treated as a dull, easily frightened schoolboy."

"Bill, do stop! You mustn't get angry!"

"Gay will behave like a bad master at school. Remaining serene, he will sting me with witticisms to make the class laugh. In a bored way he will parade his culture, his superiority, his knowledge of books, to make his nephew feel stupid and small." Bill's voice grew soft. "If he tries that game on me, my pet, he is going to cop a packet."

"No! No; you musn't! You must convince your uncle that you're the real Larry Hurst!"

About to retort that Larry was dead, and that it didn't matter whether Gay discovered his identity provided he could settle the hash of Gaylord Hurst, Bill suddenly saw the trap.

Marjorie was right, without even guessing why! If Bill failed to convince Gaylord that he was Larry, the whole scheme blew up. Gay would instantly get in touch with Amberley, already suspicious. Everything centered round that blasted ten thousand dollars.

What Bill now had in the bank meant his academic career. He could marry and support Marjorie. With Gaylord disbelieving him, even if he could prove by Joy Tennent that Larry had given him the money, Mr. Gaylord would get back every penny. And again the dream would be gone.

"Please listen!" said the anguished Marjorie. "You want to hit back hard at Mr. Hurst. And at his own game. But you've read so much that in an argument *nobody*, let alone Gaylord Hurst, could possibly think you were Larry. Don't you see?"

"Yes," Bill answered dully.

"I understand how you feel," she said with a burning sympathy. "But you've got to take whatever he gives. *I* know what you could do if you wanted. And you will behave?"

"Yes; my very best behavior." Bill assumed a great carelessness. "Now we must be there by eight. Where shall I pick you up?"

"Please don't bother. Couldn't we meet at a quarter of eight in the Green Park Underground Station? Shall we meet by the bookstall?"

"Right! Good-by, Marjorie."

"I love you," Marjorie whispered, and rang off.

Those words have never failed to raise any man's spirits. Bill sat down at the typewriter until it was time to bathe and dress. Larry's dress clothes, if you did not look too closely, fitted him to perfection. He had bought a thin watch with a thin chain—and he slipped it into the pocket of his white waistcoat.

Taking the Underground at South Kensington, he emerged at Green Park station. As the escalator took him up to the foyer, it was just sixteen minutes to eight.

Marjorie stood by the bookstall, her back turned, looking at the *London Mystery Magazine.*

Under a short white fur cloak, she wore a rich sleek gown of dove-gray, cut rather low in front, a longer rope of pearls contrasting with pink-tinged skin. She and Bill stopped in constraint. This atmosphere was not conducive to public demonstrations. Marjorie gravely extended her hand.

"Are we on time, Bill?"

"Just on time, I think." He lowered his voice. "Now remember. You are Joy Tennent, and I am Laurence Hurst. You know your life story, and you've briefed me on a good part of mine. Think you can manage it?"

For the first time Marjorie seemed poised, self-contained, like the good private secretary she was.[4]

"I can manage better than you think," she said. "If you only keep from doing anything foolish. . . ."

"I promise. We'd better go."

The sunshine was still softly bright. Walking along Piccadilly, they passed the Ritz, ducked darting motorcars, and paused at the right-hand turning of St. James's Street.

Bill began to speak as they turned into the long, broad, downward slope.

"Damn that typewriter," Bill said flatly.

Marjorie turned her head.

"Your portable typewriter?" she asked. "What *is* the trouble?"

"It belonged to Larry. Yesterday afternoon, just before I left the Waldorf, I opened it and took a quick look to make sure it was in working order. Marjorie, I could take my oath it was an ordinary Wolverine portable, with black keys and white letters."

"Well?"

"This morning I had to go out on a number of errands.

[4] In fairness, it must be stated that these footnotes are always to be taken in a strictly literal sense, meaning no more and no less than what they say. Yet the farseeing reader may have wondered whether Marjorie Blair, a secretary, might not by a long coincidence have been the mysterious and invisible "Miss Ventnor," private secretary of George Amberley, the lawyer. This is wrong. Discard answer number four.

When I came back at half past one, I took the cover off the machine and sat down to type. . . ."

"That's what I don't see, Bill. To type what?"

"First, letters I should have remembered before I left New York. To my landlady, to my boss: sent to a friend in America, to be posted with American stamps. Second, a complete account of this adventure, before I could forget a single detail. But that wasn't what I wanted to tell you. The typewriter was still a Wolverine portable. But the keys were *white*, with metal rings, and the letters were black."

He swept out his hand.

"This afternoon, from first to last, I kept wondering whether the hall porter, or Chief Inspec . . . someone else might have changed typewriters while I was out. But what would be the sense in it?"

"Wait!" urged Marjorie. "You didn't have a typewriter last night."

"No. At the terminus in New York, I left a suitcase and the typewriter to be taken by bus and stored in the plane."

"Then the typewriters might have been changed at the airport or even before?"

"Theoretically, yes," admitted Bill. "But there's only one real explanation. I was overtired at the Waldorf; I made one of those optical mistakes. It's been the same typewriter all the time, and I'm convinced of it!" He drew in his breath. "If only I could stop worrying about another question! Er . . . Marjorie."

They were almost at the foot of the street. To their right loomed up the entrance to a rather narrow cul-de-sac, its far wall bearing the sign, *St. James's Place, S.W.1.*

Whether because she saw this, or caught the unsteady note in Bill's voice, Marjorie stopped abruptly.

"Yes, Bill?"

"I want you to understand that this isn't a complaint. You made a beautiful job of telling your parents, and Eric, that I'd got here several days ago, and was staying at a friend's. But why did you give Cheever my address?"

Her head was averted; sunshine touched the dark-gold hair. "You see . . . first I had to tell my family you were here, and prepare them for—"

"A real wedding this time?"

"If you still want me. —No, please! But about Eric. He asked me why I went to America to begin with."

"Went to . . . But what difference does it make? Well, why did you go?"

"To find you," Marjorie said simply.

70

Bill stared at the pavement and wished he could drop through it.

"And today," Marjorie blurted, "I've been horribly conscience-stricken. I rather let myself go last night. I didn't mind that. But when I imagined you'd think I was throwing myself at your head like a . . . Bill, what's the matter? Why don't you say anything?"

"I can't, Marjorie. I'm too ashamed."

"Ashamed?" The word seemed to puzzle her. "Eric asked whether I'd found you, and I said yes. Then he wanted your address, because he's got something to tell you." Marjorie's mind came back to perplex itself. "Ashamed?" she said.

"Yes! That—that anybody as wonderful as you could possibly care so much for a—for a—"

Bill glanced round wildly for something to distract attention, and saw the street sign.

"This *is* St. James's Place!" he announced. "We've been standing in front of it all the time, and never knowing. In you go, Marjorie." His collar felt as though it were too tight. "Afterward, I'll try to tell you—!"

The cul-de-sac had a pavement on each side, as well as a road in which two cars might pass each other with care. The shop on the left belonged to a firm of gunsmiths; on the right a stationer and mapmaker. St. James's Place now was shadowy and damp.

This backwater of a turning had only gas lamps projecting on brackets from the walls on each side. Nearly all the houses, red brick with window frames painted yellow, showed brass plates. Marjorie saw—though Bill, blank-eyed, did not—the premises of solicitors, several estate agents, one bookie, and, upstairs, what purported to be a French night club.

Marjorie stopped and pressed Bill's arm.

"There it is," she said. "Straight ahead at the far end of the square. The back of the house is toward us. But there's a little white '68' on the side."

Only one side of the big Georgian house, dark with age, was visible at its back. It stood alone, amid blitz rubble against the foliage of the Green Park beyond. There were three floors, of long windows masked by blinds between indented columns, and a broad stone shelf under the windows on both upstairs floors. A burglar with a strong hook attached to a rope, you might imagine, would have easy access to those upper ledges.

Number 68 looked cold and repellent.

"It's no good denying it," whispered Marjorie. "We're going to meet something awful before we leave here. But what is it?"

Her companion was silent. Just round the right-hand corner

of number 68, the door to the one entry stood wide open. But inside it was so dark that Bill had to strike on the silver lighter. Its flame showed a brass plate bristling with titles and decorations.

> *Ground floor: Sir Ashton Cowdray, K.C.*
> *First floor: Vice-Admiral the Hon. Benbow Hooker,* and a string of naval honors.
> *Top floor: Mr. Gaylord Hurst, O.B.E.*

Each floor was a very large flat for a wealthy bachelor.

The flame of the lighter wobbled as they climbed steep, narrow stairs. On the top floor they emerged on a little landing at the back, faintly lighted by a long window with a drawn blind. Against the south wall showed a tall old dark-polished door with a brass knob, Gay's card, and a white bell push.

But Bill made no move to press the bell push. Marjorie's low-voiced agitation burst out.

"What are you thinking about? When you go far away, I don't like it. What are you thinking about?"

Bill, half waking into a smiling human being, shook his head.

"But why won't you tell me?"

"Because it sounds too high-falutin'. You want to know what I was thinking?"

"Yes!"

"Remember your Froissart? It's about Bertrand du Guesclin, the great champion of the fourteenth century. *'Then he saith, yet speaking but to his squire: Upon this day, by God's grace and my lady's favour, will I do a deed of arms shall ring in Christendom; not for my poor name, but for love of my lady and for honour of my friend, in the high court of all chivalry.'* "

He closed the silver lighter, and dropped it into his pocket. Marjorie's unsteady hand sought and found the bell push, and a soft buzzing could be heard inside.

"For the last time, Bill," she said, "promise me. You won't do anything foolish?"

"Marjorie, I don't know."

The door opened. Hatto awaited them on the threshold.

"GOOD evening, Miss Tennent," Hatto said in his unchanging tone of respect. "And welcome home, Mr. Laurence, if I may say so."

His head inclined very slightly as he moved aside and closed the door.

Marjorie and Bill were in a rather narrow foyer stretching almost the breadth of the house. The body of the flat ran east and west; in the middle of the wall on his right, closed double doors showed silver handles.

The walls of the foyer were a soft green. It was lighted by five tall windows along the left. Heavy velvet curtains of green figured in gold were partly looped back, though the blinds were drawn.

"Your cape, Miss Tennent?" suggested Hatto.

As Marjorie turned her back, Bill saw Hatto clearly. Hatto did have the head of a bishop; a medieval bishop. Though he showed his forty-eight years, the head was square and square of jaw: the nose straight and long, the mouth almost invisible against a pale face. Atop a high forehead his dark hair had a tinge of gray; his dead black eyes seemed turned inward in meditation. Bishop Hatto was six feet three, a giant above Bill's five feet nine. Hatto's apparent leanness was disguised by perfectly fitting evening clothes, white tie and polished shirt marred only by the black waistcoat which was the badge of his office. His height and indifference made Marjorie and Bill feel like children.

As he lifted Marjorie's cape, some movement of his elbow reminded Bill of . . . of . . .

"Your coat, Mr. Laurence? —Thank you. If you will follow me?"

Hatto pressed the silver handles, opened the green double doors, and stood aside.

As Bill and Marjorie entered the room, they gained an impression of soft yellow lights up and down the walls. "If you will wait here in the anteroom," said Hatto, "I will ascertain whether Mr. Hurst wishes to receive you."

"Receive us?" repeated Bill. "We were expected at eight o'clock, I believe?"

"Mr. Hurst's time, sir, is valuable. Yours is not. If you permit the suggestion, you may avoid discipline if you speak only when you are spoken to."

Hatto, with the coat and the fur cape over his arm, backed out and closed the doors.

"Lord Gay," observed Bill almost tenderly. "His little Order of the British Empire has swollen his head. Don't you see the game? He'll make me wait, until he thinks he's upset Larry Hurst's nerves. What did you make of Hatto?"

"He's awfully distinguished-looking. He's like a Cardinal. I think he's . . ."

"He's a wrestler," said Bill. "I may be wrong, but I noticed that trick of sticking his elbows out and his hand to shoulder height before he took your wrap and my coat."

"A *wrestler?*"

"Don't think all wrestlers are barrel round and with bulging biceps. The Cornish wrestlers look thin: until, they say, you feel the crush of the grip. But if Hatto were a boxer, for all his height, he wouldn't be more than a cruiser weight."

"What's a cruiser weight?"

"The weight varies, of course. But take it at a hundred and seventy-five pounds."

"Bill . . . what do *you* weigh?"

"I'm a welterweight. Exactly a hundred and forty-three pounds. Hatto's got a longer reach, of course."

"That's too much difference! They—your uncle keeps talking about disciplining you. What if Hatto . . . ?"

"I don't know. But don't worry. This is a battle of wits, not a prize fight. Let's see what . . ."

For the first time both looked round the room.

Having no outside windows, it could be illumined in daytime by a skylight; but dark wine-colored curtains had been closely drawn over the skylight. The walls were covered to above head height by that dull red matting you see in art galleries. Against the dull red background hung about fifty paintings or water colors, few large, and all in sober frames made rich by concealed lighting across the top.

It was Gaylord Hurst's private art collection. There was no furniture save a round armless sofa.

Bill surveyed the pictures. "Ah, God!" he said, in genuine prayer.

"They do seem rather awful," Marjorie acknowledged. "But after all, it's modern art!"

"The futilists have convinced many people the work must be modern because it's crazy."

"Stop a bit!" breathed Marjorie. "That one isn't!"

He swung round. The largest, best-placed and best-lighted oil painting was a full-length picture of Gaylord Hurst himself, an exact likeness and no work of his favorite painters.

It was just like the photograph Bill had studied, except that

74

background and pose were different. The portrait showed him seated in what looked like a padded armchair with wings. He wore thick bifocal glasses, magnifying expressionless pale blue eyes. His tousled hair, the color of grimy sheep's wool, showed heavy above the long narrow face. The Order of the British Empire was conspicuous. One short leg, with a small polished black shoe, did not quite touch the ground. Partly across the other leg lay part of a blue silk coverlet, falling to the floor in large folds, and grasped at the top by Gay's thin delicate hand, as though it were a lap robe.

Gay, if he had studied it closely, would not have been pleased. This painter, though his signature was no giddy foreign name, being only "Thompson, '50," had plucked out the hidden qualities. Greed hung round the wrinkles of mouth and forehead; cruelty—the very mild cruelty of the bored—touched the eyes and mouth; Gay's look of sad virtue was overdone.

Bill turned away, exasperated. "And now, Lord Gay has kept us waiting for over fifteen minutes. If I were to kick in those doors, for example . . ."

"Are you going to let him get on your nerves?"

"No?" Bill prowled restlessly and finally sat down on the circular red divan. Though he saw no ashtray, he plucked out a Gold Flake, lit it, and smoked broodingly.

"How I wish, my pet, I had a Leonardo to paint *you!*" he said. "Leonardo's nudes would be best. Rubens—no; Rubens far overdid what I'm thinking about. . . ."

The double doors of the foyer opened swiftly. It would be against Hatto's dignity to move swiftly. He did not seem to. Yet, before Bill could understand what had happened, the cigarette was removed deftly from his fingers, and Hatto backed away.

"Mr. Hurst, sir, does not permit smoking in this room. You were wise to give up the cigarette. Otherwise the consequences might have been unpleasant."

Bill got up from the divan, moving a little out from it. He whipped another cigarette into his mouth, lit it, and blew smoke into Hatto's face.

"Care to try taking this one?" he suggested mildly.

Bang went the first gage of battle.

"One moment, Mr. Laurence," replied Hatto. Turning with churchlike dignity, he marched into the foyer, holding the cigarette away from him as though he had never seen one. Presumably after extinguishing it, Hatto returned.

"Yes?" prompted Bill.

"To take the cigarette from you, Mr. Laurence, would not be difficult. But I might be compelled to hurt you a little."

"How you curdle my blood!" smiled Bill.

"Your uncle, sir, is deeply attached to you. I should not think of chastising you without his orders. Before I am tempted to, however—"

Hatto stopped short. From behind the closed door came the faint tinkle of a hand bell: the doors were thick.

"You will now go into the drawing room," Hatto informed them. "Mr. Hurst has graciously consented to receive you. I hope, Mr. Laurence, you will not be so rash as to let Mr. Hurst know you have been smoking."

"My rashness is proverbial." Bill, who never had addressed a servant as though the latter were a servant, dismissed Hatto briefly. "Open the doors."

Hatto obeyed and stood aside.

"Miss Joy Tennent," he announced. "Mr. Laurence Hurst."

They were dimly aware of another large square room, its skylight also muffled. Long lines of bookshelves, open and painted white, were a-gleam with fine bindings. Beside the farther double doors burned a table lamp, its shade muffled in black and white.

"I beg of you," called a soft voice from across the room, "that neither will brush against the small Adam table in the middle of the room. Otherwise you may come forward."

Despite her glance in the direction where she knew Gaylord Hurst must be, Marjorie glanced at the small table on a deep black-and-white carpet. On the table, supported by an ivory board stood a set of Chinese chess men. Each man was at least four inches high, the opposing armies being of light green jade on one side and dark green on the other, carved into elaborate shapes.

"If it should interest you," continued the melancholy voice, "they are of Ming jade, of our fourteenth century. The slightest damage would be irreplaceable. Beyond and in the front of the chess men there is a sofa set to face me. You, Miss Tennent, will move to your right, and sit there facing me. You, Laurence, will move to your left, and occupy a chair near me. Come, come!"

Just to the right of the third double doors was the table lamp muffled in black and white. A little further right, their host sat in the same chair as in the painting.

"Come, come!" he said. "This is all very gratifying."

A thin flow of hatred, controlled until now, crept from Bill to the thick spectacles and the thin mouth moving in and out like the gills of a fish, without opening. The same hatred flowed back to him from Mr. Hurst.

You may be polite, you may be subdued, you may smile: all these three did. Marjorie, sitting alone on a sofa of very soft white leather with pillows edged in black, leaned forward as though deeply impressed. Bill sat and smoked with his head lowered.

"My dear," said Gay to Marjorie, "you may be pleased to hear that I approve of you. I feared that any choice of my poor boy would prove unfortunate. Not so. You are at least socially presentable, and charming."

('Now is there any woman on earth,' thought Bill, 'whose back wouldn't bristle up at that patronizing "socially presentable"?')

But this girl was pretending with success.

"I'm awfully glad you like me," said Marjorie, clasping her hands.

"I do indeed, my dear. Yet . . ."

The blue leer behind the thick lenses would have been goatish, if it had not been for the voice.

"Yet I can only hope, Miss Tennent, that the poor boy will not bring you disappointment and heartbreak."

"Disappointment? Heartbreak? But why?"

"Alas," said Mr. Hurst, "I am now a lonely old man. Yet for years I was Laurence's tutor and mentor. He was frightened into fits by the mildest joke. He was very backward in his studies: perhaps not so much through lack of intelligence as from sheer stubbornness. It grieves me to say that he was a liar, a sneak, and a coward. To take one instance, I recall . . ."

The grisly anecdote flowed on.

Bill, crushing out his cigarette in an ashtray, studied the man carefully. Mr. Hurst, in rather sloppy evening clothes which conspicuously showed his O.B.E. as in the portrait, sat upright against a background of long white shelves and bright-colored books.

The large blue silk coverlet, outlining short legs and delicate shoes, was spread completely round from the waist: not only touching the floor, but pressed back on either side so as to conceal as much as possible of the chair's sides. Bill could see the hands, under the blue robe, plucking and plucking to draw that silk further and further toward the back. But how, Bill wondered, could Gay's fingers reach through the sides of a wing chair which . . .

Then he saw. That apparent wing chair was a wheel chair. In front of Marjorie, at least, the exhausted satyr would permit no sign of disability.

Gay's voice droned on.

"And so, my dear," he concluded, "there was the sorry chap, blubbering on the floor. Naturally his parents could not believe that I, of all people, had put on a papier mâché mask, representing the face of a victim of the Great Plague in1666, covered with blue pustules and mouth open. I cannot wonder, my dear, if you find it incredible. Sometimes I doubted his sanity."

"But, Mr. Hurst!" said Marjorie. "You tell me he was eight then. And you haven't seen him since he was sixteen!"

"True, my child."

"Don't people change? Doesn't the rabbit at games become the hero of real life?"

"A pleasant fiction to soothe the groundlings, my dear. An oafish youth may change in appearance. But his basic character? Never."

Craning his neck round, he deigned to look at his pseudo-nephew for the first time. His attitude and tone subtly changed.

Bill had already prepared his plan. He must use the gestures and speech of Larry Hurst, mingled with his own, so that a slip in the former would not be noticed.

"Ah, old chap." The thick spectacles dazzled; the voice was patronizing, godlike. "And how are you?"

"Not too bad, Uncle Gay," replied Bill, fidgeting as Larry would have fidgeted, eyes lowered. "I mean: Glad to see you, and all that."

"You flatter me, Laurence. But it is better for growing boys to tell the truth. You are not pleased to see me."

"Eh, sir?"

"You are not at all pleased to see me, Laurence."

"Don't follow you, Uncle Gay."

"In all these eighteen years, have you written me one line? Nevertheless, I have followed your career through Mr. George Amberley. Hunting heavy game! Mountain climbing! Motor racing! Now what does this mean?"

"I liked it, Uncle Gay."

"No, Laurence. With jejune feverishness you have tried to convince yourself you were not a coward. But you have found that you were the worst of cowards. You dare not face me now."

This arrow whacked so close to the target that Bill flinched.

"Yes, I see by your face I am right." The detached voice, never even showed a shade of triumph. "Well. Let us forget that. But before I offer my hand, I must insist that we settle your impertinent behavior, which—"

"Look here sir! Phoned late today, yes. Admit that. But . . ."

"You will find it wiser, Laurence, not to interrupt. Is that clear?"

Bill swallowed hard, and nodded.

"Very well. Had your famous courtesy permitted me to

continue, you would have been glad to hear I have decided to pardon another offense. You have never found me unjust. But impertinence I will not tolerate."

"No, sir."

"Then we understand each other. —That cigarette in your hand, for instance. That, I think, is your second. You were smoking the first when you entered this room. Were you unaware that I do not permit smoking in the anteroom?"

"I was at first. Hatto told me."

"Hatto told you. Then you deliberately violated my command. Why?"

Not for the first time that day, Bill pressed his temples and rubbed his eyes. He rose to his feet, making flapping gestures after the fashion of Larry.

"Look here, Uncle Gay! No rotting; tell you straight. When I came in here, I thought I didn't give a damn for you. There it is."

"At least it is frank, and what I suspected. —Now put out your cigarette in the ashtray on the table at your left. Do not attempt to argue. Put it out."

Bill sat down and obeyed. While he slowly rubbed out the cigarette, he saw what the table was, and what stood on it.

It was a Chippendale of fair size, of mahogany and square shape, with a tasso edge binding of white plaster and gilt. At one side of the black-and-white lamp stood half a dozen small round bottles, each carefully corked and with a red poison label. Beyond the lamp stood an old-fashioned policeman's lantern. Strangest of all were half a dozen pairs of old-fashioned brass knuckles.

"Have you quite finished, Laurence?" the godlike voice asked.

"Sorry, Uncle Gay. Er—aren't you allowed to smoke here either?"

"Ordinarily. Tonight, however, I cannot permit you to smoke at any time. Should you produce a cigarette, it will be taken away. Am I clear? Dinner, as usual, will be served punctually at nine o'clock. At dinner, Laurence, you will make full apology to Hatto for your impertinence." Bill gave a covert look at Marjorie. Her short, shallow breathing indicated fury.

'Get him!' her gray eyes seemed to be whispering. 'Stick him through! Don't tell me *you're* afraid of him too?'

Bill turned away.

"I can only imagine, Laurence, that you are deaf. It would be a pity if I were compelled to take certain measures. Will you apologize to Hatto, or will you not?"

11 A DEAD KING BEGAN IT

BILL rose, pressed his fingers over his eyes, and sat down again.

"It would be painful to see you blubbering and crying on the floor; you remember how? Poor Miss Tennent would pity you but perhaps not admire you. I have no wish to see you hurt. But a boy must learn his place. Therefore . . ."

Bill raised his head.

"Sorry, Uncle Gay," he said gruffly. "If you want me to apologize to Hatto, I'll do it with pleasure."

Now he did not dare look at Marjorie.

"Come, this is admirable." The royal note softened a little. "I am sure we shall get on capitally. There is only one more impertinence to discuss."

"More impertinence?"

"Yes, old chap. I confess it puzzled me. Over the telephone, according to Hatto, you sneered the quotation, 'I have been almost obliged to wait.' This you correctly attributed to Louis Quatorze of France. Curious, is it not?"

"Curious, sir?"

"Your backwardness was the despair of your poor parents. To say nothing of myself. I tried to impart to you the beauty of literature and of history. These caused your worst stubbornness. Now where did you learn this not-very-well-known quotation?"

"Dunno, sir. Must have read it somewhere."

"You are quite sure, Laurence?"

More than once Bill had wondered whether Gaylord Hurst had grown senile and really believed him to be sixteen. But behind those thick flashing lenses, he sensed, the old boy was even more cunning than he had been described.

"Look here, Uncle Gay!" Bill fidgeted. "Never could understand you. Dunno why. What's the odds about a quotation?"

"Nevertheless, Laurence, I think I must test you a little. Now concerning Louis Quatorze—"

"Looey what?"

"*Anglice,* as Macaulay wrote it, King Lewis the Fourteenth. Now concentrate your great brain and tremendous research, Hurst Minor. In what century did this monarch live?"

Bill's gaze strayed. His answer must be wrong, but not so wildly wrong as to arouse suspicion still more.

"Got it!" said Bill, with Larry's own kind of triumph. "Eighteenth century! He was followed by—you know; the fat one—who got his head chopped off."

The history master sighed, yet he looked pleased.

"It was the seventeenth century, Laurence. Had you said he lived some few years into the eighteenth, you would have been correct. And he was not followed by Louis Seize, but by Louis Quinze. Can you recall anything else?"

"Lived a hell of a long time, Uncle Gay."

"That is all. I need not further test your gigantic historical knowledge. Your impertinence must be dismissed as mainly due to ignorance."

Bill fought down rage. The greater grew his hatred of the temporary uncle, the more grimly he determined to convince this tyrant that he was undoubtedly Laurence Hurst. Everything depended on that.

Yet Marjorie spoke out.

"Really, Mr. Hurst," she said coldly, "is it necessary to speak to him as though he were a schoolboy?"

"He *is* a schoolboy, my dear. What if he has grown a few years older. Laurence is no more mature—than the pathological little sneak I knew. Permit me to deal with him as I choose."

"But . . .

"I must warn you, my child." The tone was melancholy again. "If my manner toward him sometimes seems cold, I am not accustomed to changing my habits and I fear you must put up with them. Bank managers, directors of property trust companies in which I have more than quintupled my money, have found it wise to obey my orders. It seems to have escaped you, Miss Tennent, that of late I have became rather an important man."

Marjorie remembered to act. And she acted beautifully.

"But everyone knows that, Mr. Hurst! Not only your judgment, your—your wealth, but your wonderful charity!"

"We-el!" Mollified, he directed a glance down at his O.B.E., order. "Perhaps the Government have seen fit to recognize my small efforts toward benevolence. However, this is unimportant. Let us return to our schoolboy. Despite my odd-seeming questions, I have discovered what I really wished to know."

"Oh? What was it?"

"That this overgrown schoolboy actually *is* may nephew."

There was a bursting pause.

"But, Mr. Hurst! Did you ever doubt it?"

"Doubt everything at first, my dear. But, when you have become certain, acknowledge the truth."

"You're awfully clever, Mr. Hurst. But I don't understand!"

"Listen, my pretty child. If I suspected Laurence, do you imagine I should have prepared a long list of questions about his past life?—which any imposter would have learned?"

"Well . . ." Marjorie moistened her lips.

"That would have been jejune, my dear. Instead I asked him quite unexpected questions. And the boy, who is afraid of me, answered them exactly as I expected. Physical appearance accounts for nothing; it changes too much. But his instinctive gestures, his facial expressions, his turns of speech, his cringes: these I remember vividly. This was Laurence."

Bill, averting his face to conceal relief, again stared at the Chippendale table.

"Mr. Hurst, that was clever!" said Marjorie, like a housemaid congratulating her employer.

"We-el. Let us say mature. But an old pedant, my dear, even when he sees your beauty, must not play at being Sherlock Holmes. I recognized Laurence by his voice."

"By my voice?" Bill almost shouted.

His genuine amazement, it occurred to him, had set the seal on Gaylord's belief.

"This did not occur to you, Laurence?"

Again the Olympian tones stung him.

"Curse it all, no! What I mean: don't voices change most of all, sir? After you've grown up?"

"Sometimes, but not greatly. At sixteen you had already developed a hideous baritone which nobody could mistake now. Do you recall the gramophone record I took of you attempting to recite the St. Crispin's day speech from *Henry the Fifth?* I see you have. I played that record last night. Aside from your intolerable overacting, it might have been you speaking now."

Bill wanted to ask, and couldn't: "Do you mean I've got a voice like Larry?" It seemed incredible, until memory threw light. The clerk at the Waldorf-Astoria: "Yes, sir. I recognized your voice." And further back than that! On the first night he had met Amberley, in the dim law library, Amberley had asked Bill who he was; and, at Bill's first words, had given a visible start. At the same time, through an open transom, there had been a feminine whisper. Larry, of course, did not recognize his own voice. But Amberley knew. And Joy Tennent knew.

Events now began to run swiftly.

"Hence we shall call the matter settled, Laurence. It reminds me: I have bought a trifling gift for you, as a homecoming present."

"Gift, sir?"

"Had it been of real value, I should have withheld it because of your behavior. But you may have it." The voice went up almost in falsetto. "Hatto! Hatto!"

Hatto must have been listening. The little door giving on the passage opened immediately.

"Yes, sir?" said Hatto.

"Please give Mr. Laurence the book I ordered from Hatchard's."

Even now Bill did not forget his part.

"Book?" he blurted out, uneasily.

"I am aware, Laurence, that to offer you a book may be considered a punishment. But no fear. This one will interest even you. I remember this book as both entertaining and intelligent."

The ecclesiastical wrestler handed the book to Bill. It was an old, big and heavy English edition of Theodore Roosevelt's *African Game Trails*. Hatto melted away.

"Never read it," Bill said with real enthusiasm. "Heard about it, though. Many thanks, sir. Let's have a look at it!"

Bill's left thumb went out to the edge of the cover.

Then a new, ugly thought darted through his mind, and he hesitated. Gaylord was much too eager. He had craned his neck round toward Bill. His eyes, smallish and pale blue, were little flashing daggers behind glass. His fingers plucked and plucked inside the silk counterpane. It was he who remained the small boy, with a taste for grisly jokes.

"Come, come, Laurence! Aren't you going to open the book?"

"Yes, of course! I—"

"Please observe the poor coward's expression, Miss Tennent. Alas, for my jests of long ago! He is in real terror—lest a toy snake should jump out when he opens the book. Rest assured, poor chap. On my honor, there is no toy snake inside."

"Let's see!" said Bill—and opened the book. Nothing seemed to happen. Inside was a thick end paper: a big map. Bill ran his left thumb partway down the edge of this very thick flyleaf, before putting his thumb inside to turn more pages. The next page he found blank, the third a genuine title page, the fourth, the fifth, the sixth . . .

Bill heard a soft titter, and his cheeks burned.

"Now look through your book, old chap. You will not be surprised if I find your fiancée more charming and more stimulating. Eh, Miss Tennent?"

Marjorie's voice had its former awe of their host. But there was an odd note in it now.

"I'm afraid, Mr. Hurst, you'll find me disappointing."

"You will find me only a boring pedant, my child. However!"

Lower your voice. Can you guess why I asked him those questions about Louis Quatorze?"

What was the matter with this infernal book?

Bill had searched everything, touched everything. Nothing seemed wrong; yet instinct told him it was more dangerous than any snake. Even while absorbed, he could still hear the conversation of the other two; but only far away, half-noticed.

"You see, Miss Tennent, I have more than hinted that Laurence's backwardness at school was not lack of intelligence, but stubbornness. The poor boy hates me. He would kill me if he dared."

The creepy voice seemed to hypnotize Marjorie, who did not answer.

"Particularly he hated me when I ridiculed him (good-naturedly, of course) for his denseness in literature and history. When I learned he was returning after his long absence, I wondered if he returned for revenge."

"Revenge?"

"S-s-h! More softly, my child. I do not mean revenge in any Monte Cristo sense. But how that boy would have loved to return and triumph over me in my own fields! He had eighteen years, and there were delays and long pauses between those sporting expeditions of his. He could have read until his brain almost burst. Once he could become dead to the world in some detective or red-Indian trash, just as you see him now."

It was a fair description of Bill. Finding that apparently the book was innocent of danger, he had read on in absorption.

"Oh, then that's all!" Marjorie gave a trembling little laugh. "You only mean he'd have loved to show he knew as much as you?"

"My child, do not dismiss the other matter. If I cannot keep the puppy's nose in the dirt, and one day you find my body strangled or . . . But his sweetest revenge, I fancied, might have been just what you mentioned. My notion was wrong. Even the simple historical questions I asked him . . ."

The gray head shook despondently.

"My child, I could not even question him in the modern fashion. Now your fine modern historian does not tell what happened; he tells why. He explains trends, movements, without regard to small human life."

From Bill, deeply engrossed, came a faint grunt of anger as though he half heard.

"True," the serene voice floated on, "one cannot adopt such tactics with a stubborn boy. One must intrigue him with battles and adventures, and picturesque stories. Would you believe, I could not even interest him in the story of Marie Antoinette and her diamond necklace?"

"Wasn't that," said Marjorie, with real enthusiasm now, "the enormous necklace Marie Antoinette refused to buy? Somebody else bought it without her knowledge, and it was stolen?"

"Well done, my charming one! One oaf we need not mention could not have done so well. The theft of the necklace was brought about by the so-called Count Cagliostro. . . ."

Then Bill spoke out, believing he was only mumbling to himself without even moving his lips.

"Don't talk such bloody nonsense!"

It ripped through the half-whispered conversation. The other two stiffened, and turned to look at him.

"That fat swindler Cagliostro," continued Bill, "for once wasn't guilty of theft. Read Vizitelly: still the best authority on the Queen's necklace. Read Funck-Brentano!"

The enormous silence smote him. Rousing himself, appalled, he looked up.

"Uncle Gay—" began the culprit, trying to retrieve the situation.

"I quite understand, Laurence." The voice was complacent, even a little pleased. "If you had heard what I told this young lady, you would know I had already suspected it. Do you imagine you could think of any scheme I should not anticipate?"

Bill rose to his feet.

"I see," remarked the mentor-satyr, "you have been gulping indigestible lumps of knowledge. They will hurt you, I fear. It is possible, dear boy, that in my chosen field you believe you can defeat *me?*"

"Easily." Bill, holding *African Game Trails* in one hand, noted the page number, shut the book, and put it down in the chair.

"Your impertinence, Laurence, has reached beyond insolence I shall deflate you a little with a few more questions about Louis Quatorze."

Bill, secure in his belief that Gaylord believed him to be Larry, lost his head.

"Louis Quatorze!" he snapped. "Now listen, you old swine! Your French is so intolerable that you can't even say names. Where did you learn it, anyway?"

There was a meeting of hatred like the flash of a blown fuse.

"Since your cultured ear may shudder at my accent," said Bill's adversary, smirking, "shall I again adopt Macaulay's term of Lewis the Fourteenth? I shall ask you . . ."

"Oh, no, you won't!" said Bill. "You answer *my* questions."

"By all means, dear boy."

"Lewis the Fourteenth!" Bill lit a cigarette, inhaled deeply. He fired queries like a machine gun.

"Who or what," he said, "most influenced his boyhood? Why was his brother such a trial to him? Through what female did he arrange the Secret Treaty of Dover; and why did her identity help so much? Who were his most notorious mistresses, and which led him back to religion? What was the policy of Colbert, his 'financial wizard,' and why did Colbert prove to be no wizard at all? What was the king accustomed to wear on his periwig? Name his barber. Why is it impossible that Fouquet . . ."

The face of the tutor-satyr was distorted.

"You will regret this, Laurence."

"You will learn something, Gaylord. Why is it impossible that Fouquet could have been the Man in the Iron Mask? What woman told the king that she smelled better than he did? What was the *Chambre Ardente?* Why was it set up and soon closed? In what four great battles was the king's power crushed on the Continent? Where and of what did he die? Fourteen questions for schoolboys, uncle. I will give you full marks if you answer seven."

The would-be pedant made a jerky move as though to lift his fist, but checked himself.

" 'A little knowledge is a dangerous thing,' " he murmured.

" 'A little *learning* is a dangerous thing,' " Bill retorted instantly. "If you must quote Pope, at least quote correctly."

"Ah!" There was a little gasp. "Then you have heard of Pope, too?"

Bill sat down, pushing the book to one side. He looked at his companion, whose eyes were fixed on the forbidden cigarette. Bill leaned forward.

" 'Willing to wound, yet afraid to strike.' " he quoted clearly. "Shall I continue? Or don't you recognize yourself?"

You could almost imagine the sound of the slap across Gaylord Hurst's face. He sat up straighter in his sloppy evening clothes, this crazy, childish, dangerous man.

"I informed you that you would regret this," he answered with great distinctness. "It is now time for you to be disciplined."

12 BRASS KNUCKLES IN THE DRAWING ROOM

BILL'S illegal uncle unexpectedly gaped his mouth wide open. Every one of his teeth was set wide apart in upper and lower jaw. They were decayed. The effect was that of a shark opening its jaws.

"Hatto!"

"I am here, sir," the bishop replied.

The voice was so startlingly close that Marjorie twitched her head round toward the far end of the sofa. Hatto stood well beyond the sofa, facing Bill. Beside him was a round Heppelwhite table, with a tray bearing a sherry decanter and two glasses.

"I have brought the sherry, sir. Dinner will be served in ten minutes."

"Sherry and dinner must wait. You must make an insolent boy scream for mercy."

"Very good, sir."

"But first you will take the Adam table with the Ming jade chess pieces into the anteroom. If so much as a wing were chipped, it would break my heart."

"Very good, sir." Hatto obeyed and returned almost immediately.

"Very well. Now draw back the sofa half a dozen feet. It will make a good space in front of me."

Marjorie sprang up from the sofa. "No!" she cried.

Hatto grasped the eight-foot sofa, and moved it back as gently as a perambulator on wheels.

"Hatto!"

"Yes, sir?"

"Please come round the far side of the sofa, and face Mr. Laurence from on my left."

"Very good, sir."

"Don't worry, angel-face," Bill said gently to Marjorie. "You thought Hatto was 'awfully distinguished-looking,' didn't you?"

Bill rose to his feet. He sauntered forward, a little out from the Chippendale table on his left. From four feet away he faced Hatto.

The tutor-satyr had been almost drooling with pleasure. "Hatto! Laurence! You will both take a pace forward, and shake hands."

Bill, trained from endless bag-punching and sparring in American gymnasiums, had felt a sober hope. Now he knew he was finished.

"Yes," the soft voice stabbed at his fears, "it is the ancient game of hand grip. Hatto will crush your hand and force you to your knees. I would not hurt you. A little praying for mercy, that is all."

Hatto stood like a wrestler, a lean giant above Bill. Bill stood sideways, weight on his right foot and left foot back.

"When you are ready," murmured the referee. "You will begin when I say 'Go.' "

"I regret this, Mr. Laurence," sighed the impassive bishop. "But Mr. Hurst has told you that an impertinent boy must be taught discipline."

"What about a damned impertinent servant?" asked Bill.

"Go!" whispered the referee.

Both right hands shot forward. Bill, as fast as a leopard, beat Hatto to the grip and wrenched on full pressure. Hatto's long fingers tightened round Bill's hand.

One second, two, three, four . . . At first it was less pain than excitement. Bill's lips were drawn back, the veins standing out at his temples. They stood locked, quivering, neither hand moving a fraction of an inch.

"Hatto"—Bill heard distantly—"you are not exerting your full grip. Don't play. Use it now!"

"Very good, sir."

Bill had heard of tropical fishes whose sting is agony. His grip wavered, almost gave way. His hand seemed crushed; it was as though blood spurted from under the nails.

Hatto, risking his balance, directed a vicious kick at Bill's right knee-cap. Bill staggered, but shifted his weight to his left leg. The shock cleared his wits as it cleared his dimming eyesight.

His left hand, unobserved, crept out to the table. His fingers touched metal. He slid the brass knuckles on his left hand.

Though his right hand was all but useless, his right knee buckling, he put out all strength to wrench that right hand up. It was easy. The crafty Hatto permitted it, because it would mean easier downward leverage when he broke Bill to his knees.

"My dear Laurence," cooed the referee, "distinctly I see tears in your eyes. Too much pain is repugnant to my nature. Only go on your knees, and ask for mercy—?"

"Oh, I think not," Bill managed to say. And a voice in Bill's brain whispered, *"Now!"*

His left leg and arm shot out. Bill's left fist, cased in brass and with nearly full body weight behind it, smashed into Hatto's body.

Many men, after that punch, would have bent double. Hatto did not. But his right hand instinctively loosed its grip. There was a "Whuh" of expelled breath. He bent forward, straightened, and took a few steps back.

Bill, wrenching loose his hand, threw the brass knuckles on the table and backed away with fists up.

How could you meet an opponent of long reach, except by

in-fighting? But when this opponent was a wrestler, his grip would lock your arms against your body. Nevertheless, Bill flung out his challenge:

"Now come on!"

And Hatto came on.

"No noise!" screamed the goblin in the wheel chair. "Whatever else, no noise! The flat beneath this"—even now Gay's taste must linger on titles—"is occupied by Admiral the Hon. Benbow Hooker. No noise!"

Hatto fired a left jab at Bill's head. Bill, blocking, closed in, and whacked another left into Hatto's belly. The right that followed hurt Bill, but he jolted in three more body punches before Hatto's arms found their grip. Bill tore free, danced back—and fell into the leather chair.

He was up in an instant, hurling the chair aside. From Marjorie came a small cry of triumph.

Marjorie didn't know. But Bill did. That was why nausea, dangerously near physical, sickened his throat now.

In front of him stood Hatto: unruffled, hands at his sides. Not one of Bill's body punches had hurt him, even made him breathe faster.

Bill had unconsciously pulled his punches even against Hatto, whom he hated. Even his power to hit like a mule's kick was drained away by some mental block, like Larry's fear of Mr. Hurst, whenever Bill faced a real opponent.

"Are you ready, Mr. Laurence?" asked Hatto, raising both hands to the level of his shoulders.

"I—"

Bill would be shamed and ridiculed as Gay wished. But, by God, he wouldn't back out!

"Come on, then!" he snapped at Hatto, and raised his hands.

Hatto edged forward poised for a paralyzing spring. . . .

At the same moment the front doorbell buzzed.

Hatto, straightening instantly into the pious bishop, glanced inquiringly at his employer. The employer, hesitant to break up such merry sport, nevertheless nodded toward Hatto. Marjorie stood up straight, her eyes narrowed.

Hatto, touching an already perfect white tie, marched out. All, except Bill, heard Hatto open the front door. They heard the visitor murmur questions; Hatto's grave replies; the startled queries now put by the visitor. . . . .

Bill was vaguely surprised to see Hatto march back from the anteroom, bend over Gay's chair, and whisper into his ear. The long face seemed angry and disturbed; then he almost smiled, and nodded.

When Hatto went out again, tension sang in the air like a

tuning fork. Marjorie moved swiftly across to Bill. Hatto threw open the double doors.

"Miss Joy Tennent," he announced.

13 THE GIRL IN GRAY, THE GIRL IN GREEN, AND JEALOUSY

JOY entered with a confident step. Her black hair fell to the shoulders of a long mink coat, over a green evening gown cut high and full above the waist.

Only her eyes showed indecision.

To Bill it seemed a miracle that he stood up cool and alert, prepared for trouble. Marjorie stood at his side, and he could almost feel her absolute calmness.

Joy knew that "Larry Hurst" and "Joy Tennent" were here. She had every reason to know the real Larry Hurst was dead. With a dozen words she could have wrecked everything.

But Joy's quick mind was already made up. With a firm step, and only a trace of archness, she walked toward the figure in the wheel chair and extended her hand.

"You're Mr. Gaylord Hurst, aren't you?" asked Joy, with the right blend of respect and friendliness. "Larry's shown me pictures of you, and I feel I know you already."

"Yes, I am Mr. Gaylord Hurst," replied that dignitary, who could not be bothered to shake hands. "At the same time, there seems to be—ah—some confusion here."

"Confusion?"

"Alas, madam! If there be any gay Lothario in our family, it must be dear Laurence over there. Curious! Most curious! He seems to have acquired two *fiancées* with the same name."

For an instant Joy stood rigid. Bill knew that she could ruin him in one minute. Joy was letting him stew while she made up her mind.

"Larry, you *naughty* boy!" Joy came toward him, dark-red lips pouting. "You ought to be killed for making me miss yesterday afternoon's plane." Her eyelids drooped with a suggestion not very subtle. "I ought to lock the door against you, oughtn't I? Every night for a week?"

Now Bill felt the shiver of Marjorie's shoulder against his arm. A new apprehension darted from an unexpected quarter.

'No more jealousy!' he prayed to her silently.

For the first time Joy seemed to see Marjorie. As though catching sight of an old friend, she uttered a cry of delight and threw out her arms.

90

"Why, Marjorie Blair!" she exclaimed. "Don't you remember me?"

Here Joy, as though unable to restrain emotion, threw her arms round Marjorie's neck. She stopped, as though appalled. "Darling! Don't tell me Larry—he's a *dreadful* liar when it comes to women—got round you in one day, and made you pretend to be me?"

Now Bill feared the explosion of all time. But he need not have. Marjorie was magnificent.

Straightening up in her close-fitting gray gown, she made the fashionable Joy look dumpy.

"My dear Miss . . . do forgive me if I've never heard your real name," Marjorie said gently. She smiled without offense, as at some maid who has blundered into the wrong room. "I'm certain this must be as embarrassing for you as for me. You say—er—you arrived back from America this evening."

Joy stood motionless. Hitherto she had only half noticed Marjorie as an unobtrusive secretary. Now she faced a dangerous opponent with charm, poise, and a subdued grand manner.

"Really—" Joy began, in an attempt to imitate the grand manner. She stopped. "I only came to see Larry's uncle."

"We are already late for dinner, madam. And I was not aware that my dinner engagement included you."

"Tomorrow morning, then?"

"I am never to be disturbed in the morning. Any of my many friends will tell you that."

"May I inquire," smiled Joy, still all allurement, "the name of your solicitors?"

"Madam, I cannot trouble myself to tell you. Solicitors bother me."

"At the same time," breathed Joy, "your New York solicitors are Amberley, Sloane & Amberley. George Amberley I know quite well. If he were to dig up certain information about poor Larry, and cable you, would it interest you at all?"

"Ah, that!" Glistening lenses of pure hatred turned toward Bill. "That would be different."

"I do so hate to interrupt your dinner, Mr. Hurst. But to prove I'm honest, may I ask him one or two questions? He won't dare deny them. May I ask the questions?"

"This too is different!" The other licked his lips openly. "Prepare, however, for a coward and a liar. Er—questions about what?"

"About our relations with each other."

Bill glanced at Marjorie. All Marjorie's queenly air was now gone. She stood near the sofa, the gray eyes shrinking as they watched.

'It isn't true, is it?' those eyes seemed to be saying.

Bill gritted his teeth. He dared not go outside what Joy could easily prove, but he had done nothing! Joy turned with pitying wistfulness.

"You're *such* a dreadful liar, darling," Joy observed—and that word "darling" made Marjorie jump. "But at least you can't say you never met me before, now can you?"

"No, I've met you. But only once: night before last, in New York."

Joy shook her head. "Well!" she sighed, "let's say once, anyway. At the very least. Where did you spend the night before last, and in what room?"

"At the Waldorf-Astoria Hotel. Room 932. But—"

"And where did *I* spend the night?"

"I don't know."

"Be careful, sweetheart. Now where was I registered? In the room next to yours? With a communicating door?"

"Yes! But I never saw you!"

"Was this door *ever* locked or bolted?"

"No. But—"

"Did you look into my room that night?"

"Yes, but it was dark. You—"

"We-el!" said Joy, cutting him short. "We'll allow you a bit of conscience if the room was dark and you didn't exactly see me. But"—her hand went up to his face, and caressed one cheek, "you felt me, at least. Like that? Or another way? What was the room like next morning?"

"You'd gone. Your luggage was gone. I mean—"

Joy swept in for the *coup de grâce*.

"For a man who didn't spend the night in my room, darling, you know a lot about it. And that photograph you took of me, in what old-fashioned people would call the 'altogther'? Why did you steal it?"

"*You* stole it!" retorted Bill. "It was in those papers I . . ." He stopped dead.

Marjorie, more straight and self-possessed than ever, her gaze passing over Joy, drew herself up.

"Under the circumstances, Mr. Hurst," she said lightly, "I'm sure you'll understand if I don't wait for dinner. May I have my wrap, please?"

"My dear child," said Mr. Hurst, with an evil leer, "it does you honor, and of course I understand. —Hatto! Miss Tennent's wrap! Quite rightly, you will forget my nephew. Please remember he is only an oafish schoolboy, more interested in clumsy caresses than true love. . . . Ah, here we are."

Hatto, materializing, put Marjorie's cape about her shoulders and immediately faded away to hold open the front door in the foyer.

"Yet I hope, my dear, that you will not forget a lonely man? You will call on me?"

"Well—" Marjorie began. Broken at last, she turned and hurried through the art gallery.

Bill heard the soft click of the closing front door. Then he dashed after Marjorie.

But up in front of him loomed the unruffled Hatto.

"It would be inadvisable, Mr. Laurence, to follow the young lady."

"Get out of my way, damn you!"

"It is futile, sir, to close your fists like that. You have already found that you cannot hurt me. Whereas, should Mr. Hurst instruct me to hurt you . . ."

Bill looked at his hands.

"I seem to have some kind of—of mental block," he said in despair. "But if I ever get over it, Hatto, then by the living God . . . !"

"Yes, sir," replied the bored Hatto. "You will find it safer, Mr. Laurence, to join your uncle in the drawing room."

Hatto marched away into the foyer. Bill rubbed his temples, and his eyes. Was he always to let down his friends?

With a vague idea of restoring circulation in his right hand, he began to flick the thumb against the second finger. He continued the gesture, mechanically, long after he had gone into the drawing room.

There, from the wheel chair, he heard the soft, deadly voice:

"—and I now request, madam, that you will be good enough to leave my house."

"But you're so *unreasonable!*" Joy protested archly.

Bill knew only he was so sick of Joy that he could hear her voice no longer. "You've heard my uncle's order," Bill said. "He's not to be disobeyed here. Now get out!"

Joy, hands on hips under the mink coat, gave him one of her most cryptic glances. Even now he could not deny that he thought her attractive.[5]

"Aren't you becoming a bit presumptuous, Mr. Laurence Hurst?" she asked, putting a sinister inflection on the name. "Your dear uncle isn't very nice. It wouldn't be pretty if I told what I know about . . . Laurence Hurst."

"Do what you ruddy well please," he retorted, "so long as I tell what really happened at Dingala's Bar."

Joy began to survey a point somewhat above his knees on the right hand side, and stopped.

---

[5] The lover of detective stories, than whom no nobler reader exists, may perhaps have come to suspect a too-old situation. Thus: that the hero, if we may so call the too-human Bill, believed himself to be in love with one woman (Marjorie) whereas he was subconsciously in love with another woman (Joy), thus helping in a plot twist at the end. This is entirely erroneous. Bill's allegiance, first and last, was to Marjorie and to nobody else. Discard answer number five.

"You wouldn't dare?" cried Joy, too shrilly.

Bill knew merely that he had found an advantage to get rid of Joy.

"Won't I?" he asked. "Mention this to any solicitor here, and, in good Americanese, I'll blow the town wide open!"

"You *filthy*—" Joy stopped.

"Good night. And clear out!"

Joy cleared out. The slam of the front door echoed through the flat.

"I thank you, Laurence."

"Not at all, Uncle Gay." Bill sat on the sofa.

"You would seem to have quite a way in managing your . . . tarts. I have no curiosity concerning what happened at Somebody's Bar; kindly do not bore me with it."

"I promise, thanks."

"Poor Laurence." Again the mock sympathy. "At the moment you wallow in self-pity. You have lost your *fiancée*, who is a lady and whom you do not deserve. You have been humiliated by Hatto. Now you begin to fear you will lose the game to me, and this is true. However, Laurence! You believe you have reached the last possible punishment and surprise. And you are wrong. Until we are at the dinner table, Laurence, and you learn of your last duty, believe me, you will not understand the meaning of surprise."

Hatto, from inside, slowly opened the third and last pair of double doors. "Dinner is served, sir," he announced.

Since they had been talking so much about Lewis the Fourteenth, Bill was not surprised to find the big, square dining room ornamented after the fashion of the Sun King's successor. The walls were set with gilt-twined panels of tapestries woven from the paintings of Watteau or Fragonard. Heavy gilt chairs were upholstered with damask. Over a dummy mantelpiece of marble hung a too-ornate gilded mirror. Though a glass chandelier hung from the ceiling the room was lighted only by two candles in crystal holders on the mottled-marble dining table.

This table, in the middle of the room, was set longways against two full-length windows. These windows, open under brocaded curtains, breathed in the cool fragrance of the Green Park.

Bill hurried over to one of the windows, and put his head out on its very small balcony with the wrought-iron rail.

The sky was not quite dark. He could see above the trees, to the south, the long front of Buckingham Palace, turned to pure white by floodlights. There was a murmur of voices under the tall lamps of the Mall.

"Hatto, my dear Laurence," said a soft voice, "prepares a

94

Potage St. Germain of no mean quality. It would be a pity to let it grow cold."

Hatto had already pushed in Gay's wheel chair. Setting the chair at one narrow end of the table, Hatto adjusted the lap robe and placed an open backgammon board in his master's lap.

"You will perceive, Laurence, I have before me only an empty plate and an empty glass. Between ourselves I am permitted food only once a day. My physician forbids me even wine, and says my weekly expedition to my club may kill me. Pah! We live only once—in the fleshly sense—and there I am as good as ever." His nod indicated Bill's side of the table, where Hatto had first held the chair and then disappeared through a small door.

The contents of the fine Sèvres dish had an appetizing odor. There was a delicate array of silver on each side, with two polished wine glasses and a brandy glass.

Bill found the very sight of food nauseating. But it was only common courtesy to try. The *Potage St. Germain* was excellent.

"You seem, Laurence, to have little appetite." The stab again. "No doubt you are wondering from where the lightning will strike. It will do you good to wonder. Eat."

The dining room was the darkest of all. Beyond the candles the spectacles were only large sinister blurs.

"By the way, Laurence. In those schoolboy questions concerning Lewis the Fourteenth, two were rather interesting. The lady whom you called 'his go-between' was of course the sprightly 'Minette,' of English birth and French training. She was unhappily married to Lewis's brother, the Duc d'Orléans. But she was much beloved by her brother-in-law, King Lewis, and her brother, King Charles the Second of England. After the signing of the treaty . . ."

The melancholy voice broke off. "I trust, Laurence, you did not really imagine I was floored by your futile questions?"

Bill put down the spoon.

"No," he answered honestly. "But I couldn't resist the temptation to upset your insufferable superiority. If anyone you considered an oaf suddenly fired unexpected questions at you, you would be too flabbergasted for a moment to think of the right answers. Before you could collect your wits, you made a common misquotation from Pope, and I pounced on it. You forgot anything except punishment. Admit, dear uncle, that I did a good job!"

Gaylord Hurst, as his enemies or friends could have testified, never admitted anything to his disadvantage.

From the open backgammon board on his lap, there was a

rattle and roll as "Lord Gay" threw dice from a box. Bill deduced that he kept the board hidden because he was not moving pieces; he was merely fascinated by the numbers.

"Ah!" he murmured. "Then you despise me. Is that it?"

"Perhaps it's too strong. Say rather I hold you in contempt."

Gay gave a nod. The dice rattled again.

The small door with a glazed panel opened to admit Hatto, bearing another dish and a bottle in a napkin. "Forgive me, sir." Hatto deftly removed the soup, and substituted an admirable Dover sole. The Chablis he held out to Bill; Bill finding it properly chilled, nodded.

"Admirable. Thank you."

"Thank *you* sir," replied Hatto, filling the glass and melting away.

"Now to return to our former discussion, Laurence. After the signing of the Secret Treaty of Dover, Minette returned to France. There, shortly afterward . . . ?"

"She died," answered Bill, swallowing wine before he could force himself at the sole. "For some time it was believed she had been poisoned. But later research has proved her death natural."

For a moment the scholar-satyr seemed to drop a few of his masks.

"The crime problems of history!" he whispered. "Has your cloddishness ever prompted you to study them?"

"Yes. Sometimes the story of history *is* the story of crime."

"At times, Laurence, you can make a remark almost intelligent," sneered the other. "Had you troubled to note my bookshelves, you would have found an extensive library on the subject. Had I shown you my room devoted to criminal relics . . . I saw you watching some few odd items on the table in the drawing room: some brass knuckles, a contemporary policeman's lantern. . . . Are you acquainted with a Mr. Ronald Wentworth?"

"Ronnie Wentworth? Of the Marylebone Library?"

"Ah? You know him?"

"Yes, I know him." Bill woke up.

"Quite possibly in connection with this rather absurd Sherlock Holmes Exhibition. Most of the real work has been done by a Mr. C. T. Thorne. For some reason this Mr. Wentworth, who assists when Mr. Thorne cannot be present, wrote to me. . . ."

"About your criminal relics?"

"In effect, yes. And I answered. He had the insolence to say that they already possessed a policeman's lantern; and that he could find no record in which Holmes—a fictitious character—had ever used brass knuckles. Not to have my name before the public . . . !"

"Yes. Bad luck."

The dice clattered across the board.

"My career, dear boy, will soon be terminated in a fitting manner. Do not be surprised if, in next year's Honours List," he spoke very carelessly, "you see your poor uncle mentioned as Lord Hurst of Beaulieu, in Hampshire. A somewhat higher distinction than your father's knighthood."

The spectacles seemed to become enormous, opaque.

"Meanwhile, Laurence, I wish to do something else. I have wanted to for more than thirty years. Now I am determined to."

"Oh? And what do you want to do?"

"I want to commit a murder."

Bill tried to manage a laugh, and failed.

"Rather a hazard, I should think. Have you decided on your victim? Whom do you want to kill?"

"You," the other said simply.

Quietly the dice were tilted out of their box, heard in faint rolling on the board.

"Good!" snapped Bill, a little shaken. "Don't you think I'd make any protest about it?"

"But, my dear boy. It is in the contract we both signed. —Not openly, I know. Let me state it thus. Over a period of six months, with your consent, I shall make one attempt to kill you. It may be at any time. Meanwhile, to make life amusing and trouble your nerves a little, there will be various false attempts."

"False attempts?"

"Mere trifles, dear Laurence! Some of them . . . good-natured practical jokes; just as in the old days! Others perhaps may hurt a little."

Viciously, now, the dice danced round in the box.

"A sporting proposition? For six months, your nerves and intelligence against mine. If I kill you, there's an end of it. If I fail, you inherit my fortune. Its size might astonish you."

"Now look here, Uncle Gay . . . !"

"I am a careful man, Laurence. Even after death duties and other inquities, it means over half a million. You need money, dear boy. You have almost finished the inheritance from your mother. Don't you want this money?"

Now Bill laughed aloud. "That's just the point," he said. "I don't want your damned money. You can take this fine inheritance and stick it. Have I made myself clear?"

"I cannot scare you, dear boy?"

"No!"

"I can make you feel no fear?"

"No!"

"Then you must not be aware, Mr. William Dawson, that I can get you a long term of penal servitude for impersonating my nephew?"

14 WILL YOU ROLL THE DICE FOR DEATH?

TO Bill the shock was so great that he remained motionless.

"Now if such a fantastic idea could ever be proved . . .

"Mr. Dawson, I detest bluff except when I apply it myself. I did not deduce this. I learned it for the most part from a letter, sent by air mail night before last."

Again he nodded. Hatto, carrying a salver with a few envelopes, put it down beside Bill.

"One moment. The sole is admirable, but I can't touch it. Please take it away."

"This is not to be wondered at. Hatto, you may remove the fish. But I think our guest deserves the best of our cherry brandy. I shall defy the doctor and join him. . . . Now, young man, kindly read the letter on top."

Bill saw that the thick envelope was in the stationery of Amberley, Sloane & Amberley, 120 Broadway. Amberley had remained in his office to type it himself, and, in an ominous way, he had referred to it the following morning. Again, in the secret moonlight, he heard Larry whisper, 'Mustn't make George suspicious!' And Joy's reply, 'Darling, do you think he isn't suspicious already?'

While Bill skimmed the letter, a malignant presence rolled dice and pounced on the damning points.

"You, Mr. Dawson, appearing unexpectedly to claim a small legacy from your grandmother. . . . hearing a conversation through a transom . . . Dear Laurence, stupid as ever, hearing an English voice, inviting you in. . . . Thenceforward, a baby could have seen all his questions were directed at an impersonation, since you both have light-brown hair and dark-brown eyes.

"But Laurence's last blunder! No sooner have you left than the dear boy suddenly puts all the money into a brief case, saying he is looking for a lavatory, and hurries after you. When he returns, Mr. Amberley casually touches the brief case and finds it flat. Could there be clearer presumption that you have received ten thousand dollars for impersonating him?"

"Presumption, certainly. But proof . . . ?"

"You underestimate *me*, Mr. Dawson. Do you imagine that, even before I received the letter this morning, I had not arranged for my nephew to be watched from the moment he arrived in London?"

"Watched?"

"What else? After going to the Albert Arms, Mr. Dawson, you went on a number of errands. One was to the Victoria-and-Albert Branch of the Midland Bank. There, in the office . . . do you recall that both windows were open because of the heat?"

Bill did recall it.

"My agent, of course, was outside the window. He saw, and heard, you—under your proper name—change something under ten thousand dollars into three thousand, three hundred and eighty pounds, some shillings and pence, which you deposited."

Bill saw the trap begin to close.

"Now these," mused the satyr, "were ordinary American banknotes except in one respect. In each packet was a single hundred-dollar note. Mr. Amberley—at my direction—asked the bank to take careful note of its serial number."

Yes; the trap was closing rapidly now.

"Now pick up the cablegram under the letter. It has been written but not dispatched."

The cablegram, addressed to Amberley and signed Gaylord Hurst, put the last touch to it.

PLEASE HAVE BANK CABLE SERIAL NUMBERS OF HUNDRED DOLLAR BILLS GIVEN MY NEPHEW TO HATFIELD MANAGER VICTORIA ALBERT BRANCH OF MIDLAND BANK LONDON POSSIBLY STOLEN AND MAY BE CRIMINAL MATTER SIGN CABLE NOT ONLY WITH YOUR NAME BUT NAME OF ANY LEADING POLICE OFFICIAL OTHERWISE KEEP MATTER QUIET.

"And," the soft voice gloated, "you may remember that for an offense like yours Arthur Orton, the Tichborne Claimant, received a sentence of fifteen years. And your money will go too."

Bill drew a deep breath.

"Well, you'd better call the police," he said. "My ineptitude deserves a few years in jail, anyway. But I can't understand that infernal contract!"

"No?"

"No! The only two conditions were that I—Larry, I mean—should return immediately to England, and visit you once a week."

"To study his reactions, Mr. Dawson, as week by week I played my little jokes before the kill."

"Yes. This escape-me-and-inherit-my-fortune business couldn't have been included by any lawyer; it would have been compounding a felony. Stop a bit! I did notice Mr. Amberley looking very doubtfully at the end of the last page."

"No. It was merely a harmless clause, in small print toward the beginning. Should any dispute arise between myself and my nephew, over conditions expressed or unexpressed, it stated I should be sole arbiter."

"In other words, if Larry refused to play clay pigeon in front of your gun, you could withdraw the inheritance?"

"Crudely expressed, but accurate. I hoped his real adventures had given him courage to reverse his role from the stalker to the stalked. But he is still a coward. He sent you. By the way, where is he?"

"I don't know," Bill said truthfully. "I never got a note of his last address."

"No doubt he is lying low. If found, he would stand in the dock with you."

Bill flung off the mood. In front of him—mysteriously since he had not seen Hatto—was brandy. Another glass stood in front of his host, a decanter between. Snatching up the glass, Bill rose and prepared for a wild toast.

"Before you speak," the torturer interposed, "let me analyze your character, Mr. Dawson. You are overimpetuous. You are overquixotic. From my knowledge of men, I should have judged that you cared even less for money, as such, than you said you did."

Bill lowered the glass.

"And yet . . . this rather trifling sum, which you gained from impersonating Larry, must mean a great deal to you?"

"It means everything in the world," said Bill. Then embarrassed, he swung up the glass. "Here's to crime!" he cried. "And when do you ring for the coppers?"

"One moment," the other said softly.

The dice rattled gently out of their box, and were snatched back again; as though Gaylord Hurst were again at cat-and-mouse.

"Forget your troubles," suggested the older man. "Suppose there were a way out?"

"Suppose there were a way out?" Bill repeated.

"Suppose you were never prosecuted by me or by anybody else? And that you were permitted to retain every penny of your money in the bank?"

"How could I get that chance?"

"Easily. You could play the part I originally assigned for my shrinking nephew."

The dice rattled softly in their box.

"For a period of—come, Mr. Dawson, I'll make it easier —for three months you would pit your wits against mine. You would try to outguess me, to outmaneuver me. I will kill you, be assured of that. But keep your life—if you can. Of course, the matter of an inheritance is finished. But, if you were sure of freedom from prosecution and sure of keeping your money, would you agree to my proposition?"

"Would I!" Bill breathed. "Like a shot! —But what assurance have I got?"

"My word of honor, for instance?"

"Sir," returned Bill in his most polished manner, "you must concede that your word of honor is, if anything, somewhat less reliable than that of the late Adolf Hitler."

"And yet I accept yours without question. However, you are right. I must give you proofs. Will you be good enough to take the next envelope from the salver? Thank you. Now open it; it is from Amberley, Sloane & Amberley. What is it?"

"Why . . . this is the original contract! The one I signed in Amberley's office as witness. Come to think of it, you usually sign duplicate copies. But we didn't!"

"Come, Mr. Dawson, you are not very observant. No: in case my nephew later attempted to make legal trouble, I asked for one copy only. —Now burn it."

"Burn it, sir?"

"I trust I make myself clear. Push away the last remaining envelope, and burn it in the salver." Though Bill's lighter at first had difficulty with the backing, the document presently whirled into a sheet of fire, and was reduced to black powder in the salver. "Now! The only contract is gone. Though a dozen witnesses swore to it, you could not be prosecuted for anything arising out of it. Any solicitor will tell you that."

"But the money?"

"Please open the last envelope. Even though I knew that 'William Dawson' was an impostor, I presumed him to be a man of some mettle. I instructed my London solicitors to draw up two copies of the document inside. I have signed both. Please examine both; there is no trick."

And there was no trick. Bill opened the top copy.

I, Gaylord Hurst, do depose and state as follows: 1. That I have caused to be paid through (name and address of Amberley's firm) the sum of ten thousand dollars ($10,000) to my nephew, Laurence Hurst; that the said Laurence Hurst, through my instructions and full consent, has paid the said sum to William Dawson, only son of the Rev. James Dawson, of Sandsrun, Sussex. 2. That I, Gaylord Hurst, give to the said William Dawson this sum of ten thousand dollars ($10,000) without any claim, condition, or attachment whatever.

"Do you find it satisfactory?" asked the lord of subtlety. "Take one copy; leave one for me. It will be perfectly harmless should either copy be found, yet it assures your money."

"Then it's accepted as from now. Are you prepared for everything, Mr. Hurst?"

"Are you prepared for death, Mr. Dawson?"

"If you can manage it, Old Satyr. Like a side bet of ten to one you can't?"

"Your offer is foolish, Mr. Dawson. You will assuredly die. Of course, there are certain conditions in the original document: that you will call on me once a week, so that I may see your nerves shredding away bit by bit?"

"Granted. And you'll find nothing wrong with my nerves."

"I wonder! However, second and last: you will mention no word of our little pact to anyone?"

"Granted. We've compounded a real felony this time."

"And yet, I fancy, you must have said some word to your delectable former *fiancée*, Miss Tennent."

Bill, startled, remembered Gay meant Marjorie.

"She knows me as Bill Dawson. I told her I was impersonating Larry, and nothing else."

"Excellent. I must warn you," the murmur grew even softer, "I mean to take her from you. You smile? But it will happen. In any case, you cannot much longer enjoy her charms. You will be dead.

"However, in fairness, I grant you one condition. When you come to die, it will be no crude performance. No hired thug will shoot from ambush. No one will strangle you from behind. My legs are in good shape. At the end you shall see *me*, and know me.

"True," the torturer continued offhandedly, "I cannot trouble to deliver my . . . pleasant jokes, or the like. That would be fatiguing. The post, a messenger, some unknown lounger who does not know what he is doing . . . these will suffice."

"Oh?" said Bill. "Then what about your Scotland Yard man? Chief Inspector Partridge? The agent you employ in the Victoria Arms, just across the road?"

The other's face lengthened with what Bill could have sworn was genuine astonishment.

"Scotland Yard?"

"Yes! Watching my window with field glasses from across the street?"

"I am sure that your nerve strain must be working already. I give you my solemn word that I employ no agent whatever in the Victoria Arms or anywhere near there." [6]

"But—"

"Mr. Dawson, is your ignorance of police procedure so great that you imagine a Chief Inspector would watch windows at the request of a private person?"

Bill looked at the man's mouth and wondered.

"Tell me something, Mr. Hurst. I'm not your nephew; I'm a stranger. Yet you seem to hate me more than Larry himself!"

The voice grew all the more deadly.

"Rather more, Mr. Dawson. If anything, much more."

"But why?"

"This evening, Mr. Dawson, though I knew you for an imposter, you almost deceived *me*. And that, Mr. Dawson, is not done to me with impunity."

Bill gave him a disgusted look, but said nothing.

"Finally, you attacked me with an unexpected burst of historical questions. You upset my dignity. On several occasions, by accident, you bested me in repartee. No man makes a fool of me and lives."

Bill wished he could see behind the spectacles, at what really crawled in the eyes. Gaylord Hurst might be a plain lunatic. Yet he was clever, ingenious—and he meant business.

"In that case," said Bill, "I'd better cut along now; it's nearly a quarter to ten; and let you plan my murder."

"That? It was planned long ago."

"Oh?" Bill was not quite jocular. "Is it . . . quick?"

"In a sense, yes. In another sense, no."

"Hardly matters, does it? Look here, I must rush!"

"Already, then, your nerves are on edge? . . . But, before I summon Hatto, may *I* give you the toast?"

"With great pleasure!"

"Then—a good death to you, young man!"

"And to you, sir," Bill replied suavely, "a more comfortable damnation than you are likely to receive."

He swallowed about half the cherry brandy, which was-

---

[6] This may be accepted as true. The jaded reader, finding Bill bewildered among so many apparent impossibilities, must have suspected that he was the victim of a long string of lying witnesses all bribed or coerced to deceive him. This device is so easy as to be contemptible. It is the essence of fair-play detective fiction that one guilty person shall deceive a dozen innocents, not that a dozen guilty shall deceive one innocent. In the plot involving Bill, there was one master criminal, and only one. Though this criminal may be said to have had an accomplice, the accomplice knew nothing of what end was in view. All other characters speak innocently or unwittingly; in short, without knowing any plot existed. The reader must be warned, however, against any obvious choice for one criminal murderer. Discard answer number six.

sharp, with a bitter-sweet odor which reminded Bill of . . . of . . . Glancing across the table, he saw that the other glass had not been touched. It seemed to him that Gaylord wore a faint smile.

"Oh . . . Hatto," said Gaylord, as Hatto appeared beside the table, "I regret that Mr. Laurence must leave us. Would you mind finishing Mr. Laurence's brandy?"

"Not at all, sir, if you wish it." Taking the glass by the stem, Hatto swallowed the brandy and put down the glass. Did Bill only imagine that Gay's smile was now sardonic?

"Pick up the dice, Hatto; put them into the board; leave it here. You may then push my chair out to the front door."

In the drawing room, Bill looked instinctively at the Chippendale table as they slowly moved.

"On your next visit, Laurence," the Clever One was prattling, "you must see my room of criminal relics. You might fancy my air guns: Not the doubtful air gun used by Colonel Moran in these Holmes fantasies; but the modern Spandau, devised for German Commando raids, with very high velocity at short range, and only a sharp click to . . ."

"Ah! No! Stop!" Here Hatto ceased to push the chair. "You are looking, Laurence, at my brown poison bottles with the formula on each bottle."

"Er—haven't I a topcoat somewhere?"

"I think of issuing a slender volume (perhaps five hundred presentation copies when I am Lord Hurst) concerning popular ignorance about poisons, especially those which act on the bloodstream."

"But there's no misconception about potassium cyanide, is there?"

"No, none." The Clever One was impatient. "Now, that bottle on the extreme right contains one of the most misunderstood poisons in fiction. Our old friend curare. And how small a quantity, they think, is needed to kill! Talk of poisoned pins is laughable."

"Look here, sir—"

"Suppose you wished to murder a friend, let us say, by smearing curare on his safety-razor blade, in the hope he might cut his finger. Curare is a thick dark-brown liquid. One blade could not suffice. How could you manage two, three . . . Am I boring you?"

"I should rather like to get home."

Bill hurried forward. The wheel chair suddenly stopped again.

"Come, Laurence! Aren't you forgetting your book?"

"Book?"

"The copy of *African Game Trails*. I bought it especially for you."

Bill dashed back to the chair and picked up the thick volume. Then his eyes narrowed. For a long time it had lain unattended in that chair. Time for somebody . . .

Conscious of eyes, he opened the book and leafed through it with the most careful scrutiny. It was quite harmless, just as before. Nevertheless, gripping the book, he resolved it should not leave his hand again.

"How suspicious our dear lad has become!" tittered the trickster. "Forward, Hatto!"

With strong relief Bill found himself in the foyer at the front door. Hatto held his topcoat, and he thrust both arms into the sleeves. His now discredited uncle, making no move to shake hands, seemed drowsy.

"Oh . . . Hatto," he remarked. "What is a week from today?"

"I make it the 21st of June, sir."

"Then shall we make it the 21st, Laurence? At nine o'clock? Would that suit you?"

"Perfectly," returned Bill, still gripping the book.

"As I think I remarked, you are one of these nervy, highstrung people. It will be a pleasure to watch your reflexes a week from tonight. *A'voir.*"

Bill, emerging from the house into the cooler air of St. James's Place, allowed only one thought to enter his mind, the inconsequential rambling idea which had struck him when he first saw 68. 'With those wide window ledges and flimsy long windows,' he decided, 'a man with a good hook at the end of a rope could burgle that house quite easily.'

He hastened under the gloomy gas lamps of St. James's Place, turned left into St. James's Street, and arrived at the bus stop just as a number 8 rolled in and stopped. Bill, swinging aboard past an old-fashioned bus conductor, clattered up the stairs to the top deck.

It was deserted. Bill sat down halfway up. The starting bell pinged; the red monster rumbled and nosed out. Bill sat back.

As soon as he reached his flat and a telephone, he would find Marjorie's address, think of a plan of campaign, and see her tonight.

Opening *African Game Trails*, he automatically ran his left thumb down the edge of the thick end paper, put the thumb inside and suddenly stopped.

His left thumb and the palm of his right hand were partly covered with blood.

Despite the shock, he felt calm. He looked closely at the end paper down which he had run his thumb. Concealed to sight

105

or touch from the side by the very thick paper, ran the edges of three safety-razor blades set in line. There were traces of some brownish substance. . . .

"Curare is a thick dark-brown liquid."

Automatically, since his palm was thick with blood, Bill gasped the covers, flicking the book forward and holding it out so that drops should not fall on his clothes. A white card like a visiting card—covered with microscopic blue handwriting—fluttered to the floor.

Bill put the book, closed, on the seat beside him. His right hand whipped out a handkerchief, swabbed his left hand, and fastened the cambric as tightly as possible round his thumb. He reached down and picked up the card, which read thus:

> No, the razor blades are not poisoned. But they might have been. You see how easy it is to take you off guard? Having . . .

Bill had not heard footsteps approach along the aisle.

"Anything wrong, guv'nor?" asked the bus conductor, both sympathetic and conspiratorial.

"No! I cut my thumb on some sharp paper in a book somebody gave me. This is the card that went with it."

His eyes returned to the card.

> Having twice examined a harmless book, you were determined not to let it leave your hand again. Yet you suffer from a mental blind spot common to many. No man can keep a book in his hand when he thrusts both arms into the sleeves of a coat. Seldom . . .

Bill twitched the card over.

> Seldom does he even notice when someone behind him—myself—slips the book from his hand as the arm goes through the sleeve, and in the same flash returns it on the other side. What I returned was a different and already prepared copy lying under my lap robe. No poison; but can you have any hope of matching wits with me?

Bill put the card into his waistcoat pocket. The bandaged thumb was crimson.

"Yer thumb, eh? Naow you tyke my tip, sir. 'Op orf at a chemist's and 'ave it seen to properly. Yer never knows."

Cold reason told Bill that the lunatic Gay would not attempt even a near kill on the very first night. At the same time . . .

"But what chemist would be open at this hour?"

" 'Seasy! There's the orl-night *Boots*' in Piccadilly Circus. Don't wyte for a stop. I'll tyke a penny fare and drop yer off 'eere. *Come* on, naow!"

Catching up the book lest it should hurt someone else, Bill clattered down after him.

The big, quiet shop was half deserted. A cheerful chemist in white coat and pince-nez swabbed the wound while he heard Bill's—partial—story.

"Nothing much wrong here," said the pince-nez. "You won't even need a stitch."

"But those . . . razor blades. That dark-brown stuff you see there—?"

"That's iodine. You've got a damn silly friend, but he wouldn't let you be infected."

Bill's pulse slowed to normal. With deft fingers the chemist dealt with everything.

The chemist looked up automatically at the clock, whose hands indicated one minute to ten o'clock. "Wish I'd got off tonight. Program on the wireless they've been shouting about for weeks. *Fateful Lightning*: ten-thirty . . . what's wrong?"

Back to Bill flashed a promise he had forgotten. They expected him at the B.B.C. Walter Kuhn, producing *Fateful Lightning*, wanted him to vet a part of the script. In the listening room he was to meet the oily Cheever, and afterward meet Cheever for a talk about Marjorie.

Catching up *African Game Trails*, paying his account, Bill ran for the street and hailed a passing taxi.

"Broadcasting House," he said.

15 THE STALKER ON THE STAIRS

BILL, who had not gone through the revolving door of Broadcasting House since the end of the war, moving a-clatter across the silent temple, selected a reception girl with a friendly eye and gave his name.

"Oh, Mr. Dawson! Of course!" She flicked cards. "You're to meet Mr. Cheever in the listening room in 8-A." The girl cast a look to the right. "But I'm afraid the lifts aren't working." Her look suggested that something always went wrong. "Studio 8-A is on the top floor. You'll have to walk up."

"Oh, I'm in good health."

"Then you don't mind? The stairs are over there on the left side of the lifts. Follow them straight up."

The stairs, of ringing marble, were enclosed on the right by the opaque lift shaft and on the left, after the first curve, by a wall which shut you in. There was an open space only when you emerged at a floor—and crossed to take the next staircase on the far side to the floor above. Your steps rang. Though a few glass panels were illuminated, their light might have come from torches inside a pyramid.

Bill, walking slowly, wished he could get rid of *African Game Trails*. But to tear out the razored end paper and throw it into a litter bin would be as bad as throwing away the book itself. As he moved upward, Bill allowed himself to consider the last little joke of Gaylord Hurst.

Whether you opened that end paper with your left thumb, or your right thumb, or even your right forefinger, poisoned blades would have caught you. Cripple-minded Gaylord read your every thought.

How many men, even if they noticed a book had left them and been returned after the dart of an arm through a coat sleeve, would dream it was not the same book? Gay found the blind spot.

"Can you have any hope of matching wits with me?"

Theoretically, for sheer crazy ingenuity, no. Yet Bill swore to manage it, if only by adjusting his brain to think like Gay. For some reason this revolted him, as did the remembrance of Gaylord himself; old satyr Gay, who had calmly announced that he meant to seduce Marjo . . . stop! To imagine Marjorie in Gay's grasp was nauseating. To think personally of Gay, without merely studying to outwit him, would be fatal.

Bill grew suddenly alert, hesitated, and then went on without a break.

Somebody was following him up the stairs, with a new stroke of danger instantly to follow the other.

True, the follower might be innocent. But the rhythm of the footsteps, exactly matching Bill's, was suspicious. When Bill deliberately hesitated, so did the stalker.

Alert to complete coolness, Bill meditated plans as he went on. 'Got to get a look at the blighter,' he reflected. 'Got to fetch him into the open. Haven't been counting floors. But the next must be the sixth. Can't dash back; he might get away. No: cross the sixth floor, use Old Snuffy's trick on the stairs to the seventh, and then catch him—flat-footed—when he comes to the seventh floor.'

Bill went up to the sixth floor. There he ran swiftly across the strip of carpet to the far side, where the next flight ran up. Sitting down on the third step, he removed one shoe.

'Good old Snuffy!' he thought. The late Mr. Horace Snufferley, an unpopular housemaster at Bill's preparatory school, had been fond of catching small wretches out of their cubicles, following lights-out. Beginning at the end of the corridor, he would remove his left shoe and then run toward a suspected card game at the other end. His stockinged foot made no noise. The sound of his shoe, spaced out, was that of a man walking heavily but slowly. . . .

With his left shoe in his left hand and the book in his right, Bill raced up the stairs. In the stillness the right shoe seemed to have a trampling beat. Below him the slow, light tread of the stalker kept its rhythm.

Only a second to go, now! Then Bill's stockinged foot slipped on the marble. He all but pitched backward, righting himself only by a stamp of both feet. The step of the stalker hesitated, as though wondering. But it came on. Every echo was magnified.

Bill gained the seventh floor long ahead of the pursuer. Stooping down to put on and lace his shoe, he glanced round.

Facing each line of lifts, with their marble enclosures and stairwell on both sides, Bill saw what looked like a block of offices with corridors on each side. Pale light from the corridor on the left, past which the stalker would have to go if he followed, lay just ahead of the concealing marble round which he must appear on his way up. The whole space behind Bill was almost dark.

Backing away toward the next flight, Bill moved out to the middle of the carpet. Though it was shadowy on the far side, he could not fail to see the stalker.

Though his topcoat weighed him down a little, and his collar was wilted, Bill found his muscles loose and easy. Softly he put the book on the floor, to have both hands free.

That ominous footfall, never changing pace, drew near the top of the stairs.

Now it stopped dead at the top. Bill, watching from a distance of thirty feet, with his back toward a wall more than thirty feet behind, could see anything which appeared round the corner.

And nothing appeared. The stalker knew. He was waiting.

'Got to rush him,' Bill decided. 'I can cover thirty feet in nothing flat. Then . . .'

Now something did appear, only a foot above the floor. At that distance it was like a small oval shape: with a faint gleam as it moved back and forth, side to side, and then vanished.

A mirror, of course! The stalker, looking sideways, could

discern Bill's outline as the latter stood in a space not altogether dark.

'Quick, now!' Bill lowered his shoulders, tightened his muscles, and crept forward. 'A long jump when I'm close. Grab him and hold. If he's too big, chuck him down the stairs. He'll . . .'

Suddenly, and apparently without co-operation of hand or body or head, there slid round the corner at waist height a press camera fitted with flash bulb. The lens turned to seek Bill, who leaped forward.

The flash glared out, blinding and momentarily paralyzing him.

Past Bill's right arm a jab and hiss of compressed air jolted his arm and shoulder. At the same moment he heard the sharp click from the camera a shade after the smash of the bullet into the wall far behind him.

Snatching up the book, Bill leaped for the next stairway and raced for the floor above.

"The modern Spandau air pistol, devised for German Commando raids, with a very high velocity at short range, and only a sharp click to . . ."

Bill, breathing hard, remembered those words as he reached the floor above. In an open street, with an air pistol concealed inside a camera—no flash from the lens, no report, a click unnoticed in traffic—any alleged press photographer could kill without suspicion. Especially if he let the flash bulb go later, while apparently photographing somebody else. . . .

Bill looked round wildly. This floor—it must be the top floor, with Studio 8-A not far away!

But it wasn't the top floor. That he always recognized. Either they hadn't adopted the usual process of failing to count the ground floor, or he had miscounted on his way up.

Slowly, never ceasing, the footfalls of the stalker were coming up behind him. Bill didn't want to plunge into the studio out of breath. He went up at a quick but moderate pace. The other footsteps exactly matched his.

'You—cannot—escape,' those steps seemed to beat. 'I—shall—find—you. I—am—death.'

Galvanized, Bill ran to the next floor. This was the right floor at last. Straight down a long and lighted corridor, the swing door to the studio faced him, with its round glass panel. At right angles, in the wall to the left, was the same kind of door to the listening room.*

If the stalker meant murder, and Gay's assurance meant anything, the stalker could be only one person.

---

* In America called "control room," just as the English "producer" is the American "director."

16 STUDIO 8-A—AND THE BLACK PHOTOGRAPHER

BILL heard the inexorable steps reach the top of the stairs. He raced down the corridor and swung left at the large, heavy door of the listening room. Glancing through the glass panel, he pushed open the door.

There was a haze of tobacco smoke and the air of nervous hilarity which precedes a big broadcast. Four faces turned toward Bill, with pleased recognition.

"Bill Dawson, you so-and-so!" A girl's voice.

"The old Squadron Leader himself!" A *basso profundo*, tuned to friendliness.

"Bill, you should have taken up radio!" A baritone, quizzical yet serious.

"Bill, what's wrong? Have you been in a fight or something?"

The last voice was another girl's, Bee Roberts, the Programme Engineer, who sat at the control panel, dark eyes dancing.

Beside her was the broad back of Walter Kuhn, he of the quizzical yet serious voice. Beyond Bee Roberts, on the other side of the control panel, sat Walter's secretary, Norma, with stop watch, red pencil, and marked script. All three were listening to loud-speaker strains of "Dixie."

The listening room was long and wide, because of the immense studio outside. In the far corner, in a chromium chair, sprawled the muscular length of Del Durrand, of the deep voice, the best narrator in radio.

"Dixie" faded away. Walter Kuhn snapped the switch of the talk-back. "That's it," he said. "Take a short break, everybody. But don't leave the studio."

He clicked back the switch. A confused murmur and orchestra tuning flowed in. Automatically he glanced at the clock. It was ten minutes past ten.

Walter got up and turned round, displaying a square face with an engaging smile. He shook hands with Bill. "Here, Bee's right! What sort of fight have you got yourself into?"

Bill, very conscious of his bandaged thumb, saw for the first time that the sleeve of the topcoat had been ripped open above the right elbow. Though the bullet from the air pistol had not grazed him, its drive past had left a painful abrasion.

"Now listen," Bill told them in deep earnest, "I haven't been in a fight. But some crackpot photographer has been following me about. This crackpot may look in through the glass panel of the listening room. If he does . . ."

Bill moved backward, and bumped into another person.

The girl, in a white shirt and khaki shorts, was one of those Junior Programme Engineers better known as Jeeps. She presided over a long "gram-bank" set with moving turntables for records.

Bill apologized and backed away. The girl, grinning, shuffled records in a rack above.

"Er—this is Felicity," smiled Walter, nodding in paternal fashion. "Now let's get this in order, Bill. A loony photographer is chasing you. He may look in here. If he does, what then?"

"As soon as I see him, if I do see him," pursued Bill, "I'll duck low and run for the door. I'll pull it *inward;* got that?"

Del Durrand sat up at full height, his long face animated.

"You're considerate, Bill. You mean you don't want to bat him silly?"

"No, that isn't the idea. As soon as I get outside, I want to prevent him from running back toward the lifts. You and Walter follow me instantly. The game is to force him through the other door and into the studio."

"But why into the studio?" demanded Walter, his forehead furrowing as he looked at the clock.

"I'll explain later. —No, it won't be during transmission, Walter! If that happens, I'll ease him away and let him . . . photograph me."

Walter's taste for devilment triumphed over his seriousness. "We-el!" he said, quizzical though a trifle dubious. "If this should come soon, perhaps we have a bit of fun and jump on the loony's camera, eh?"

"Norma!" said Bill. "Bee! I'm very sorry about this. . . ."

"Do you think we should miss it for anything?" whispered Norma. "Besides, it ought to be much funnier than . . ."

"Norma!" warned Bee, looking stern. "But isn't there any way we could help, Bill?"

"You might, at that. I hope I spot this bloke as soon as he turns up. But if anyone else spots him—I mean, any face you don't know—; go on with your work; but just say . . . say, '*Black Whiskers,*' so that I hear it."

"Has he got black whiskers?" Durrand asked quickly.

"No; he's more likely to have bifocal spectacles. But I'm not sure. Walter, I'm sorry to have bothered you with all this. Now what is it you want me to do? Vet part of the script, isn't it?"

Now he knew there was something wrong here.

"Yes. Oh, yes!" Walter nodded quickly. "It's only a very

short scene, but it's at the very beginning. It's a meeting of Lincoln's Cabinet, just after Beauregard has fired on Fort Sumter."

"What's the overall timing on that?" Bill heard Walter ask Norma.

"The whole business is two-fifteen."

"Let's run through the lot just once more." Walter consulted his watch. "It's not quite ten-fifteen now. Plenty of time. Bill! Got to leave you a moment. I must make sure everybody's there. No, don't bother with a script; we'll do the first two minutes and fifteen seconds." Walter almost bolted out of the door.

Bill for the first time looked properly out of the glass panel into the studio. The main microphone stood some distance out in front of the window. Near it was a high wooden stand bearing the green bulb for a cue light. Studio 8-A, very large, had at times a bad echo. Padded screens were on either side of the main microphone.

Down the loud-speaker into the listening room flowed the plunks and twiddles of tuning instruments, the buzz of conversation.

Bill looked past the screens and saw the full twenty-piece orchestra. For the Drama Department to get any orchestra was like drawing teeth. Still, this show was Cheever's baby. Del Durrand, as narrator, had a screen-enclosed booth with table mike and small green bulb. But there were other open mikes, at one of which two absorbed Jeeps were snapping the breech bolts of ancient rifles.

At Bill's side loomed the giant figure of Del Durrand. "Got any use for this?" Del murmured.

From his right hip he pulled out a .38 revolver almost as big as his own hand.

"Where'd you get that?"

"It's mine," said Durrand. "We live in the country, and my wife is nervous if I'm late. Come to think of it, *she* ought to have it. Any good to you?"

"Could I borrow it until the end of the show?"

Bill slipped the .38 into his topcoat pocket. Del, hurrying out script in hand, almost cannoned into Walter. Walter—never out of temper, endlessly patient, now had faint sweat on his forehead. An instant silence followed his departure. Walter sat down and clicked the switch.

"Stonewall Jackson!" he shouted at the talk-back. "Where the hell is Stonewall Jackson?"

The switch clicked again. Whispers, through which clove the clear voice of a young Jeep.

"I'm sorry, Mr. Kuhn. He's down in the canteen having a coffee with George Washington."

A small hypodermic of dread struck Bill. "Look here, Walter. You haven't by any chance got General Washington in the Civil War?"

"No, no! He's a spirit. He speaks kindly both to Lincoln and Jefferson Davis."

The talk-back clicked again, while Bill drew up a chair closest of all to the door.

"Sorry for being impatient," Walter's good-nature flowed out through the talk-back. "He's not in the first scene, but be sure he's here. Ready now?"

Various "readies" came back, including that of a well-dressed careless-seeming man, the announcer, at one side of the main microphone. Nobody else was there.

"For the last time, please," Walter spoke almost gently. "President Lincoln! William H. Seward! Edwin M. Stanton!"

Three men wheeled abreast round one far end of the padded curtain stand, and marched like soldiers to the microphone.

For the last time Walter addressed the talk-back.

"I'll give you a hand cue, Franz," he told the orchestra leader. "Now. We go in—" he looked up at the clock—"five seconds."

The switch clicked for the last time. There was no reason why Bill should tremble in anticipation. Yet he did.

Walter, rising and moving over, gave a hand cue to the orchestra leader. Norma's stop watch clicked for a timing. Clearly and sharply, a bugle call rattled out.

A green cue light flashed on by the main microphone. The announcer leaned forward.

"Tonight," he said with no mean sense of the dramatic, "we present Monica Carslake and Robert MacTavish in . . ."

Felicity, the girl at the gram-bank, whipped down a record to the turntable, held the needle ready for the yellow pencil mark which told the exact band, and dropped the needle. A long peal of thunder from the record was instantly faded by Bee's expert hand to an angry growl through which the announcer's voice rang clearly:

"*Fateful Lightning*," he said. "The Story of the War Between the States."

Walter threw another cue. The music took up rather slowly, with a tinge of sorrow, the strains of "When Johnny Comes Marching Home." A green light flicked on beside Del Durrand's table mike. And Del's superb voice touched every line with sympathy.

114

" 'By the flow of the inland river, whence the fleets of iron have fled . . .' "

Del, altering tempo, gave so short, vivid, and accurate an account of the causes leading to the war that—paradoxically—Bill's attention began to wander.

For this stuff was magnificent! Where could anybody suggest an improvement? Bill's eyesight felt dull and strained. He had been rubbing his eyes or knuckling them with his fingers all day. His temples felt hot.

Suddenly he darted a look at the panel in the door. The stalker couldn't keep away forever. Bill's right hand dropped into the pocket of the topcoat, and touched the .38. If Gaylord Hurst were lunatic enough to kick open the door and fire point-blank, then he would pump every bullet into the loathsome old goat if he hanged for it.

As a result, Bill missed the end of Del's first narration. He missed the rap of the fatal date in April, 1861; and the boom of the opening gun against Fort Sumter.

Brooding, feeling very hot, he was faintly conscious of more music, and of Del's fine voice describing the Cabinet meeting at the White House, and the great gaunt President sitting at the head of the council board.

Bill woke up with a start. The music was "The Battle Hymn of the Republic." That Mrs. Howe had not written it as early as 1861 was an easily pardonable artistic license.

The announcer had stepped back, leaving one side to the youthful President Lincoln, ready to sound like fifty-two.

"Now get this, you mugs!" grated out President Lincoln, in a voice suggesting Edward G. Robinson in one of his tougher roles. "They've muscled in on Fort Sumter, lamebrains. And I'm the Big Shot of this outfit, see? I'm gonna have war if every doggone one of you votes against me!"

Bill fell backward in his chair; literally.

"You said it, Mr. President!" piped up William H. Seward, Secretary of State, played by a little wizened man with a testy voice. "It's a cinch! Grant will go through them Confederates like a dose of salts!"

"Nuts, Mr. Secretary," retorted the rich baritone of Edwin M. Stanton. "Don't be too cocky. They say this guy Lee has got plenty on the ball."

From the loud-speaker rang out a long flourish of trumpets.

"Mr. President!" called a dapper young man.

"Now look, Hay! I can't have my sekkatary buttin' into a private conference that . . ."

"*Stop!*" cried Bill. He staggered up and clutched at the air.

Walter threw the switch. "Hold it, everybody." Walter lifted a heavy eyebrow at Bill. "Do you . . . find much wrong in that?"

"Wrong in it? The trouble is to find anything right in it! I say nothing," declared Bill, "of mere facts. In 1861 nobody had ever heard of Grant. Stanton was not even a member of Lincoln's Cabinet, until January of '62. But, listen, Walter—!"

"Easy. Easy. Am *I* ever upset?"

"I concede that John Hay really was one of Lincoln's secretaries at that time. But the rest of it, Walter! Seward was a cultured lawyer, a platform speaker with a fine voice. Stanton was a fussy, angry little man, but also an experienced lawyer, even pedantic in his speech. Do you really think Americans talk like that?"

Del Durrand lumbered back into the listening room.

Walter pursed his lips. "You do not think we can get away with this, Bill?"

"Definitely not."

Walter threw the switch. "Final corrections!" he called. "Page two, speeches three to twenty-two inclusive. Strike out dialogue written in, and use the original. Stanton becomes Seward, as before. John Hay as in the original. This affects only page two. All other speeches as before. But no gangsterese, except battle scenes. Thank you."

The switch clicked. Norma raised a tear-stained face.

"Oh, no!" she cried. "Oh, Cheeseman, you this-and-that!"

"Never!" cried Bee, straight-backed. "Oh, Cheeseman, you unspeakable!"

Walter, though showing sympathy, nevertheless felt he ought to be mildly stern.

"He's not a bad sort, no! I am not fond of him, and yet —honestly, I don't know why. This Cheese . . . sorry, Bill. His real name is Cheever."

"Yes, I know that," said Bill. "I called him Cheesecake." Bill sat down, dull-witted. "Do you mean that whole crazy scene was a trick to fool me?"

"No, Bill! Cheever. We knew better, of course. But if you *had* passed it—no; I couldn't have done it. I don't give a curse for Cheeseman. I can't ruin a fine show to hurt anybody."

"You're quite right." Bill looked at the floor. "Even as a joke I didn't like it."

"I can't say I like it either," rumbled Del, whose length was again stretched out.

"Now, now!" soothed Walter. "We're not far from transmission time. Listen to that roar in the loud-speaker! They're keyed up; they'll give the show of their lives. Something is going to happen; something big!"

Norma turned and made another red line on her script. Clearly, casually, she spoke.

"Black whiskers," she said.

17 PANIC AT THE B.B.C.

FOR a time in which the second hand of the clock might have traveled four paces, nobody moved or spoke.

There was no noise except a dim clamor from the loudspeaker, the dance of Felicity as she shuffled records, and a click from the black hands of the clock.

That clock showed the red second hand within fourteen seconds of ten-twenty: the nervy ten minutes before a belauded, expensive show goes on the air.

Bill, nearest the door and least likely to be seen by anyone through the glass panel, shifted round.

The stalker was not Gaylord Hurst; he had been foolish to imagine this. The stalker was Hatto, so tall that he must peer downward, a figure of frozen cruelty. . . .

"That's our man," said Bill, who knew no sound could be heard even outside that door. "Are you ready for me to duck out first?"

Walter, apparently studying the clock, spoke.

"Bill, this must not be done! Ten minutes to the red light, and a potted picture taker in the studio? Another time, yes! But now . . ."

Del Durrand dragged his chair close to Walter and spoke as though referring to the studio.

"I think I'll follow Bill," he rumbled. "Ready, Squadron Leader?"

"I am a dumbhead," said Walter. His flawless English showed the slight trace of Teutonic inflection when he was angry. "Yet I will do this because I have no sense. Very well."

"Right!" said Bill, who had twisted round. You could see the reflector of the camera held high. Bill plunged for the lower part of the door—and found no way to pull it inwards.

"What're you waiting for?" mumbled Del.

About halfway up the door Bill saw a metal insertion. He reached for it, flung the door inward, and dashed out.

His fear had been that Hatto might bolt down the corridor. But Hatto backed to the left and stood against the door to Studio 8-A.

"Why, hul-lo, Mr. Hatto!" Bill said cordially. "It was good of you to keep the appointment so promptly!"

He crowded his left shoulder against Hatto's left side and showed Hatto the .38. Walter and Del appeared at Hatto's right.

"This, gentlemen," said Bill, "is Mr. Hatto, the famous photographer, of Bond Street."

"It's a great honor, Mr. Hatto," intoned Del, letting his great left hand fall on Hatto's right shoulder and towering above him.

"You must see our studio, Mr. Hatto." Walter fastened a powerful grip round Hatto's right arm.

"Keep away from his camera, gentlemen," Bill said genially. "We don't want him to 'shoot' a picture before we're ready. Into the studio!"

"Into the studio!" thundered Del.

Hatto's flying entrance into 8-A resembled a chucking-out. Hatto remained utterly impassive.

They whipped him well in along the wall of the studio, before Bill's signal stopped them.

"Well, what do we do now?" Del asked Bill. "What you want him here *for*?"

The buzz of talk beat round the great white walls of the studio, amid the plunk of tuning instruments. Bill dropped the .38 in his pocket.

"Ladies and gentlemen!" he shouted. "May I have your attention, please?"

About fifty persons suddenly appeared from among screens or behind pianos.

"Ladies and gentlemen," shouted Bill. "I speak by kind authority of your producer, Mr. Walter Kuhn."

("Bill! Twenty-two minutes past ten!")

"No doubt you have all heard of Mr. Hatto, of Bond Street. Mr. Hatto does not as a rule condescend to press photography. Tonight, however . . ."

Hatto, in short black coat and striped trousers, wing collar and black tie really did seem to be what Bill professed. Negligently Hatto held the camera, its back draped with a large black silk square: either to hide the gun trigger or for artistic effect. Nobody could know of death concealed in that black camera, or in the gun in Bill's pocket, or that in an instant each might cut loose at the other. Bill found himself entirely willing to commit murder.

"As I was saying, ladies and gentlemen . . ."

"Better say it damn quick," muttered Del. "Cheeseman himself is coming in."

Bill braced himself as he turned round.

Eric Cheever was a tall, slender man in his early forties. He radiated efficiency. Most of his head was covered with a

118

dark-yellow fuzz which became flat fair hair at sides and back. Underneath a high forehead he wore glasses designed not to look like glasses.

"You're Mr. Dawson, I'm certain," he said, and shook hands too cordially. "It was splendid of you to help us to-night! Splendid!" He lowered his voice. "In the listening room I've got the radio critic of the *Times* and C.P. himself. But—er—aren't you keeping the cast rather long for final notes?"

Bill ostentatiously drew him aside, and at the same moment caught the eye of the studio attendant. Nodding toward Hatto, tapping *African Game Trails* against his head to suggest high eccentricity, Bill nodded toward the door. In understanding, the studio attendant moved in front of the door and folded his arms. Hatto saw this, and remained bored.

"Mr. Cheever," Bill said so loudly that most could hear him, "I may have done a very important thing. But, since this is your program, I wanted to help."

"My dear fellow!" said Cheever. Clearly he was both taken aback and touched.

"That man is a famous West End photographer. I've taken the liberty of hiring him, under the auspices of the *Daily Mail*, for a small group picture of the principals."

Cheever shook his head.

"Mr. Dawson, our policy is to discourage any publicity of the vulgar sort. As I have explained even to my superiors . . ."

Bill cut him off.

"The principals," he said, "with yourself in the center. The picture will appear tomorrow on the front page of the *Daily Mail.*"

Cheever's mouth opened, and slowly closed. You could see him look at his own picture on the front page of the *Daily Mail.*

Bill cast a wild glance at the clock. Twenty-five past ten. If he were to work out his full purpose against Hatto without losing the game, he must have time inside ten-thirty!

"True," declared Cheever, "there can be no objection to dignified publicity. I myself, of course, must not appear in . . ."

"Yes! I insist! That's one of the conditions!"

"Well! If you override me, my dear Dawson, I have no choice." Cheever overdid his martyr's air. "What other persons had you considered for the group?"

"The producer on one side of you. The lady star, Miss . . ."

"Miss Monica Carslake."

One of the Jeeps, undoubtedly inspired by Walter, darted in front of Bill, showed her wrist watch, and darted back.

"Miss Carslake, then, on the other side of you. President
119

Davis at one end and President Lincoln at the other. —Walter! Walter, can you arrange the group? The background of that screen this side of the main microphone will do."

"One moment!" Cheever interposed loftily, following Walter's glance at the clock. "Couldn't we do this afterward, and not cut the time so fine?"

Bill's heart seemed to shrivel.

"Mr. Cheever," he said, "you know that the artists leave here as soon as their parts are finished." (They didn't on a program being recorded, but he prayed Cheever was too busy to remember this.) "We can't stop them. And to miss the *Daily Mail*—"

"My dear fellow, you're right. Well? Well?"

Walter had raced out.

"Miss Carslake, please!" he called. "Rabbie! Joe! —The rest stand by for transmission at any moment."

Cheever followed Walter at a dignified stride.

" 'This is your storyteller, the Man in the Dark,' " intoned Del Durrand. "What do we do with the photographer now?"

"If I might be moved toward the center of the group, sir?" Hatto spoke for the first time. "And a trifle closer? Thank you."

"Now, Del!" said Bill, moving close against Hatto's side. "Go back toward the group on the right as we face them. I'll join you in a moment."

Del sauntered away. The group against the screen were still shuffling, since an overexcited Walter was shoving people into the wrong positions. Twenty-six minutes past ten.

Bill crowded close to Hatto's left side, and rammed the muzzle of the .38 against his ribs. Hatto seemed to be arranging the large square of silk across the camera. His vicious whisper was heard only by Bill.

"If you have given away my identity, young man, or told anything of Mr. Hurst or the bargain you made . . ."

"I haven't said one word. I'll keep my pact with the old goat."

"Then you will instantly release me."

"Oh, no! That's not in the bargain. By the way, my name tonight is Bill Dawson."

He was certain Gaylord Hurst had let drop no hint to Hatto about the changed identities. Hatto undoubtedly knew of the plot, but still believed he was Laurence Hurst. His next remark confirmed it.

"How interesting," murmured the bishop.

"Isn't it?" said Bill. His left hand, holding open *African Game Trails* from underneath, whipped up the book. Bill let

120

the first end paper drop on the back of Hatto's left hand, and drew a light cut from the base of the fingers to the wrist.

Hatto wrenched to swing the camera lens toward Bill. Bill jammed the pistol muzzle closer. Hatto could not make it, and knew he couldn't. Yet his right hand still fumbled under the side of the silk which must conceal a trigger. The cut on his hand was shallow; he wrapped several folds of silk round it.

"No, Rabbie!" they heard Walter shout. "You don't want a beard for Lincoln! You must be as you are. Take it off. And hurry! It is now . . ."

Hatto's voice drifted down to Bill.

"I begin to find a young pup most boring, Laurence," he murmured. "When I see you next week, I will give you a disciplining you will never forget."

That word "discipline" had begun to blur Bill's eyes with red.

"Listen, you swine." His voice was soft. "You're caught. Get that into your thick skull? That's not a camera. You don't dare fire the gun, in front of fifty witnesses, or you'll hang. Even if you tried, I'll put every bullet into you. You can't get out."

"Really?" the whisper was unperturbed.

"And you can't fake a picture. They'll want to know what's wrong. When they do, it means the police. Now get out of that—or try."

The voice of Eric Cheever clove across the studio.

"My dear Dawson, we are ready. Please let Mr.—Mr. Hatfield get on with his work."

"Right!" said Bill, and quickly backed away from Hatto standing there alone, with a white wall behind him. Hatto glanced left toward the door, now guarded not only by the studio attendant but by a male Programme Engineer.

Bill took the .38 and held it at practice position, lower arm up, ready to whip out straight and fire. Twenty-eight minutes past ten.

"Shoot your picture, man!" bellowed Walter. "We have just time if you hurry!"

"Yes!" cried the now-shaken Cheever. "For heaven's sake, shoot!"

Hatto, trapped at last, stood motionless over his death camera.

The studio was deathly quiet.

Now there was a very light click, not from the right side of the gun camera.

"There you are, sir," announced Hatto in his most deferential tone. "The picture is finished. I hope, ladies and gentlemen, you will find it satisfactory."

"Here, stop!" said the astonished Cheever. "That bulb should have flashed! But it didn't!"

Then out spoke the tall man who played President Davis. "As a matter of fact," he said, "the bulb is half black. He had no new bulb in the socket."

"What's more," spoke out President Lincoln, "the view finder of those cameras is usually at the back, and he's got the back covered. Or, if it's the front—he's got that covered too."

Behind the long glass panel, Bill could see Bee Roberts making anguished gestures. Two other men, whom Cheever had called the *Times* radio critic and the Controller of Programmes, were close to the window. One looked at a wrist watch; the other held a pocket watch face outwards. The red second hand had just passed the black hand which showed twenty-nine minutes past ten.

"We'll damn soon find out," roared Walter. "Mr. Hatfield, let me see that camera!"

Walter's step clacked out on the floor, to bear down on Hatto.

Then for the first time the gun camera really moved. Hatto swerved it diagonally to his right. For an instant the lens-eye was full on Bill. Bill whipped his right arm straight forward: he drew the sight steadily on the middle of Hatto's chest, as Hatto's fingers began to creep under the silk on the right-hand side. . . .

Walter's footsteps clacked. As the seconds raced, camera gun and .38 faced each other. Then Hatto's hand fell away from the silk. Bill knew Hatto, inspired by a gust of hatred only momentary, would not shoot him, being too coldly sensible, nor dare fire at anyone else.

"Now, then!" said Walter, at Hatto's side. "The camera, if you please."

"Come, my man," cried Eric Cheever. "Come, Hatfield. We must have a look at this camera."

Hatto backed away.

"It is of my own design, sir. I should prefer not to—"

"*For God's sake,*" screamed Bee Roberts through the talkback, "*the red light's flickering! It'll be steady in a second! Places, everybody! Walter, if you want to . . .*"

Then came sheer turmoil.

Walter dashed for the listening room. At the same moment the two men, who for so long had expostulated with watches, chose to hurry out of the listening room into the studio after someone's blood.

The watchers of the door, bewildered by these sacred presences, flung the door open and held it wide. Bill, rousing himself, dropped the .38 into his pocket and ran for the door. But he knew again the bitterness of despair.

As the two dignitaries hesitated in the badly lighted doorway, Hatto moved out so skillfully between them that the confused guards did not even see him. Through the studio floated the bugle notes of "Assembly," hardly two seconds over time. Hatto looked at Bill with a sneer and tapped his camera before he faded away. Bill plunged after him—into confusion worse confounded.

Running toward the studio two actors, evidently slothful General Washington and Stonewall Jackson, determined to rush in. From the inside fought Norma, who had crept out to see the affair and must return for her timing. Cheever piled up against Norma, and into them all crashed Bill.

Though every person was too well-trained to make a sound, anger locked them in a silent wrestling match at the door.

Bill solved it. Kicking Cheever in the shin, dragging Norma behind him, he butted the Controller of Programmes full-tilt in the stomach. Bill tore through, discarding Norma by the listening room. Not much more than halfway down the narrow corridor, the unbeatable Hatto sauntered at that soft, unhurried pace which Bill should have recognized on the stairs.

Bill raced straight down the corridor: or so he thought. Up in front of him, mysteriously, loomed a door which should have been on his right. He saved himself from collision with an outthrust rigtht hand.

Suddenly his eyesight dimmed, his temples throbbed. His left arm and hand seemed so thick and painful that *African Game Trails* dropped to the floor. Bill staggered back against the wall, feeling pain in the right hand, swaying.

Well, he'd lost Hatto. Always nothing but defeat.

"Mr. Dawson!" said a sharp voice.

Up over him, dimly seen, was the unsmiling, yet not unkindly face of Eric Cheever.

"I hope, Mr. Dawson, it was not you who were guilty of bringing that lunatic photographer Hatfield to our broadcast?"

"No," Bill managed to say clearly, though his arms were weakening. "Didn't bring him. Hate him. I was chasing him now."

"Nevertheless, I fear there must be a full investigation."

'Don't try it, old son,' Bill was thinking hazily. 'You're not a bad sort. But . . .'

"Mr. Dawson," said Cheever, in a less sharp tone, "there is every reason why I should wish us to be friends."

"Eh?"

"Let us forget this unpleasant incident. I—er—noted your eyes and forehead. Let us say you are merely drunk."

123

"I'm not drunk, you fool. I'm poisoned."

"*Poisoned?*" The word rang like a yelp in the hushed corridor.

"You won't understand this," said Bill, trying to wag a finger, "but listen. That camera gun was never intended to kill me, even wound me. The bishop had a dozen chances to kill me on the lower stairs, if he'd wanted to. When I got to the top, he was so close behind he could have drilled me through the back as I ran down . . . yes! . . . this corridor."

"Dawson! Steady! You're ill! I didn't—"

"Good old Cheesecake! Gay kept my attention fixed on a harmless air pistol to distract my attention so that I wouldn't notice the symptoms. Take care of that book! It's got poisoned razor blades in the end paper. By keeping my attention off the blades, Old Goat-face caught me with the poison after all. I . . ."

Bill's hands slipped on the wall. He fell heavily on his side, mildly surprised that it did not hurt.

"Steady!" said Eric Cheever. "Here; let me help you up. Dawson, I apologize! I don't know what all this means, but—"

"I'm all right," said Bill, and struggled to his feet. "But could I get a taxi?"

"Of course, old man! Don't worry about the book. I'll get the taxi and take you home myself."

But, in the taxi, Bill collapsed.

18   IN WHICH BILL WAKES UP

"WELL," said the doctor comfortably, "you've been a very good patient, on the whole. You've kept those bandages on your eyes for—let's see: it's the twenty-first today—yes, for exactly a week."

"But—" Bill began.

"I know, Mr. Hurst!" The voice of the invisible doctor had that underlying note of pleasant security and deep interest in your case which is a gift of Providence. "The greatest torture, of course, was not to be allowed to ask any questions until today. But there were good reasons. I had to keep you under opiates for three nights. . . ."

"Was it as bad as that?"

"No," chuckled Dr. Pardoner. "But it helps. The effect has gone long ago. You've been eating like a horse, and you'll be fighting fit if your eyes are in reasonable condition when

124

the bandages come off. Are you ready to have them taken off?"

"Am I?" Never had Bill felt so refreshed, so active of brain, so—he hoped—freed from a certain incubus. Out of horrible nightmare had come the fragment of memory which, if he could get all events straight, might put together the problem instantly.

"You say it's the 21st of June?" he demanded. This night, heaven willing, he had plans for Hatto and Gaylord Hurst. "I can tell through the bandages there's some light in the room. But I've been sleeping. What time is it?"

"Seven-twenty," Dr. Pardoner told him. "Your night nurse arrived at seven. Don't you want to see Miss Conway, Mr. Hurst?"

"See Miss Conway?" exclaimed Bill. "It's one of the things I've been wanting most to do!"

"And why," said Miss Conway rather coldly, "should he wish to see me? I'm sure Mr. Hurst has other things to look at."

"Still, if you don't mind," suggested Dr. Pardoner, "you might lower the blinds, Miss Conway. Now sit up straight, my dear sir. Keep your eyes lowered at first."

To Bill it seemed an age before the unwinding was finished.

"Ah!" Dr. Pardoner remarked to himself, pleased. "Not a trace of the burns at the temples."

Bill felt the last touch of gauze go free. Even against the muffled evening light he opened his eyes cautiously. Slowly opening, the eyes, though a trifle sticky, gave no pain whatever. Clear outlines emerged. Very slowly he raised his head.

At the other end of the sofa, he saw a nurse's cap from under whose upper edge curved a small semicircle of red hair. Miss Patricia Conway had a pretty, rather broad face, with a faint touch of freckles and dancing brown eyes. Bill grinned at her. Miss Conway instantly became aloof and austere.

"I think the patient needs no more attention, Doctor," she said.

Dr. Pardoner, a short stoutish man, twinkled satisfaction from behind shell-rimmed spectacles.

"You're more or less as I imagined you," said Bill. "But you—" he turned to the nurse as in wrath. "You're prettier! You're a thousand times prettier!"

Miss Conway turned away aloofly. Yet the back of her neck, so to speak, did not seem displeased.

"Get used to things for a moment," said Dr. Pardoner, "before I put a light on your eyes. You'll want to ask some questions, I daresay?"

"Questions!" roared Bill. "I've got a million questions. But they say a man who's blinded for a week or so can't enjoy

125

smoking. And that's true! Miss Conway, acushla, would you be after bringing a cigarette?"

"'Deed and I won't!" Miss Conway appeared instantly at his side. "Not a cigarette shall you have," she continued, putting one into his mouth, striking a match, and lighting it. She moved quickly away, lest his grin should disturb her unsevere mouth.

"First!" said Bill to the doctor, swinging round fully in pajamas and dressing gown, "you saw that book Mr. Cheever had? Or didn't you?"

"Oh, yes. Mr. Cheever rang me up."

"Then what poison was on those accursed razor blades?"

"Mr. Hurst, there was no poison on those razor blades."

"What?"

"In fact," said the doctor, "it almost sent us in the wrong direction. Fortunately, I had seen a few cases like this. When the needle began going all over the place—"

"What needle?" demanded Bill, who could think only of the radio control needle.

Dr. Pardoner, taking up the poker from among the fire irons, went over and tapped the cover of Bill's typewriter.

"How long have you been using this machine, Mr. Hurst?"

"The typewriter? Only once, on the first day I arrived here a week ago. I typed steadily for one afternoon and part of an evening."

"Ah, that accounts for everything!"

"But how the devil was I poisoned by a typewriter?"

"The keys were smeared with radium paste."

"Radium?"

Dr. Pardoner, slowly wagging the poker in the air as at a class, was thoughtful. "The specialist . . . I hope you did not mind when I called him in?"

"No, of course not!"

"This method is not new. In a book by Mr. J. C. Goodwin, *Sidelights on Criminal Matters,* you will find it happened in Czechoslovakia before the war. Some jealous man wanted revenge on a typist; not to kill her, but hurt her. This radium paste is still used commercially; but it is so very weak that you could look at it for days without effect on the eyes. It must be smeared on *white* keys. It must not show, or be felt by touch when it dries. The real effects are burns, carried by the fingers. And it must be renewed. The typist, exposed for some days, did not die but had an unpleasant experience."

Miss Conway could not restrain herself.

"And Mr. Hurst there," she said, "had it for only half a day, without a double dose. And he told you and Dr. Lambert (didn't he, Doctor?) about his habit of rubbing his eyes and temples? And the stuff didn't get far into your bloodstream from the cut thumb, so your symptoms came on quick and the doctors caught 'em."

"This thing's not dangerous," observed the doctor, absent-mindedly putting down the poker on the typewriter case, "if you keep the cover on. All the same, I should get rid of it. And —er—it would be better if I didn't learn too much."

"Yes. I see."

"In fact," mused Dr. Pardoner, his eye on a corner of the ceiling, "I had to report this to the police. At first there seemed to be some confusion about your name. Mr. Cheever insisted it was William Dawson. I put it down as that, though later I learned differently. Since everyone insisted you had brought the typewriter from America, I suggested," here his little eyes rolled round, "you had been the victim of a crude joke by some friend on the other side. The police officer lost interest. He will not trouble you again."

"Thanks," grunted Bill. "This is a private feud."

"At the same time," the doctor frowned at the ceiling, "Dr. Lambert and I did some very discreet detective work. All your luggage, including a hat which didn't fit you, bore a tie-on label of the B.O.A.C.—except that typewriter. Dr. Lambert pointed out that the white keys, which didn't go with the machine, could have been exchanged here."

Bill glared at the typewriter desk. Never before had he noticed above it a water color of the Grand Canal, with an almost invisible cream-painted wire running vertically below.

"Unfortunately," murmured the doctor, "both the hall porter and a boy named Tommy insisted that no person had come in with any luggage except a commercial traveler with his sample case on this floor, and an old gentleman with a suitcase to the floor above. I am afraid that the foyer is empty a good deal of the time. Any person could have changed typewriters. No more, now! I'd better not hear it." He bustled over toward Bill. "Now a final examination under light, and we've finished."

Turning on the bridge lamp, Dr. Pardoner directed its light downward. Round his head went some apparatus with a large round reflector in front, while a shaft of light worked round Bill's eyes, and under the eyelids.

"H'mf, yes. Excellent. Do a lot of reading, don't you?"

"Incessantly."

"Ever thought of reading glasses?"

"Yes. But I won't wear 'em!"

"Many people don't like glasses," chuckled the doctor. "But long ago they invented little shells, unbreakable but paper thin, which go underneath the eyelids and fit on the eyeball.

Nobody can tell they're there, because they move with the eyeball. If you don't like the appearance of glasses—"

"It isn't that. I've tried reading glasses, but the damned things never stay where I put them down."

"That's absent-mindedness. If you weren't so absent-minded, you'd see better in more senses than one." Chuckling, Dr. Pardoner clapped him on the back and replaced his apparatus in a black bag. "In any event you're passed as fit. No more doctors or nurses. While I wash up, Miss Conway can tell you about your messages, phone calls, anything of that sort."

Dr. Pardoner smiled on his way out. "And, of course," he added, "the terrible things he may have said in his sleep."

Miss Conway did not reply. But her eyes suggested matters so shocking that Bill squirmed.

Bill, swinging his legs back on the lounge and pulling up the coverlet, pointed beside the sofa. Primly Miss Conway took a chair, put it there, and looked aloof.

"You and your women," she said, not angrily; only with a kind of detached shame that such as he existed.

"Now listen!" said Bill, rearing up. "I'm no sultan with a harem. What women?"

"I'm sure it's no business of mine. But, the second night you were under opiates, no less than two of them kept ringing you up one after the other. And both trying to get in at the front door. And each calling herself Joy Tennent. And you, in your shape, raving most disgustedly of another called Marjorie. Sultan, is it? The Grand Turk himself."

Bill realized this was the first time in which both Marjorie and the real Joy could have heard of his illness.

"Did you see either of these two women who called themselves Joy Tennent?"

"Really, I hardly noticed. But there was one," said Miss Conway, "with black hair and blue eyes, and foul temper when I would not let her in. She said she was your widow, as if 'twas a joke, and she had her marriage certificate, and could go to your uncle . . ."

"My widow?" said Bill. "She's not; I'm alive; it's a damned lie!"

"And did you think I could not guess that?"

Bill's cigarette was burning his hand; he put it out.

In an instant's illumination, he saw everything that had been mysterious about the real Joy Tennent. Joy was what the French called a *demi-vierge*—the English had a coarser, more accurate term—whose cold good sense would never allow favors before marriage.

Bill felt that Larry had married her and that the elaborate business of separate rooms had been kept up until Joy was certain Uncle Gay approved of a fiancée. When you learned that, you understood Joy's mannerisms, and actions.

But this marriage license could not affect old Goat-face. Gay knew Bill was not Larry Hurst; Gay was concerned only with a private kill.

"Listen!" said Bill. "You saw the other young lady, too. The fair-haired one. How did you like her?"

"Well!" The voice was a little less aloof. "I can't deny she has a way with her. I can see why a man would . . . would . . . I invited her in. She spent two nights with you."

"She . . . *what?*"

"Now the low minds of some people! She sat in a chair and talked all night at me." Miss Conway's brown eyes were almost tender. "You've been nice to me. And I'll not tease you any longer. I know your real name is Dawson, not Hurst. I know the girl is called Marjorie, the same you raved about. You're in some danger, but she wouldn't or couldn't tell me, because I've got a brother in the C.I.D. You're most awful in love of her, and she is with you, and why shouldn't the silly girl be? But there's a reason why you can't . . ."

"Thanks," Bill said dully. Miss Conway seemed relieved to stop. "There's only one other matter: these ravings in my sleep."

"Ah, bad luck to me bad temper! There was nothing. Only how you hated somebody called Hat or Hatter or the like. You said you'd faced him with guns and he didn't dare fire; and now you'd broken a block or something. . . ."

"Yes. I hope I have." Bill moved his shoulders.

"And how you'd got the clue, because two persons said the same thing. And something about a thumb flicking against a finger."

Bill hadn't got it all, but he would have when his memory reassembled the facts. "Any messages or phone calls?"

Miss Conway went to the desk, picking up a list.

"There's a Mr. Ronald Wentworth, of the Marylebone Library," she said. "He's phoned three times. He wants Mr. Dawson."

Bill leaped off the couch and into slippers. It was good to feel sound legs; he had been walking for four days, and even sparring under bandaged eyes, with gloves, at a punching bag Tuffrey had rigged up in the bathroom.

"Got to stop Ronnie now," he said. "Otherwise he'll come barging round, and mixing up this Dawson-Hurst business worse than it is."

Letting up both blinds, Bill obtained the phone number and gave it to Tommy downstairs. It was a relief to hear Ronnie's real voice, since Ronnie's power of mimicry often presented him as anybody from Mr. Churchill to the latest radio star.

"Bill Dawson, you dog! Why haven't you been round to see our Exhibition? Oh! Sorry! Forgot! Hope you didn't mind my little item about you in the press."

"Item in the press?"

"Yes. I just said that Mr. William Dawson, noted expert on Sherlock Holmes, was on his way to the Holmes Exhibition when stricken by some Sumatran disease suggesting Mr. Culverton Smith's fanged box in *The Dying Detective*."

"What the devil are you talking about?"

"Of course," you could almost see Ronnie's long face, and his large black Raf mustache, "I know from a police friend—he gave me the tip, after some doctor gave it to him—that it was radium poisoning. But that wouldn't have suited the story so well."

"I understand you've been in touch with a certain Mr. Gaylord Hurst?"

"Believe it or not," Wentworth declared, "I am actually a member of his club. That little blighter, with his thick lenses and his weak legs, dispenses his erudition every Thursday regularly in the Prince Regent's Room, over a group of the select. He's got pots of money and no relative except some nephew in the States, and openly admits he hates the chap. When I approach him about a Holmes relic, I have to write. He's got plenty of usable stuff, but won't exhibit it without a price we can't . . ."

"That's not it, Ronnie. Is he sane?"

"Certainly not. But you can't get him certified. He's too rich."

Miss Conway's voice struck in.

"Two phone calls from a Rev. James Dawson, in Sussex, for Mr. Laurence Hurst."

"It's my father," said Bill, putting his hand over the mouthpiece. "You won't give me away, will you?"

The expression on Miss Conway's face said that this was too much.

"Listen, Ronnie," Bill turned back to the phone, "don't ring again until I can ring you. Where can I get you?"

"Several places." Ronnie rattled off numbers. "They're all in the book. But I've just had a terrific idea. You know we've got a complete reproduction, furniture and gadgets and all, of Holmes's sitting room in Baker Street. Well, my idea is—"

"Later! I'll ring you!" Bill put down the phone and turned round in his chair with relief, almost brushing the heavy poker across the typewriter.

"No letters or telegrams," continued Miss Conway, now at the small occasional table, "but a parcel of books from the Rev. J. Dawson. The Vicarage, Sandsrun, Sussex."

"The old Dad never fails," beamed Bill. "Open it, please?"

The door to the small foyer of the flat opened and closed. Dr. Pardoner bustled in with hands which appeared to shine from cleanliness. He hurried over to his hat and medicine case.

"Well, that's all finished," he said. "By the way, Mr. Hurst, I shouldn't be surprised if you had visitors. Tuffrey, who's been taking down your punching bag, was just opening the front door as I went past."

Miss Conway, who had been attacking the parcel with a small knife, cried out.

"Mr. Hurst! This looks like books, but there's something moving inside!"

Bill jumped to his feet. "Stand back!" he cried. "Don't touch it!"

Miss Conway dodged.

Then, amid a rustling of paper, the great tarantula crawled in bloated slowness to the upper edge of the box. It squatted there, its furry black legs crooked up.

Its horror lay not in poison, since it probably contained little or none. Its horror lay in the obscenity of its appearance.

Bill had heard of a variety of this tarantula to be found in parts of Texas; it could leap across the room. He didn't know this was the same kind, yet—

The door to the foyer was flung open, parallel to the wall where stood Bill's sofa. In the opening, facing the obscenity on the edge of the box, appeared Marjorie Blair, dressed in a blue which deepened the color of her eyes. Eric Cheever, beside her but a little back across the lintel, swung a heavy folded magazine in his right hand. Both saw the thing at once.

The obscenity, its furry legs quivering, seemed to spring straight at Marjorie's face.

An instant before, Cheever had shown strange presence of mind. Moving in front of Marjorie, his right hand holding the heavy magazine across his chest, in mid-air he caught the obscenity with a savage backhand.

The tarantula was flung back against the wall beside which stood its box. It scrabbled and fell to the floor.

Bill, seizing at the heavy poker on the typewriter, found that Dr. Pardoner had anticipated him. Six times the poker whacked down. Then Dr. Pardoner, less ruddy, straightened up.

"I don't think there was much harm in it," he said mildly.

131

He looked at Bill. "You might get a newspaper and cover up the remains until Tuffrey can get it away. It isn't pretty." ·

Bill picked up the few sheets of an evening paper and did as he was told.

"You might discover whether there's a card in that box," he added. "I'm going in to get dressed."

He did not dare to look at Marjorie as he passed. Eric Cheever now seemed half paralyzed at what he had done. Bill slapped him on the shoulder with a, "Well done, old man." In the foyer outside he met Tuffrey—and his own father.

"Only another joke," he said to the hall porter. "Unpleasant bit of cleaning up, I'm afraid." He turned to his father. "Sir, I've been wanting to talk to you. . . ."

"So have I," smiled the Rev. James. "Where do we go?"

"Straight ahead. That's the bedroom, much like the sitting room."

The bedroom had two windows on the same side. Between them stood a chest of drawers. The double bed, somewhat wobbly and covered with a faded orange counterpane, had its head pushed against the far wall. Over it hung a water color of the Bridge of Sighs, with a cream-painted wire running down under.

Bill sat down on the bed, motioning his father to a fairly comfortable rocking chair beside it.

The Rev. James might have been Bill's elder brother except for the scanty sandy hair brushed across his skull, and the deep kindly lines in his face. He wore a clerical collar with heavy gray tweeds, bulging with books and brier pipes.

"Bill," he began, clearing his throat, "Marjorie has come down to see your mother and me."

"Yes, Dad. I gathered that. You sent your telephone calls to Laurence Hurst. I wanted to phone you the first night I arrived. But . . ."

"I know that, Bill. It doesn't matter. But—"

"One question," snapped Bill, "I've got to ask you. It concerns you and Mom too." Still he did not look up. "I know you can be very evasive when you've given somebody money you can't afford."

The Rev. James looked guilty. From his pocket he drew out a brier pipe, unscrewing the two parts.

"Here's the question," said Bill. "How much do you and Mom need to make yourselves comfortable?" The Rev. James's astonishment could not have been assumed.

"Bill! This is extraordinary! It was a question I wished to put to you. Never have your mother and I been so affluent. I give you my word! Surely you . . ."

Here he put the pipe stem into his mouth the wrong way. He regarded it with an air of injury.

"Dad, are you sure of that?"

"My word of honor, Bill," answered his father. "Yes. Now I understand why you . . ." Words failed him. "My only important question. This so-called 'game' you are playing . . ."

"Well?" Bill froze instantly.

"From what I could see a moment ago, and from what Marjorie has told me, you do battle with very dangerous playmates. Danger? Well! At times it may be necessary. But your motive for this impersonation?"

"Yes, sir?"

The Rev. James stood up. "One side Marjorie knew, or seemed to know. It was to help this Mr. Hurst, because he is your friend. But let me ask this. Are your other reasons as good? If I knew them, should I approve them?"

"You would approve them, sir. You might even do the job yourself."

"Well, then!" All doubt cleared from the Rev. James Dawson's forehead. In radiance he dropped the two pieces of the pipe into different pockets. "All I ask is: come to see us as soon as you can. Marjorie . . . I—er—promised to deliver a message from Marjorie."

"You needn't bother, sir. If Marjorie has any message for me, she'd better bring it herself. I shall stay here."

"Yes, Bill. I told her that was best. Well . . . er . . . I'd better be going. Your mother sends her love. Keep fit, you know."

The Rev. James, who would have been more embarrassed to show affection toward his son than the son to the father, wandered toward the door.

"We're . . . we're rather proud of you," he muttered, awkwardly slapping at Bill's left sleeve.

Bill, sitting on the edge of the bed, glanced round at the water color of the Bridge of Sighs, not needing closer examination to know what it meant. He looked also at another writing desk set at an angle in one corner of the wall, with all Bill's possessions, including watch and lighter, set in a line.

He would have known Marjorie stood near him, by presence, by animal sense, even if she had not sat down beside him.

"Bill," her voice stabbed him, "your father said . . . my message . . . that is . . ."

He would not look at her. Staring straight ahead, he tried to lock up every shade of feeling.

"It's fairly obvious, isn't it? You're going to marry Cheever."

"Bill, you don't understand!"

"I not only understand; I deserve it. Last week, near this

133

time of night, I had shown myself for the worst kind of failure and weakling. You said Eric Cheever was solid and dependable. It doesn't matter whether you put more faith in being solid and dependable, or couldn't stand my jealousy. It's good enough."

Bill moistened his lips. "You couldn't marry anybody I admire more than Cheever. When he knew I was down and out, did he have one word of triumph? Oh, no! All he said was that there was a reason—why he wanted us to be good friends. Well, he can count on me."

"Bill, no! You still don't understand! There's no question about jealousy! I admit I thought there was, at first . . . I felt, really in my heart, I was never going to have you."

"Fair enough. That was what I felt too."

"*No,*" pleaded Marjorie. "Won't you at least turn and look at me?"

"Sorry; no. That's too dangerous."

"Then I've *got* to tell you the story, Bill. Please don't look at me either; I don't think I could bear it." Marjorie paused a moment. "I practically had to force you to ask me why I went to America. Darling!" she said with sudden emotion, and controlled herself. "Why did I come back?"

"How should I know? For the Festival, I suppose."

"No, Bill. You see, my father's getting old. His mind is—well, not so quick as it used to be. In signing contracts with private persons . . . Anyway, there's a clause that by a certain date the builder must put down a whacking sum of money: with the stipulation, of course, that this is null and void if he can't get the materials. The other man, as financial backer, is to put down a sum five times as big, but with no stipulation. Well . . ."

"Go on," said Bill, pressing his hands together.

"But if you're dealing with what they call a warm man, or the backer isn't entirely convinced about the project," continued Marjorie, "then the clause about the builder 'guaranteeing to find the materials' goes in, but the part about 'in case of the Government departments agreeing to provide them' goes out.

"My father missed that part of the clause. It's legal-proof; we've tried. He can't *get* those materials, Bill; he *can't.* But unless he pays that enormous sum by next Monday, we're ruined. And he can't pay; that's that."

"The warm man, I take it, now thinks the project was no good and wants his money on the nail. Who is this warm man?"

"That's the silly part!" Marjorie burst out. "And yet it isn't coincidence at all! Who is the one man who's known to put

134

every penny into property trusts, large and small building of every kind? Who's a philanthropist, but a skinflint who's pleased to do you down? Who would you naturally go to?"

Bill's hands locked together. "Not my dear, good Uncle Gaylord?"

"Yes. You can understand why I wasn't keen to meet him, even under another name and to help you? You must have seen many times how I broke down, and showed I loathed him? I was the one who let *you* down. But—"

"Just a minute. How does Eric Cheever fit into this?"

Marjorie hesitated. "Eric's been awfully decent, as you've said yourself. But, Bill! Have you ever wondered why I've put you off, every time you asked for my address? First I said we weren't living at Highgate any longer. Then I said I was phoning from a public call box, to avoid telling you where I was. I wouldn't give you any address, because I didn't want you to know. Bill, do you know why?"

"Well?"

"Because I've been living with Eric. —No, no! I mean at his house, with my parents. Father's got to save every farthing, because—that thing threatens prosecution for fraud if he doesn't pay."

"But let me hear a little more, please, of the gallant Mr. Cheever?"

"Bill, he *is* nice. On the day we arrived he said—very nicely —that he thought he could raise the money to pay off father's debt, if we'd accept the offer."

Bill unconsciously lifted his right arm. "The provision being, I imagine," he said, "that you marry Eric at once."

"Bill, no! No! There's absolutely no 'Heh-heh' or mustache-twisting nonsense about it. He *is* a gentleman. Salaries aren't too large at the B.B.C., and it's wonderful how he can raise it. Bill, it's three thousand, two hundred and fifty pounds."

"Go on."

"All the same, of course, it'll be just the same thing; only not in a Victorian way. I shall feel mother's eyes boring into my back. She hates you, Bill. My father's always liked you. But I'm 'expected' to marry Eric. Everyone expects it. And why not? If Eric's paid my father's debt, why not?"

Marjorie's voice ended in a little sob. "Anyway," she said. "The money must be paid to Gaylord. Bill, I hate to hurt you."

Bill felt like a giant. Never had a man been so elated when he saw in the air before him his bank passbook, glowing with the sum of £3,381.11.6d.

Bill arose, turned round in stately fashion, and spoke like the hero in an old-fashioned melodrama. "And is that *all?*" he asked with ringing contempt. "Is that all, dear Marjorie, which disunites us?"

Marjorie sprang up, flushed and lovely and bewildered.

"Wh-at?"

"Shut up," said Bill, dropping his lofty tone. "Then you didn't really think me a failure or a weakling after all? You don't mind if I'm not dependable like Cheever? Your fits of jealousy were because you feared to lose an unspeakable ass like myself?"

"Failure? Weakling?" Marjorie's face blazed. "When every time that foul old man dug at you, you dug back so much harder that he hated you worse than ever? And—have you seen last week's newspapers?"

"Er—my reading has been somewhat curtailed."

"Well, somebody they can't find because they call him Hatfield, when I bet you anything it's that Hatto, chased you into the B.B.C. with what the police think was a gun inside a camera. You outwitted him, outmaneuvered him, then chased him out of the studio as a laughingstock."

"Do you know," muttered Bill, "that version never occurred to me?"

"Darling," burst out Marjorie, her gray eyes open. "I don't want you to be solid and dependable. I want you to be as you are."

"In short, you really love this bungling fool? Come here!"

The next two minutes were chaotic. Marjorie drew away.

"Oh, what's the good?" she said bleakly. "I'm going to marry Eric; and that's that."

"You may forget this business of marrying Cheever. Your father's debt to Gaylord will be paid in full tonight, and he will get a receipt tomorrow morning."

Marjorie backed away.

"Bill, *please* don't joke."

"Be a good girl, and run into the sitting room. Tell Cheever gently you're going to marry me. Ring up your father, and tell him the debt will be paid. Or, if you still think I'm out of my senses, wait until he gets the receipt tomorrow. I shall not see you again tonight, my dear."

Marjorie believed him now. The expression on her face wrung his heart, even in the mood upon him. Marjorie rushed out of the bedroom doorway, darted into the bathroom for necessary repairs to tear-dimmed eyes, and, finding the hall porter at work on the punching bag, flashed out again and darted into the kitchen.

Soft twilight now fell through the lace curtains at the windows. Bill did not notice. Shifting his feet, he brought up his fists to guard.

Miss Conway had long been waiting in the foyer just outside, having overheard much of the conversation. Her pretty face showing sympathy, she entered now with a small white card in her hand. She called Larry Hurst's name several times before Bill woke up.

"You wished to know, Mr. Hurst, if there would be any card in that box with the filthy baste. This was all we could find."

Bill held out his hand as though he were touching the tarantula itself. On the card was printed in ink only, *Compliments of J. Hatfield.*

Bill crushed the card and threw it away.

"Thank you, Miss Conway. That's all. I—er—wish to dress."

Hastening to the wardrobe, he quickly exchanged clothes and shoes. Then he went to the desk catercornered between one wall and the left-hand window. He took from the drawer his passbook and checkbook. He noted by the loud-ticking wrist watch that he was fifteen minutes late for his appointment with Gaylord.

No matter! Carefully he wrote a check for three thousand two hundred and fifty pounds to the favor of Gaylord Hurst. Seldom had be known such delight. On a sheet of paper he wrote out a receipt, and affixed a stamp across which Gaylord could sign. At the foot of the check was his lawful name.

While he put on the wrist watch and dropped the lighter into his pocket, Bill made mental calculations. His doctors' and nurses' fees, he estimated correctly at about a hundred quid. This left him the proud sum of thirty pounds, eleven shillings, and sixpence.

His parents, through what miracle he did not understand, were well off. His promise to his friend, that he would settle Gaylord, he hoped would soon be paid. He could marry Marjorie; and, though he disliked the work, he was still a first-rate motor mechanic. As for anything that concerned him or his academic career, that could go whistling down the wind.

"Mr. Hurst, sir!" called the hoarse, persistent voice of the hall porter from behind.

Bill in his dream did not even hear.

"Mr. Hurst, sir!" shouted Tuffrey, and tapped Bill on the left shoulder.

Bill, roused by that tap on the shoulder, whipped round and up in a movement that almost baffled eyesight. His left fist flashed up. The hall porter leapt back, staring at Bill, obviously terrified.

"Oh, murder!" whispered Miss Conway, who had materialized behind Tuffrey. "But what have you against poor Mr. Tuffrey, now?"

"I . . . I don't know," replied Bill, still in a daze.

"Now listen, Bill Dawson!" said Patricia Conway, as no nurse should ever address a patient. "There's me address and phone number. Ah, and not for nursing! But if you get into trouble—and ye will, you crazy loon—then I'll come from China itself to help you, so help me!"

"I shall be glad to give you assistance," Bill told her politely, shoving the slip into his pocket. Then his voice became harsh. "In the meanwhile, Miss Conway"—he explained what he wanted, and grew impatient as she groaned. "Yes! At once. Tonight I will administer some very bad-tasting medicine to a couple of swine!"

19 HOW THE MING JADE CHESS PIECES WERE SMASHED

IN the flat of Gaylord Hurst, all double doors were set open to the least breath of air, except those of the foyer leading to the anteroom picture gallery. The windows of the dining room were wide open to the soft depth of the Green Park.

It was not quite dark. A breath of air stirred from the park. Yet it was so still that you could almost imagine, far away, the whisper or vibration of Big Ben.

In Gaylord's drawing room—with its white shelves stretching to the ceiling and book sets carefully arranged for contrasting colors except an artistic gap where one book could lean against another—only the black-and-white lamp burned.

The lord of the evening himself, in evening clothes and decoration much less sloppy, had drawn his wheel chair close to the Chippendale table. His blue lap robe swept across the wheels of the chair.

The knuckle-dusters and policeman's lantern were gone. The little brown poison bottles had been pushed to the other side. Gay, body twisted sideways, was laying out a game of patience.

The black-and-white leather sofa, together with black-and-white chairs or other tables, had all been pushed back. The big room made a large open space: except where, on the ivory board, stood the Ming jade chess pieces.

Across this space, with impeccable dignity, came Hatto.

"It is half past nine, sir," remarked Hatto. "I do not think Mr. Laurence will honor us tonight."

The other did not even look up.

138

"You need not worry, Hatto. He will be here."

"Very good, sir. Then, for his impertinence in being late, have I your permission to give him some discipline of a rather severe kind?"

The bifocal spectacles shimmered with pleasure. "You have it, Hatto! You may discipline him as severely as you like."

Softly, but with thick insistence, the buzzer of the front doorbell began to sing.

"Sir," asked Hatto, "I have your permission to deal as I wish with Mr. Laurence?"

"Better still!" whispered the other. "I have ascertained that the two flats below us will be empty until midnight. If you were considerate enough to close the dining-room window, they could not even hear him scream."

"If you please, sir. A little later, perhaps?"

At his employer's nod, Hatto turned toward the outer door. The wheel chair was facing almost outward through the open line between the open doors between drawing room and art gallery, to the closed doors to the little narrow foyer. Closing up the cards, the torture master stacked them on the table. Then he thrust his hands under the lap robe, to touch something lying hidden. He was happy.

Hatto had disappeared behind the double doors of the foyer, closing them, on his way to the front door. The ordered world of the night remained serene.

"'Chess,'" the man in the wheel chair misquoted from Lafcadio Hearn, "'an invention of the learned Wu Wang, which is an imitation of war.'"

There was a crash. The double doors to the foyer had crashed flat against the wall on either side, smashing one of Gay's pictured horrors and swinging another loose on the far side.

And Hatto, flung back from those doors as though catapulted, went reeling through the art gallery, to pitch head-foremost on the carpet of the drawing room.

Bill Dawson, carrying a large square cardboard box over his left arm, walked through the gallery into the drawing room. Hatto instantly rose, brushed his lapels, drew tighter his shirt front, and waited with a tight smile on that side of the doors.

The man in the wheel chair might have seen the alteration in Bill Dawson's appearance. Bill's whole body seemed heavier and more coarse. But this was an optical illusion. All good nature was gone from his look. Since Hatto was just inside the door on one side, he took a step in at the other side.

"Now, J. Hatfield," he said, "can you only wrestle, like a dog? Or can you box?"

"I can do both."

"Will you fight, scum?"

"Yes, puppy!"

From the cardboard box Bill took a pair of boxing gloves. He flung the gloves straight into Hatto's face.

Bill threw off coat and waistcoat. A belt rather than braces gave him freer play. Ripping off his necktie, he opened his shirt collar, flung the discarded articles across a chair. His own gloves snugged closely to his hands and wrists.

The voice of Mr. Hurst rose serene and almost bored.

"One moment, Hatto. You will be good enough, first of all, to carry into the next room the ivory board and Ming jade chess pieces. I cannot repeat too often that the slightest injury . . . Hatto! Do you hear me?"

Hatto did not. He could not lower his dignity by removing his coat. But his gloved right hand was now murderously settling down the glove on his left hand.

"Hatto, I think you must have taken leave of your senses. The chess pieces are exactly in the center of the room. I must *command* you . . ."

Neither heard.

Bill was on the left of the broad double doors, faced toward the gallery. Hatto was on the right. Hatto, his long left arm moving out, his right fist cocked, shuffled out slowly.

Bill, head low, guard high, prowled as softly as a panther. . . .

Mr. Hurst shrilled like a banshee.

"The chess pieces!" he screamed. "More precious than any jewel ever . . ." Suddenly the voice dropped to nothingness.

Bill waded in. What happened happened in three minutes and four seconds.

Not a man spoke during the fight. In the heavily carpeted room sounds seemed small and muffled in the thickness of hatred. If any voice spoke, it was only in Bill's imagination.

'Now ya doin' it, kid! Now ya doin' it! Smear the son-of-a-bitch all over the canvas!'

Hatto, for the third time floored by Bill's right cross, staggered up. Hatto, so riddled with body blows that he could neither lock Bill's arms nor protect his own sagging head, bleeding heavily over his right eye, groped for his balance and stood up.

Mr. Hurst screamed again. Hatto was standing near one end of the board, when Bill brought up the long right uppercut. Hatto's head snapped back, his bloodied face and shirt front flung upward. He swayed; then, as though something had jerked loose every sinew, he fell straight backward. There was a heavy crash as his full weight landed on the chess pieces.

Bill, dazed, looked down at his gloves, then at Hatto, who

lay across the board with his head hanging over one end and his feet dangling over the other.

After that first crash which had all but destroyed both chess armies, there were more cracks as other parts flew: a jade head, fragments, a whole green figure flashing out, so that Hatto seemed to writhe.

Again Bill looked at his gloves, and shuddered. He tore them off and threw them away. "A cheap victory!" he said. "After all, my main business here is with Gaylord Hurst."

He did not think Hatto had done him any damage, though he knew the worst punishment is only felt afterward. But the breeze chilled his damp shirt. Without a glance toward the wheel chair, he went back to the doorway, where he donned necktie, waistcoat, and coat.

After a glance round—he saw, as he had not seen before, that there was a door of dummy books in the north wall, as well as the ordinary door in the south wall—Bill strolled toward the source of mischief.

"And now," he said, with a smile, "we must deal with *you.*"

"Indeed?"

Two of Gaylord Hurst's paintings had been damaged. His undefeatable manservant had been slaughtered. His most prized possession lay in ruin.

And yet you would not have thought he minded the damage at all. The bifocal lenses shimmered, opaque. His face was without expression, even when he nodded toward Hatto.

"As you remarked," he said, "a cheap victory."

"I couldn't agree more," said Bill, his smile a little too broad. "Some days ago I told myself that no problem was ever solved by a fight with fists. And this is true. But I forgot the underlying truth."

"Your philosophy bores me."

"It won't, in a moment. The underlying truth is this. Every man, a few times in his life, must burst out physically, or mentally, or spiritually—and for a brief time he must riot; or else he will go mad."

"If you make any stupid threat of physical violence . . ."

"Violence? Great Scott, no! Did you imagine I intended to treat you as I treated Hatto?" Bill beamed. "No, no! I've been working out something to settle you when the time comes. But not physical punishment; you're too old. And not just yet."

"My deepest thanks."

"I'm serious! I think you must have misunderstood what I said. When I said my business was with you, I meant a business matter."

In one hand Bill held up a check. In the other he held up a receipt.

"Here," he shook the gray slip, "is a check for three thousand, two hundred and fifty pounds, made out to you. No, I'm not backing out of our bargain. You're still free to kill me, if you can. You're a businessman. All you need do is sign this receipt in my other hand. You might even do it as a favor."

"As a fav . . ." the other began very softly, and stopped.

His dull blue eyes wandered out in a look at the smashed fragments of the chess set. He strained to discern the two damaged paintings. Bill knew, in his bones, that Gaylord Hurst —alone, apparently helpless—had never been so dangerous as then. But the calm spectacles merely turned back.

"Give me the check and the receipt. Also a fountain pen, if you have one."

"Yes, I've got one. Here!"

"Gently, Mr. Dawson. Don't come closer!"

"Eh?"

"Despite your cheerful mood, you have been brushing your hands together, slowly, while you looked at my neck. On the chair nearest to me you will find the backgammon board. Put the check, receipt, and pen on it; and hand it to me at arm's length."

Bill complied.

Lifting the lap robe with the finger tips of his right hand, the ex-uncle took the board, lowered it behind the robe, and held up the lap robe with his right hand. He seemed to be hiding something toward the right.

"'The sum of—' Yes." His voice was emotionless. "'In full settlement . . . monies accrued . . . John Blair.' I remember the matter now. What have you to do with John Blair?"

Bill, who had dropped the wrist watch into his pocket before the fight, slid it on again.

"It's now two minutes to ten o'clock," he said. Here, he noticed, Gay's eyes slid round the edges of the bifocals. "Sign that, and you can be rid of me by ten."

The lamplight showed every movement in silhouette, and gave Bill a shadow play. He saw Gay's right hand uncap the pen, sign the receipt, and cap the pen. The hand picked up the check, and presumably put it in his pocket. The backgammon board was returned in the manner in which it had been received.

"Good night," said the immovable one.

Bill, taking the receipt and the pen as he put away the board, could have cheered. There was no deception about this signature, either. He knew it well, since he had studied that money promise note, and seen Gay's signature at the foot of the document in Amberley's office.

"Well, good night," Bill answered, and started to turn away.

"I'll leave the gloves as a souvenir, for Hatto. Better ring up a doctor at once, and have him look at Hatto."

"Is he hurt? He does not look hurt from outside."

"He's damn well hurt inside. Three knockdowns and a knockout in that space of time—well, it hasn't done him any good. Our usual meeting next week? Until then, uncle!"

Bill sauntered toward the door of the gallery. In his pocket was the receipt for the money Marjorie's father owed, and he had given Hatto about a week in a nursing home. If Gay had objected to signing the receipt, there was a manner to deal with him. But Gay had signed without fuss. That was better.

His companion's voice spoke behind him.

"One moment," it said.

Bill whirled round. Having just circled the chessboard where Hatto twitched and groaned, Bill faced his Puckish host about ten paces away in a straight line.

The blue robe was now up almost to his enemy's chest. Through a slit, a little above the waist, and to the immovable one's right, projected the nickeled steel barrel Bill had been given some experience of.

"Yes," agreed the other, "it is the Spandau. But I have not the slightest intention of using it, unless you attack me. Merely stand and listen."

Bill glanced down. Hatto, sprawled in front of him like a barrier, prevented any sudden move. And the distance was too short for the worst shot to miss.

The lenses flashed as that calm voice continued.

"We all make mistakes. I imagined my game of stalk-you-and-kill-you, with its intervals of shaking your nerve, would provide enough amusement for six months. Last week I altered the time to three months. Now I know I cannot endure you for much more than a week.

"Frankly, I dislike you too much." The voice did not alter. The hand holding the air pistol and hand outlined behind blue silk were steady. "Even more frankly, your counter-attacks fatigue me. So I give you fair warning: I am terminating our bargain. You will receive your death sentence within twenty-four hours."

What struck dread into Bill was the change he saw in Gaylord Hurst. All his craziness—of eye, of lip, of nose, of ideas, of grandiloquence—was fading away. This was the Gaylord Hurst who saw bargains and got them. All his flamboyance had been put on to shake the nerves of his victim.

"Do you mean," demanded Bill, "that if I can dodge for another twenty-four hours, I'm free of you?"

The other nodded gravely.

"But free for what, Mr. Dawson? Your money is gone. For

143

some reason you have returned almost all. But don't worry: I shall not fail."

"Don't be too sure of that! If *I* get *you* instead . . ."

"Now how shall I do this? If you had read more deeply in the history of crime," he jerked his head toward the wall of books behind him, "you would know how a man may commit murder with complete safety."

As the other's head had nodded toward the wall, Bill's long eyesight was fixed on a row of works of toxicology. With several he was himself familiar. Bill's gaze dropped to the little brown poison bottles.

His companion smiled very slightly.

"One question, anyway!" snapped Bill. "Do you know somebody called Bradley Somers?"

"I do not know the man." The reply was so flat that Bill believed him.

"Under another name, then? He's a commercial traveler in electrical supplies. He took a flat on the same floor as mine at the Albert Arms, on the same day. All I could discover is that he's tall and fair-haired and wears spectacles. Is *he* one of your spies?"

"I do not know the man. And I am growing tired. Now be good enough to leave my house."

Bill took one last look. His host was leaning forward, his eyes glittering in the light. His face had that composed look of one who has decided to kill. But, most terrifying, his eyes were those of a perfectly sane man.

"*You will receive your death sentence.*" he repeated, "*within twenty-four hours.*"

20 AN HOUR AND A HALF TO LIVE

AS Bill put the key into the outer door of number C-14, it was eight-thirty on the following night. An hour and a half to go, and still no attack.

At his shoulder, Marjorie shivered both at events and at the weather. The small landing was normally lighted by a glass roof above the lift shaft. But this was now dark, and rustled with a Scotch mist: which merely soaks you without one honest raindrop.

Marjorie put her hand on the arm of Bill's soaked topcoat. "Bill, what's he going to *do?*"

"For the eighty-fourth time, I don't know. Whatever it is, it'll be something we don't expect. Gay's pride and joy is his ingenuity." Bill groaned. "On the other hand, he may try to outdo ingenuity by doing the obvious. . . . Got it!"

The lock clicked, the door partly opened on a dark entry. From the right hand pocket of his topcoat Bill took out Del Durrand's Webley .38, still loaded. All day he had been glad he hadn't returned that gun.

"In that case," begged Marjorie, "why on earth are you coming back to your own flat? This *is* the most obvious place to get at you!"

"I know. But I've got to pick up some gear I bought this morning. Before you began following me."

"Darling, what else could I do? When I saw you hurrying out of the National Gallery, and you wouldn't stop, I had to follow you! When I did run you to earth in the Museum . . ,"

Bill, whose nerves had been on edge all day, looked at her.

"Now listen! I'm going in alone to make sure the place is empty. You stay here: got that? Don't move. That is," he nodded toward the door of C-16, "unles you see that door begin to open, or see somebody stick his head up over the staircase round the lift. Then yell like blazes. Otherwise, quiet!"

Bill, the .38 against his side, slipped into the flat and left the door about an inch open.

For a few moments Marjorie, nervous and damp and yet wildly exalted, thought she didn't mind being left alone. For that afternoon Bill had told her the whole story, beginning with the meeting in Amberley's office and ending with last night. But he omitted all reference to the ten thousand dollars and why he wanted it. When Marjorie had pointed out that a receipt for three thousand, two hundred and fifty pounds, made out to her father and signed by Gaylord Hurst, had arrived anonymously in this morning's post, Bill knew nothing about it. When she further said the receipt was in Bill's handwriting—a bad slip—he turned the air so sulphurous with denial that she said no more. But Marjorie knew. She loved him still more for this foolishness.

She could hear Bill's soft, quick tread and the faint snapping of light switches as he explored. No, it wasn't so *bad* waiting here alone. . . .

The skylight roof had grown darker. The Scotch mist thickened to a patter of rain. Over toward her right was the door of C-16—and behind it might be the mysterious Mr. Bradley Somers, commercial traveler in electrical supplies.

If a head did appear above the staircase, Marjorie thought, her knees might give way. Quickly she looked at the door of C-16. Unless the line of shadows had changed, that door was slightly moving. . . .

"It's all right," muttered Bill's voice, so close that Marjorie jumped. "I'm certain there's nobody in the place. Come in."

Seeing the lighted foyer behind him, she felt better.

"But," he insisted, drawing her in and double-locking the door, "don't go into the sitting room or bedroom. We go straight into the kitchenette."

He hurried her across into a kitchenette, with white tile and enamel and cream-painted wood. Its one small window, above the sink, faced the street on twilight and mist. A globe lamp shone against the ceiling.

"But why h-here?" asked Marjorie, uncertain whether she had seen that other door move. "Why not the sitting room or the bedroom?"

"Over the desk in the sitting room there's a watercolor of the Grand Canal; and over the bed in the other room there's a watercolor of the Bridge of Sighs."

Bill locked the kitchenette door on the inside. He studied the rustling window. Then he stood, weighing the revolver in his hand.

"Under each of those pictures," he said, "there's a wire running to the baseboard. There's a microphone behind each of them."

"Microphone," Marjorie said slowly. Her thoughts went instantly to that commercial traveler next door, yet she did not speak, preoccupied with a notion that had been haunting her half the week.

"I had a good look at 'em late last night. The microphones are very sensitive. They'd pick up a good deal said in the room; especially phone conversations in the living room, where the phone's directly underneath. But it's no good theorizing. What we want is action." He whipped off his topcoat and sodden hat. Putting these on the drainboard, he juggled the revolver.

"All day, my drenched Venus, I've given Gay the opportunity to stalk me. But I've kept to public places where there's always a small crowd: so that I was always near people, but never so many that I couldn't spot somebody closing in. *You* know what a dance I've led you since afternoon."

"But I didn't mind!"

"Anyway! Gay, with his weak legs, couldn't follow me, even if he'd used a taxi. Probably, he had me followed by 'Chief Inspector Partridge,' the fake policeman across the street—"

"Or Bradley Somers, the commercial traveler in the flat next door—"

"Or anybody you like! The point is that nothing's happened today. Now: what does that mean?"

Marjorie moistened her lips. "That Gay will wait until the last minute!"

"Yes. Exactly. Those are Gay's tactics every time. If this trick murder method is tried on me, Gay will be there to use it. That's his character."

"Now what's my play? This. From now on, Gay or his confederates cease to stalk me. *I* stalk Gay."

"Stalk him? How?"

At one side of the kitchenette, cream-painted cupboards were built above an enameled shelf with drawers below. Putting the revolver on the shelf, Bill opened the first drawer.

From the drawer Bill took a considerable length of thin rope, wound into a loose coil. To the end was fastened a medium-sized sharp-pointed iron hook.

"Several times I've thought how easy it would be to burgle one of those flats at 68 St. James's Place. Throw up a hook on a rope: those wide ledges make it simple, and the windows are so old they can be opened with a penknife. I used to do that hook trick every time."

"But, Bill! If you mean——"

"Yes! I'm going to burgle Gaylord's flat. If he's home, we'll have a showdown before ten o'clock."

Bill, oblivious to her protests, began to coil the rope round himself, from left shoulder to right side. He remembered something else, he reached into his inside breast pocket, and took out the bundle of papers, Larry's and his own.

He could not tell Marjorie. But, if Gay's murder device worked before Bill could stop it, what could he decently leave in his pockets?

He opened Larry's passport. Here was his card of instructions. A press cutting. The old photograph of Gay and Larry. Then four or five business cards. Despite himself Bill grinned.

"And what is so very funny, please?" asked Marjorie with an edge of hysteria.

"It's not funny. Larry carried these cards and penciled remarks on the backs. Each is a comment on the card owner's wife. The wife of Edward J. Riley, a Greenwich Village printer, is described as: 'Dora R.; pushover; any time; WA 4, 0071.' With the good spouse of H. F. Thompson, Los Angeles studio address, Larry didn't succeed: the comment is wicked, phone number scratched out. Presumably he had no interest in the steam pumps manufactured by Harry T. Pinckney, but Mr. Pinckney's wife——"

"I still don't think it's funny," said Marjorie. "Bill! Did *you* ever . . ."

She stopped. Bill's attention had become fixed on another document, his agreement with Gaylord Hurst, presenting him with the nearly gone bank account on condition that it should revert if Bill died within three months.

"Oh, to the devil with it!" he said, and stuffed the whole lot back into his pocket. "That swine isn't going to get me. Why bake the funeral meats now?"

Swiftly, he bound the rope round him, slipping the hook beneath; nobody could have seen the bulge under his topcoat. Marjorie, who had been watching hopelessly, ran toward him. Despite the rope, he held her close.

"I know," he said miserably. "In your heart you're thinking all this is foolish and unnecessary; and why can't you and I forget it and get married and be happy? Aren't you?"

Marjorie nodded violently.

"And you're right! After tonight, my dear. I'm still a damn good motor mechanic; and I can support you. I don't mean to kill Gay if I can outwit him. But there's got to be a showdown."

Marjorie stood up straight.

"You don't mean to kill . . . Then listen, darling! Please! I've been terrified by something that's made me wonder all this week. You've been puzzling at what a man might do under this or that circumstance. Will you let me tell you what a *woman* might do? And ask a question?"

"Yes, of course."

"Well," said Marjorie, "what has Joy Tennent been doing for the past week? No, no, it's not jealousy! Did Miss Conway tell you how she and I sat up for two nights, while you were under drugs, and—well, got rather confidential? Did she tell you how Joy tried to get into the flat Friday night, and what Joy said?"

"Yes! Joy was still pretending I was Larry Hurst. She said she was my wife."

"No, Bill. Joy said she was your *widow*, Larry Hurst's *widow*. And that she'd go to your uncle with the marriage certificate."

"By the Lord, she did say 'widow'! I was thinking about the marriage lines. . . ."

Marjorie caught him by the shoulders. "Now you think. Try to think like a woman! Joy said she meant that 'widow' business as a joke. But it wasn't a joke. What was it?"

"I give up. What was it?"

"It was a threat, Bill. The worst she could make. You see, I didn't know Larry was dead until you told me today."

"Well?"

"By that time, after the rebuff she'd had at Gay's flat when you and I were there, Joy meant business. When you were under opiates she tried to see you. By this time she was furious, and turned nasty just as she said.

"Bill, she went straight to Gaylord. That horrible woman wants money, and nothing else. She meant to show Gaylord her marriage lines, tell him Larry was dead, and ask for money as Larry's widow. But Gay, who didn't like her—"

"Gay wouldn't see her?"

"Yes, yes! Bill, I can't prove this, but I *know* it. I can read her mind. She'd run straight to a solicitor. He'd tell her she wasn't entitled to any money just because she was Larry's widow, and he'd advise her to do something else. That's why I ask what she's been doing all week. I can tell you what she'll do, if she hasn't already."

"On the solicitor's advice, you mean? I still don't see it!"

"She'll go straight to Scotland Yard," Marjorie answered calmly, "and denounce you and me as conspirators to swindle Gay. She'll tell all about Larry's murder, and accuse you of poisoning him to take over his life and get Gay's fortune."

Marjorie shivered. Her outward calmness covered hysteria. "Darling, I—don't know much about police and things. But, if we're accused of being conspirators, which we are, then the police have to get in touch with New York, won't they? About Larry's murder. If his body hasn't been identified . . . Joy can tell them in the same cable to see this firm of Amberley, Something. They can identify him like a shot, can't they?"

"Yes. They've known Larry for years. But—"

"And, on top of all this duel with Gay, you'll be accused of Larry's murder too. That's what Joy'll do, Bill! If she hasn't already."

Marjorie began to sob. "Anyway," she added, with a wild triumph, "I can be in it with you. I'll say I was!"

"Listen!" roared Bill.

He shouted at her as he might have slapped her to cure a dangerous mood. Marjorie raised her head.

"A good deal of what you say about Joy," he told her carefully, "is true. Otherwise you're off. I can tell you every move she's made and why. But that's all I remember, I knew the whole solution a week or more ago."

"*What?*"

"Put it like this. I had a fragment of memory. Possibly under those opiates. But if you put two pieces of evidence together, and I knew what they were, you might unlock the whole box at once." Bill pressed his hands over his eyes. "I was thinking of it when I woke up from ordinary natural sleep early yesterday evening, just before the bandages came off. The whole thing seemed to be . . . Snap! Off with the bandages. From that moment to this I've had such a series of mental shocks

149

that by midnight the whole solution was clean gone. If something would just remind me!"

"Try, Bill! Try to remember!"

"But at least I can tell you about Joy Tennent. Joy hasn't gone near Scotland Yard; Scotland Yard hasn't got in touch with George Amberl—"

Shrilly, the telephone in the sitting room began to ring.

Bill whipped on his wet topcoat, noting again how well the rip of the air-pistol bullet had been mended, and fitted the coat so that there was little sign of the rope inside. He put on his hat, and picked up the revolver.

"I want you to answer that phone," he said. "Never mind why! But remember: there's a microphone close. Whoever is calling, don't say too much. Are you all right again, angel-face?"

"Yes. I love you." Marjorie's eyes and hands were quiet. His revelation had shocked her from the edge of hysteria. Out of the open drawer Bill took a small flashlight, rubber gloves, and a heavy penknife.

"Now," he said, dropping these into his topcoat pocket. "Stay close to me."

That telephone, as Bill unlocked and opened the kitchenette door, seemed to scream. Every room, every lamp, was blazing with light as they hurried into the sitting room. As Marjorie reached out for the phone, Bill suddenly caught her arm and drew her back. His whisper at her ear was so very soft that no microphone could have caught it.

"Don't touch that phone yet!"

"Why not?"

"Gay is too tricky with poison. Let me handle the phone first."

He ran his hands over every surface of the phone, which yowled, and the baseboard. He could hear the voice of Tommy, at the switchboard, but paid no attention. Finally, satisfied, he handed the phone to Marjorie.

His whisper, if possible, was even softer. "Sing out the names."

Marjorie addressed the phone. "Yes?" she said. "Mr. William Dawson? Who wishes to speak to him?"

There was a silence. Then Marjorie's eyes moved toward Bill. "Mr. George Amberley."

Bill fashioned careful syllables, soundlessly, and Marjorie lip-read them.

"Is Mr. Amberley phoning from New York?" Pause. "Thank you. One moment, please."

Marjorie put down the phone, seized Bill's arm, and dragged him over to the door of the sitting room.

"Mr. Amberley's in London," she said. "He flew here today. He's at Claridge's. He says he's got to see you."

The revolver loosened in Bill's hand. His deduction about Joy might have been wrong. It seemed to him that on all sides they were closing in steadily to drive him into a corner.

And, at the same moment, there was a soft, insistent knocking at the outer door.

"That's all right!" Bill instantly assured Marjorie. "There's somebody I'm expecting now."

Bill hoped it was the man he was expecting. But he kept the revolver steadied at his side. He undid the double locks and slid the door a little way open against his foot.

Yes, it was the person he expected, Tuffrey, his chest thrust out under a black topcoat. He held a bowler hat across it.

"Come in!" Bill closed the door behind Tuffrey, and beckoned Marjorie to conference.

"I must leave now," Bill went on, "if I've got any hope of cutting off Gay." He could hear the telephone squawking. "Marjorie, go speak to Amberley. Ease him along, find out what he wants and what he knows; use your best secretarial manner. —No; don't go yet! I want you to hear the rest. Tuffrey?"

"Yessir!"

"As soon as Miss Blair has finished telephoning, take her home in a cab. Don't let her out of your sight until she's at home. When you leave here, leave all lights burning. Right? I'll phone as soon as I can. That's all."

"Bill!" Marjorie said. For a long moment they looked at each other, neither able to speak. "G-good luck," whispered Marjorie, and hurried toward the phone.

Bill slipped downstairs, unseen by the page-in-buttons, and out the back entrance. He turned up his collar and pulled down his hat. Nobody could have recognized him in that mist.

Twenty minutes later a taxi set him down on the north side of the Mall. He approached Gay's flat from a different direction. The monuments and façade of Buckingham Palace were not floodlit. The streetlamps loomed as drowned, whitish smears.

Bill turned left through a gate—still open—in the wall of the Park close to its eastern end. A broad path ran north of the front of number 68 on the right. To burgle Gay's flat from the front of the house was the only reasonably safe way.

In this weather there would be nobody in the Park, fewer prowling policemen. Following the path, even through mist, Bill spotted number 68. Once spiked iron railings had closed off this road. But blitz damage had turned a length of the railings into a little low fence you could step across.

Stepping over into the half-replanted little garden of number 68, Bill looked round and listened.

Darkness; silence; only a stir on drenched foliage. According to all rules, he—a hunted man in a misty city at night—should have dodged back to his own flat, locked the door, turned on all lights, and waited with weapon ready. If Gay had put a tracker at his heels, as Bill hoped, the tracker could have reported Bill cornered at the Albert Arms. At the last moment, in a taxi or his own car, Gay might well drive to Bill's flat.

But you couldn't foresee what Gay would do. If Bill could catch him here, off guard . . .

A quarter past nine! Three quarters of an hour to go.

Bill, crossing the garden, craned his neck and cupped his eyes to look upwards. The front of 68 was invisible except for blurry chinks through or under drawn curtains; they made bright patches on the broad stone ledges.

Bill flung off his topcoat and hat, putting them at the base of the wall between windows. He had transferred penknife, torch and gloves to his jacket. The old .38 he wedged in his waistband. Then he began to uncoil the rope.

On the ground floor, in the flat of Sir Ashton Cowdray, heavy curtains were drawn, though several windows showed quivers of light: especially the one near Bill. From the curtains of the flat above, much more light spilled on the ledge for which he must throw. But the light was distorted by mist: uncertain, hard to judge.

Distance up? Just fourteen feet; allow a little slack. With hook in hand, Bill quickly unslung the rope. If the light deceived him, or that hook smashed a window . . .

Bill took two steps backward, calculated again, and threw. There was a faint *clack* as the flattened end of the hook struck across the ledge. Bill yanked the rope taut. The hook skidded, slipped, and flung outward and downward at him.

The flat side whacked against the stone edge of the window nearest him, and dropped into grass. Four inches to the left, and it would have smashed the study window of Sir Ashton Cowdray.

Bill stood up, his heart bumping. He thought he could hear a radio inside. Perhaps that smothered the sound. He caught up the rope, measured it, and instantly threw with a kind of ferocious recklessness. This time the hook held firm. Hand over hand, using knees and feet, he was up that rope in seconds. Once he thought he heard music above. Then, holding tightly with right hand and knees and feet, he swung his left arm over the ledge and hauled himself up.

Only one more ledge to go. The rope tied round his waist,

Bill quickly hauled up. He turned rain-bleared eyes upward. It seemed that Gaylord Hurst's flat was dark, except for one very faint little spot which scarcely touched the ledge.

"Got to throw for it anyway," Bill muttered. "Can't stand back to throw, either. This ledge is . . ."

He stopped. He had heard music. Inside the flat of the Hon. Benbow Hooker, from beyond muffling curtains, issued the loud tuning of a piano, saxophone, and accordion. Voices smote out at Bill, mainly young and female voices. A cork popped. The Admiral was having a high old time.

Bill flung the hook upward. At the same time piano, saxophone, and accordion crashed into song. A young soprano rollicked into a semi-bawdy ditty:

> I'm Jen-ny Wren of the Wrens, you see,
> A friend of all the King's Na-vee . . .

Bill could not hear the hook land. But the rope seemed taut. Again he swarmed up. The revolver seemed forcing itself out of his waistband, to fall and be lost. But there was nothing to do but climb or be flung off the ledge.

A few moments more, and he scrambled over the ledge outside Gay's flat, dirty and bruised, but he had done it. He saw that the dining-room windows—by which he hoped to enter—were tightly fastened by shutters presumably bolted inside. Every window was shuttered except the one just opposite him, from which had come the dim light.

Rewinding the rope round him, hook inside, Bill settled the .38 and peered in. This was a full-length sash window, the junction of its sashes so loose that the blade of a knife could turn and open the catch.

Bill peered through. A narrow carpeted passage ran straight ahead. On the right stretched what seemed a blank wall. On the left four small doors ran to a larger door, evidently a front door, with a light and a bell buzzer. At right angles to that, you saw the edge of a green-and-gold curtain in a foyer.

What seemed a blank wall was the wall of Gay's three large rooms in the central block. This was the passage on the north side, with doors to small bedrooms or the like.

Trying to put on his rubber gloves, Bill split one down the middle; he cursed and threw both over the ledge as useless. A closer look showed him that the window was not even locked.

Easy, then. —Too easy? Gay lurking inside?

With the gun in his right hand, Bill eased up the lower sash and ducked his head inside. Not a squeak as he closed the window.

First taking a handkerchief to clear his eyes and face, Bill

153

substituted electric torch for handkerchief in his left hand. Gay should be in his drawing room: that room he had indicated, his only study. And there was a door to the drawing room on this side. Bill had observed it only last night, a door of dummy book backs: without knob, discernible only from the too-high varnish on the books and the small hinges. Such doors usually pushed outward; on this side there must be some catch or knob.

Bill moved forward. The beam of the torch easily found the outline of the door as well as the little knob.

Bill, trying to keep the gun steady, pulled slightly at the little knob. A vertical thread of dim light showed. These old walls and floors must muffle sounds; he could hear no whisper from the party downstairs.

Ready for an instant's showdown, Bill stayed his hand and looked. Throwing away caution, he opened the door.

The Chippendale table, as usual back against the wall of books near the closed doors to the dining room, seemed even more feebly lighted. On the table were only three innocent-seeming things: a Bible, a small desk calendar and a brandy glass Bill remembered because he had drunk from one here before, empty, except for purplish dregs.

Beside the table stood Gay's wheel chair. The body of Gaylord Hurst lay on the carpet, partly on its back and partly on its left side, the unmistakable face toward Bill. The great robe of blue silk was entangled round his head and down his left side like an Oriental costume.

Gay's bifocals hung from his right ear up over his forehead. The blue eyes were half open. His short little legs were drawn up toward his stomach. Death had caved in his long face, making him look older even than he was, preserving a look of endless hatred. The whole place reeked of potassium cyanide.

Then, thick walls and floors or no, there burst out from the flat underneath voices screaming the song.

> Roll—out—the—bar-rel,
> We'll have a barrel of fun!

The revolver dropped from Bill's hand. He forced himself to touch Gay's body. He guessed Gay had been dead about an hour.

Bill examined the brandy glass without touching it. This reeked of cherry brandy; and, since Bill had drunk cherry brandy at Gay's house, he recalled how its flavor and odor resembled that of the poison; and could completely cover the potassium cyanide.

Bill's instinct banged the bull's-eye: this *was* his glass. It would have a full set of his fingerprints. Hatto, humorously compelled to drink from the same glass, clasped the stem; no prints at all. But, superimposed on those of Bill would be a fine set of Gay's.

And now Bill realized how Gay was going to kill him.

Every one of Gay's statements had been a twisted truth. He had not said, 'You will die within twenty-four hours.' He had said, 'You will receive your death sentence,' meaning the police would get him. He had said . . . 'You will see me before you die,' because Gay foresaw Bill's every move and knew he would do just this.

And what was the weapon that never failed? The hangman's rope.

Gay, old and exhausted, had poisoned himself, but left enough evidence to convict and hang Bill.

"Well, you haven't done too badly," muttered Bill.

Downstairs they had almost finished rolling out the barrel. Bill, desperate, stood with his back to the wall of bookshelves, a man literally with his back to the wall.

The odor of potassium cyanide seemed everywhere. Bill, as has been stated, had met one case of poisoning by this means before Larry's death: that was how he knew what had caught Larry. Just ten years ago, when the Jerries shot down Bill over France, and the French Underground hid him for four months, a British Intelligence Officer, who posed as a French peasant and went about under the name of Picot, had shown them the little capsule he was to crunch and swallow if Jerry ever rumbled him. It contained two and a half grains of the stuff, he said—Larry's dose. The Jerries swooped down on "Picot" as he sauntered beside the barn for a message, but he got the capsule into his mouth. Even as they tried to take him the poison struck; he fell down and rolled.

The Jerries ran for a car to take Picot to a doctor; he must be saved for questioning. But Picot was dead within three minutes.

Bill realized that he was standing with his back to a row of books on toxicology; he had seen them last night, and knew several.

Snatching down the small but authoritative *Murrell*, Bill fumbled with the index and turned to page 86. Dull-eyed, he read three lines at the foot of the page and perhaps eight or nine on the next page. . . .

Abruptly he lowered the book, and remained motionless.

Since all sounds had ceased from the flat below, Bill could have sworn he heard somebody moving in Gay's flat.

Listening, head bent, he was staring straight down at the

Chippendale table, and at one of the innocent-seeming objects on its top. No; that noise must have been imagined. As his attention cleared, he looked at that one object on the table. He looked again.

Then, in his mind, it was as though a door had clanged open or shutters were flung wide. That so-called "trifle" had unlocked his memory. He now knew the solution to the whole case.

Dropping the book somewhere, he thought hard for a few seconds. Every piece of the nightmare dropped exactly into place. All he needed was time—to prepare his defense. Now he was certain he heard noises. Bill went over quickly and picked up the revolver.

'You fool!' spoke one side of his brain. 'Aren't you going to wipe any fingerprints off that brandy glass?'

'No!' retorted the other side of his brain, which knew the whole truth. 'They'll help me.'

'Where are you going now?'

'Into the dining room. I'm certain those noises come from the passage on the other side of this room. There's a door with a glass panel, and I can look into the passage on the other side.'

'Take care! What about fingerprints on the handles?'

'They won't matter . . . unless the police nab me within a few hours; and *they* won't!'

Quietly sliding the handles on the doors to the dining room, Bill moved into the dark, wicked room and closed them. Near the end of the wall toward his left, discreet light shone from the panel in the door which led to the other passage.

Bill, tiptoeing toward the door, heard a voice. That door wasn't sound-proof, as he had imagined! Hatto, waiting on table that night, must have known Bill wasn't Larry Hurst, whatever Hatto had said—or hinted—to Gay.

From behind the door, very clearly, issued a decisive young voice.

"That's the lot, Chief Inspector," it said. "Like to hear the case against Dawson? Told partly by Miss Tennent, partly by Mr. Hatto, and backed up with information received?"

The police had been here for more than an hour.

21 "ADVENTURE YET PROWLS IN BAKER STREET!"

THIS was the time to get out of that flat. But Bill couldn't go. Whatever the risks, he must hear how strong a case they had against him; what he must and could counter if he were given a few hours.

"Go ahead, Sergeant," said the heavier, deeper voice. "But make it short."

Bill crept forward. If he kept a few feet back from that panel, nobody inside could see him. As he did so, his foot brushed some object on the floor; if he had kicked it fully, he would have brought down ruin.

His exploring fingers found the old-fashioned policeman's lantern, of the nineties, which Gay had kept on the table in the other room. Evidently some curious-minded police officer, finding it, had left it here. Not daring to bang into it again, Bill picked it up and held it.

It was in his hand when he looked through the shoulder-height panel. The Sergeant's sharp, decisive voice had fallen into that sing-song with which they recite evidence in the witness box.

". . . L. Hurst and J. Tennent retired to the floor below that of G. Amberley's office, where they met W. Dawson and discussed . . ."

Just inside the door, a tallish heavily-built man was leaning his shoulder against the right-hand wall of the other narrow passage. His soft hat was pulled down; he wore a belted raincoat still damp; he was presumably the Chief Inspector.

A little beyond him, facing outward from the kitchen doorway, the Sergeant was still singing out from a notebook, with a bowler hat on the back of his head; he was smaller and thinner, and looked like a clerk.

Beyond these two, Bill saw on a stretcher supported by wooden crosspieces, and with blanket drawn up to neck, a damaged but apparently articulate Hatto. Beside him stood a middle-sized, wiry young man. He wore a good-natured, cynical smile—Bill was certain he had seen the face before—and held a batch of short reports that seemed like a large pack of cards.

On went the Sergeant's voice. Bill felt something very close to horror. With Joy, with Hatto, and with "information received," the police knew as much—well, not quite as much—as he knew himself.

Now the Sergeant looked round and spoke to his chief in a natural tone.

"By the way, Mr. Partridge. Do you know what Miss Tennent's, or Mrs. Laurence Hurst . . . do you know what her profession really is?"

"Don't be funny, Green," said the Chief Inspector.

Bill shied back. There couldn't be a real Chief Inspector Partridge! In the Victoria Arms across the street, with a flat opposite?

"The point is," persisted Sergeant Green, "that she's a full-fledged research chemist. During the war she worked in California, overseeing the manufacture of the cyanide capsules the death-and-glory boys swallowed."

"I heard it. Well?"

"She says she kept several capsules as souvenirs."

"Sort of damn-fool thing everybody does. What about it?"

"But look here, sir. She also says she's known this Dawson a long time. When they all met at the solicitor's in New York, the Tennent girl pretended she'd never met Dawson because she was now Laurence Hurst's wife. But she also says she saw Dawson a month or more ago. She says Dawson asked for a couple of cyanide capsules as a souvenir of her; and she gave 'em to him. Sir, can you believe that?"

Chief Inspector Partridge was inclined to be irritable.

"When you're a little older, Green," he said, "you'll learn people *like* to keep and show off to their friends anything that's got death stuck to it. They kept Jerry helmets and bayonets and grenades. You tell me this capsule business is scatty? I hear scatty stories every day. And most of 'em are true. The Tennent woman is a born liar. Any b.f. can see that. But this time she's telling most of the truth, because her story squares with everybody else's. I won't swear how Dawson got the cyanide capsules. But he had 'em ready when he dropped in at the solicitor's office and got his chance to play Laurence Hurst."

"H'm," muttered Sergeant Green.

"He was sitting beside Hurst in Dingala's Bar. Nobody else was near them; nobody but Dawson could have done the dirty. Drop one capsule in a drink; it dissolves like that."

"Well," admitted Green, looking at the good-natured young man who held the sheaf of reports, "we know Old Hurst didn't make a will. But, sir! Dawson couldn't have gone on impersonating the young fellow, to get the fortune. Mr. Hurst knew he wasn't Laurence. So did Hatto. So did other people. Dawson couldn't have done it!"

The old, wise Chief Inspector spoke with weary bitterness.

"Course he couldn't! Use your head, Green. Old Hurst

threatened to expose Dawson for fraud. That's eyewash; you can't convict anybody unless he's tried to get money under false pretenses. But Dawson didn't know it. Old Hurst offered to let him keep the original ten thousand dollars if Dawson would go on with the murder-me-if-you-can game. Ask Hatto. Take a dekko at the money agreement you found in the old man's pocket."

"Bull's eye!" muttered Sergeant Green.

"Sure it is, Frank! But Dawson wasn't having any. It was too dangerous. So he knocked off the old sugarer with the other capsule. Goddelmighty! You got Dawson's dabs from his own flat, didn't you? And you found a set on the brandy glass in the other room. And that's that."

Bill, unconsciously and dangerously, was pressing closer to the glass panel. When a woman like Joy becomes blind furious, she can tell a string of lies verging on insanity. Bill thought he could meet her evidence. Yet . . .

'Get away from here!' whispered that silent voice from one side of his brain.

'Yes,' whispered the other side, 'but they'll have your flat taped by now. They'll have covered Marjorie's house too. Where the devil can you go?"

Sergeant Green, pushing his bowler further back, took a breath of relief.

"That two-capsule business was all that bothered me," he said. "By the way, sir, you did cable New York about the murder of Laurence Hurst?"

"Sure I did! The woman only came to us yesterday afternoon. I cabled in the evening. Their time is five hours behind ours, and I got an answer the same evening. They report death from cyanide—victim unidentified—of a young man in a telephone box at Dingala's Bar on the night, close to midnight, of June 12th. They wanted twenty-four hours for complete identification—these American solicitors will do it—and full details. I'm expecting that cable in twenty minutes. They'll phone it from the Yard. And then the general alarm goes out. And then, as for Dawson . . ."

Chief Inspector Partridge extended his arm, and slowly closed the fingers.

Bill, wits whirling, turned again to go. If caught, he musn't be carrying a firearm. Putting down the .38, Bill slid it across the carpet.

Abruptly the Chief Inspector's voice changed. Bill stood up, so close to the panel that his face almost touched it. Mr. Partridge was pointing, without favor, toward the smiling, well-dressed young man beside the stretcher on which Hatto lay.

"Let's see, now," said the Chief Inspector. "You're new to the Metropolitan Force, Inspector Conway?"

Conway! That was why the man's face had seemed so familiar. Bill's nurse had told him of a brother in the C.I.D.

"Yes, sir, I'm new," replied Inspector Conway. "That's why I wondered whether I'm allowed to tell the truth to a superior officer."

"You can, Conway. Spit it out!"

"Your case," answered Inspector Conway, "is full of holes."

"And what case isn't?" the other asked, "with the guiltiest man that ever walked? Get this, my lad: we play straight. If we can prove a man's innocent, we don't say a word. But if he's guilty—"

"For instance," interposed Conway, holding up a report. "I suppose this man who calls himself 'Chief Inspector Partridge,' in the flat opposite Dawson's, isn't really you? The policeman on the round has been taking quite an interest in him for some time.—No; I can see by your face the man isn't you."

Mr. Partridge was silent with rage.

"Across the street," pursued Conway, "the same policeman was already interested to hear of a flat where two men were supposed to be staying but only one was ever seen. He tipped off C-1; a plain-clothes officer took over. The hall porter wouldn't say a word, but there's a boy named Tommy who becomes boastful after about five lemonades. That's how we knew about Dawson long ago."

Bill, rooted to the carpet, realized how invisibly can fasten the nets of the police.

"But that doesn't matter now," said Conway. "What does matter is that a commercial traveler, Bartley Somers, moved into a flat next to Dawson's on the same day. Somers is tall and light-haired and wears spectacles. Why don't we investigate him?

"Last night, the 21st, Dawson burst into this flat in a mood which Hatto, here," Conway bent down and touched the stretcher, "calls murderous insanity. Dawson tore into Hatto and knocked him cold. . . ."

"I was taken off guard, gentlemen," quavered Hatto.

"Anyway, Hatto can't remember anything until he woke up, in his bedroom, with a doctor bent over him and Old Hurst in the wheel chair. He can't even remember who the doctor was."

"And what's wrong with that?"

"Wait! Let's take Hatto's statement for tonight, the 22nd. At seven-thirty he was lying in his bedroom, in the north passage over there," Conway gestured, "just opposite a door of dummy books leading into Old Hurst's drawing room.

"At this time Hatto hears somebody burgling the window at the end of the north passage. In spite of his injuries, Hatto manages to crawl to the door, in time to see Dawson slowly opening the door of dummy books into the drawing room. Time, say seven thirty-two.

"Hatto," continued Conway grimly, "knows he's of no use if Old Hurst is there. And so he crawls along the passage to the telephone. It takes time. He phones us: ten to eight. We're here: eight o'clock. Old Man Hurst is just dead, and Hatto fainted beside the phone.

"Chief," Conway said, and pointed his finger at Partridge, "let's take last night. Suppose you're a murderous lunatic and you want to smash Hatto. Would you come here with boxing gloves? We found 'em hidden, you know. The police surgeon said it was a glove fight. He also said Dawson hadn't struck one low or foul blow. Further, if Dawson's a lunatic, why didn't he dispose of Old Hurst after he'd knocked out Hatto? He didn't even take the keys."

"He's been through a lot, poor devil." The Chief Inspector eyed Hatto.

"Finally, tonight!" said Conway. "It's true the north passage window is unlocked. But there wasn't a trace of breaking or entering when we saw it. And Hatto says Dawson cracked that window at seven-thirty, when in spite of this rain it was broad daylight, and anybody could have seen him. Next—"

"That's enough, Conway," Partridge said mildly. "There's not a single thing you said that a good prosecuting counsel wouldn't shoot to pieces in five minutes. Unless you've got a whole new solution of your own?"

"Maybe I have, sir."

"Oh, ah?"

"In those little brown poison bottles we found in the old man's 'Criminal Relics' room," said Conway, the freckles standing out on his white face, "one of 'em contained real cyanide, partly used. The old man was still at his battle-of-wits with Dawson. Suppose he poisoned himself, so that Dawson would hang for it?"

Bill, at long last about to hasten away in obedience to that voice which bade him run, again stopped. He heard Inspector Conway outline the theory which—at first—he had outlined to himself.[7]

There was a heavy little chuckle from the Chief Inspector. "Fair's fair, Conway," he said. "You're a good copper; I know your record. Sorry if I cut up rough a minute ago."

[7] The very astute reader, who is the writer's joy, may have thought of this the instant Dawson found Gay dead. But Partridge's objections are sound and human. And Gay, the ingenious, would never have used so old a trick. Gaylord Hurst did not kill himself. Discard answer number seven.

161

"Forget it, sir!" said Conway mollified.

"Well, we've heard a lot about old Hurst too, from his eternal complaints to Traffic. He'd stick to life as he'd stick to his money. And here's another straight tip. Would he kill himself before they made him Lord Hurst of What's-its-name?"

"Well, sir . . ."

"You bet he wouldn't! No! Dawson's our man. In seventeen minutes our general alarm goes out. Dawson can't hide; we'll get him in three hours. Because he can't think of a place to hide that we haven't thought of already!"

Bill glanced down at the old policeman's lantern in his hand. He remembered for what purpose Gay had intended it. The shout he uttered was entirely in his imagination.

'Will you think,' he silently yelled, 'of a furnished room smack in the middle of London? Will you think of Holmes's and Watson's sitting room at the Baker Street Exhibition?'

Sergeant Green, turning round from the kitchen door, looked straight through the glass panel.

"Mr. Partridge," he said, "there's somebody outside that door."

Bill took off as though at a starting gun. He was through the dining room into the drawing room, shutting the doors so that not a gleam crept out or a lock rattled, before he heard the Chief Inspector's voice.

"There's nothing in the dining room!" he bellowed. "Stop a bit, though! Somebody's left a revolver on the carpet. We'd better . . ."

Bill, slipping the lantern under a chair, darted across the drawing room, out through the dummy-book door, down the passage to the window. Softly he slid up the window, squirmed outside, closed the window, and swiftly unreeled his rope. With a few hours to hide after that general alarm, he could prove his case. More than that! He might even . . . !

'No,' protested that cold thought. 'That's only a thousand-to-one chance. But no harm in trying it. You've got to reach a telephone anyway; try it!'

The descent was much easier than the climb. On the ledge outside the flat of the Admiral, whose party seemed to drowse, he troubled with climbing no longer. Whisking loose the hook from the ledge above, he unfastened it all and let it drop. Swinging by his fingers from the ledge, he let himself go and fell without even a shaking into the soft wet grass. By the chinks of light from Sir Ashton Cowdray's windows, he could see his topcoat and hat against the foot of the wall.

He was bending over to pick them up when he saw a hazy outline standing before him.

It was George Amberley.

Mr. Amberley was dressed in what was once a fine tan topcoat and a pearl-gray hat with an upturned brim. At the moment he resembled something imagined by the late H. G. Wells.

It would do the lawyer no harm to sleep for a time in the rose garden. Bill, loosening his shoulders for the belly left and right cross, found that Marjorie—his drenched but beloved Marjorie—had thrown her arms round him.

"Bill, no!" she protested. "Mr. Amberley hasn't come here because of . . . He doesn't know anything about it. He told me on the phone, but I was too late to catch you. So I had to bring him here. We found where you'd gone up, by that coat and hat. Mr. Amberley has something . . ."

"Eh?"

"Are you in trouble again, Bill? Are the police after you?"

"Yes! No! I dunno." He struggled into his topcoat, and disappeared under a cascade from his hat. He glanced upward. "Every second I expect to see those windows open, and hear a police whistle. Marjorie, where's the nearest telephone box?"

"I—I'm not sure. Wait! In the Underground."

"Good!" said Bill, leaving rope and hook behind as he leaped over the little wood-and-wire fence. "Come on, both of you!"

And he set off at a genuinely impressive stride, with Marjorie on one side and Amberley on the other. The lawyer seemed to jingle at every step.

"Mr. Dawson," he said, "if you will allow me . . ."

"Villain!" said Bill, in a mood for high-flown speech. "You wrote that you suspected me of impersonating Larry."

"A lawyer's first duty, sir, is to his client. I *did* suspect it. But when Gaylord Hurst replied by air mail that Larry was here, and you had decided to accompany him, I forgot the matter. I am here only as a visitor, to see the Festival of Britain."

"Oh, by the by—when I had dinner with Gay, he seemed surprised that I needed money. He had some notion that old Gran was wealthy."

"Oh yes," said Mr. Amberley.

"Then my father! I asked him whether he and my mother needed money. But he said they'd never been better off in their lives. He seemed surprised I should ask it. Anyway, I told Gay the truth. Poor Gran never had more than enough to live on. My late grandfather was crackers, and kept pouring money into loony investments."

The lawyer spoke with reverence.

"Never again, Mr. Dawson," he said rather emotionally, "refer to your late grandfather as—as crackers. He was one of

163

your financial wizards. Long ago, when men laughed at him," *jingle-jangle*, "he invested heavily in British oil refineries. Do I need to say how high those stocks have gone? The fortune is now your father's, and will ultimately come to you."

Marjorie faltered. "Bill, I'm afraid you're going to be rich someday."

"Er—that's fine," said Bill. "Thank you very much." Then a glance at his watch galvanized him. "Come on, you two! Hurry!"

Catching each by one arm, Bill plunged them forward.

Amberley could control himself no longer. "God!" he said. "The boy's nuts!"

"Darling," gasped Marjorie, "doesn't it thrill you even a little?"

"Frankly," said Bill, pacing them still, "I couldn't care less. If the Aga Khan left me every penny, what good would it do me in clink on a murder charge?"

"Murder?" exclaimed Amberley, with a heavier jangle.

At this point, three abreast, they shot out of the park entrance into crowds.

Flinging his companions to the left, Bill rushed them down the stairs of the Underground.

He could have cheered when he saw four telephone boxes against the wall, only one occupied. The clock said a quarter past ten. According to his estimates, the general alarm would go out in fifteen minutes.

"Now!" he said, exploring his pockets and finding only silver. "I want pennies! As many as you've got. The price of a phone-call is now threepence. Pennies, please!"

By his white face both the others saw that trouble was flying toward them fast. Marjorie searched her handbag and produced three pennies.

"And you, Mr. Amberley! You *must* have pennies. You sound as though you'd robbed a toy bank."

"I am quite at home in your country, young man, except for the currency. You try to think what it means in American money, and go crazy. The safest procedure is to tender a banknote and get the change. —Hold out your hat."

Bill did so. His companion poured out a double-handed shower of silver and copper. Bill selected fifteen pennies.

"For four phone calls," said Bill, "that's enough and six over if the phone turns nasty and wants to fight. Mr. Amberley . . ."

How they got rid of their guest Bill and Marjorie never quite remembered. All the lawyer wanted was a word of thanks for his good-hearted gesture in flying to tell them. They overwhelmed him with thanks. Presently an apparently very happy man was on his way back to Claridge's Hotel, with the assurance of a phone call in the morning.

Marjorie and Bill faced each other. All that running had flushed Marjorie's complexion. Her dark eyebrows, the dark wet eyelashes trembling over intense gray eyes, the short nose and half-opened mouth: all gripped Bill with such plain physical desire that his nerves were jerking as he put his hands inside her mackintosh.

Why bother with all this cut-and-run? He knew of a cottage in the country, belonging to an old friend who had left the key under the mat. He saw his feelings reflected in Marjorie's eyes. But they both knew it was impossible—yet; Marjorie wrenched away.

"Four phone calls," said Bill harshly. "If I talk as long as ten-thirty, rap on the glass. Then I shall be on the run like hell, and so will you."

So that Marjorie could not hear, he pulled shut the door of the telephone box.

Marjorie was not a girl intended for celibacy. All her pent-up feelings went into hatred for this vile trick of closing the door. Her soft voice cursed him with every hair-raising epithet. An old lady, examining *London Razzle* at the bookstall, turned in horror.

Even though Marjorie watched the dial, his first call was to a Regent number she could not identify. The call took a long time: Bill wary, low-voiced, and grunting relief at the end. Next, to her astonishment she saw him pick up a classified directory and flip its pages.

Marjorie turned away. She glanced at the clock. Twenty-six minutes past ten.

Though Marjorie had no idea of what had happened, she knew they were racing the clock. The receiver in Bill's compartment went down with a bang of satisfaction. Bill, now smoking a cigarette, could no longer breathe in that stifling air. He pushed the door halfway open. Marjorie flew across. He was speaking to the switchboard at his own flat.

"Tommy . . . yes, Mr. Dawson. Is Mr. Somers, in C-16, at home tonight? . . . He's just come in? . . . No, no, I don't want to speak to him; don't ring. Where's Tuffrey? . . . In my flat? With a shotgun? . . . No, switch me to Tuffrey."

Bill drummed impatient fingers on the side of the phone. "Tuffrey? . . . Yes, that's right. Now don't speak a word until I tell you. There's a microphone nearby. It can't pick up what I say, but it can pick up what you say. I'll give you instructions, and you repeat them aloud as though you were making sure. Right!" He deliberately dropped his cigarette and closed the door.

"Beast! Brute! Ba—" Stopping herself, Marjorie ran back for a glance at the clock. It was twenty-nine minutes past ten. When she returned, Bill had the door open and was studying a page of the directory.

"I'm sorry, my sweet," he said with a white face. "But, in case something *doesn't* happen, I don't want to let you know what might happen. Forgive me?"

Marjorie's heart melted. "Darling!" she said. "I never meant—"

"This last call," continued Bill, dropping in pennies, "is to Ronnie Wentworth. Don't look so surprised! If Ronnie's not at his home address now, we may be finished."

He pressed close to the phone, tensely. The clock moved to ten-thirty. A familiar voice, audible even to Marjorie, popped out of the receiver; and Bill sighed as he clanked home Button A.

"Ronnie? . . . Bill Dawson here. Yes, yes, I know!" Marjorie could hear the burble of pleasure in the receiver. "Listen, Ronnie. You offered to show me the Sherlock Holmes Exhibition. Could we see it tonight, for instance, when it's not crowded with visitors? It fits in with your terrific idea? Ronnie, for God's sake stop sputtering! Have you got keys to the place? Can you meet me there in fifteen minutes? Thanks. That'll do!"

Bill leaped out of the telephone box.

"It's twenty-five minutes to eleven," said Marjorie.

He saw her gaze wander toward the several ways out, and interrupted the thought. "No, angel-face. We can't get a taxi in the West End in this weather. We could walk, but the alarm is probably out. No; the Underground will be best."

Without further words they tore down into the Underground. At Piccadilly Circus they changed, and presently emerged into the big booking hall at Baker Street Station. Seizing Marjorie's arm, Bill took her out by the west entrance and diagonally across the north end of Baker Street, where it runs toward Regent's Park. On the far side was a great, square, very modern building, of white stone and with a lighted cupola at the top. Bill hurried her to the entry of this building, and glanced inside.

"But what are we doing *here?*" asked Marjorie.

"What did you say, Marjorie?"

"Sherlock Holmes," said Marjorie, still looking southward, "was supposed to live at number 221b, wasn't he? I always used to think it was one of those red-brick fronts. And didn't somebody say, or write, it was number 111?"

"There are Canonical objections, my pet. Among them that the area, in Holmes's day, was called York Place. Never mind." Bill tapped his foot on the marble entry. *"This* is number 221b; or, at least, a part of it. The premises belong to the Abbey Building Society."

"This modern building?"

"Why not? Anyway, it's where they're holding the exhibition. Blacker and thicker yet! And what the devil's delaying Ronnie?"

As though in reply, a taxi with phantom lights skidded and splashed round the corner. It slurred to a stop in front of them.

Only dimly could Bill see Ronnie's length unfold out of the taxi. But he could imagine Ronnie's long chin under the large mustache, and his twinkling eyes under an ancient green hat.

Also, in a street with probably several policemen, Bill's nerves twitched at the possibility of Ronnie's approach. He might greet you with the cry of the old clo' man, or Sir Laurence Olivier playing Richard the Third.

"Heigh-ho, John Openshaw!" he thundered. "Good God, Marjorie! My own Irene Adler, though far more beautiful."

"Listen, Ronnie." Bill's voice was hard and the other instantly stopped.

"Let's drop the Canonical business. This is serious. Is there any way we can get in without being seen?"

"Of course. Side door. In a hurry, eh? Let's go!"

As Ronnie dashed round the side of the building, Bill saw that he was carrying a large camera of the Graflex type, with flash gun. Ugly associations went with it.[8]

In the narrow street beside the building, Ronnie was fumbling with keys as well as camera. "Got a torch?" he asked.

"Yes!" said Bill, feeling for his inside pocket and finding a flashlight. But sickeningly he remembered he had left Del Durrand's .38 in Gay's flat.

A lock clicked. Bill and Marjorie followed Ronnie's gesture to go inside, and Ronnie clicked shut the spring lock behind them. The beams of two torches prodded round a small concrete stairwell, with a small iron stairs ascending to a small landing, then turning back on themselves to the first floor above.

Though Ronnie might be efficient, you could not stop him talking. "Now about this idea of mine, it's terrific. Twice I've tried to tell you on the phone, but you've rung off. I want to get some photographs. . . ."

Bill cut him off, throwing the light into his face.

"Ron, this is a matter of life or death. Is it true that a wooden partition completely hides Holmes's sitting room, with

---

[8] The king or queen of readers, those alert to catch the tiniest detail, may have remembered Ronnie's talent for mimicry, his large mustache to hide another sort of face, even a possible motive; and they may have suspected Ronnie himself as the criminal. This is erroneous. Discard wrong answer number eight.

only a narrow little way-in at one side and way-out at the other? And curtained, so that even imitation gaslight can't be seen outside? Ron, I've got to hide in that sitting room: possibly until morning. There's a general alarm out after me."

"Shades of Blessington!" Ronnie said. "What have you been doing?"

"Nothing. But you may get into trouble; you've got to know. The charge is murder."

In the crossing lights Ronnie did not seem upset. In his eyes gleamed the light seen only in the eyes of the journalist born.

"What a release for the press!" he said hoarsely. "Lord alive, what a story! I know you didn't do it, Bill, but . . . slayer caught in Sherlock Holmes's sitting room. Crikey!"

"I understand, Ron. *If* they nab me here . . . Marjorie wants to stay . . . you photograph as much as you like. But I'm betting this is the one place in London they won't think of. Will you let us do it?"

"Let you do it? A hundred times over, old boy, even if nobody wanted to nab you. Adventure prowls yet in Baker Street! Now be quiet and follow me upstairs."

At the top, Ronnie stopped before a dark glass-paneled door. "This," he said, "opens into a big office all the way across the building at the back. Parallel with it, not so long and with some partitioning, the Sherlock Holmes exhibition runs along the front of the building. Got that?"

"Yes. Well?"

"Follow my light. Keep your torch down, though I don't think a copper would spot it. Forward, by the black pearl of the Borgias!"

The great office, as they moved after Ronnie's light down the aisle, had its drawn blinds painted black by the mist. Everywhere stood small desks, some with shrouded typewriters. Bill's imagination felt out. Many times he had heard the violin behind the lighted window, and the clatter of a hansom with fog-bound lamps.

Ronnie had stopped, and was waving the light. The three turned right, under what seemed a long arch. Unhooking a velvet rope, Ronnie stepped into the main exhibit room. Recklessly he flung the beam of light round, snatching out of darkness a glimpse of many glass cases, while photographs, paintings, drawings leaped out.

"Easy with that light!"

"H'm," said Ronnie, lowering. "Now turn left and follow me straight down this aisle to the sitting room; it's at the far end facing out."

They followed. "Ronnie," whispered Marjorie.

"Yes?"

"That wax figure sitting in the wheel chair. What story is it in?"

Ronnie wheeled round. "Marjorie," he said, "we have every possible relic of Holmes's cases, from the bicycle of Miss Violet Smith to the Giant Rat of Sumatra, but no figure in a wheel chair! Where did you see it?"

"I'm not sure. I thought I did."

"Anyway, here we are."

The light shone on a small, narrow door, gray and almost invisible against the left side of the wall.

"Now we're going backstage," continued Ronnie. "On your right is the long partition that hides the sitting room. But don't go in for a look over the railing; the room's dark."

A very thin key scratched at the lock of the small narrow door before Ronnie opened it. They followed him inside.

"You see?" he demanded. "There's not much space to turn round in. The sitting room is like a stage set, inside the outer wall of the building. That big window on the left gives on an airwell. That door on the right goes straight into the sitting room."

"Do you know," whispered Marjorie, "I'm afraid that if I opened that door now . . ."

"Old Holmes," supplied Ronnie, "would be sitting back in his armchair and looking at you? But Holmes and Watson were characters in fiction! You can't have the ghost of a man who never existed!"

"Get on with it!" said Bill.

"Got to get the lights on in there," protested Ronnie. "They wouldn't let us use real gas. But the lighting effect's just the same. Mustn't turn on the sound track with the street noises. But lights—now!"

A thin yellow line sprang up under the door.

"You're first, Bill," squawked Ronnie. "Go in!"

Opening the door part way, Bill breathed the stuffiness of carpets and furniture, leading him back into the late Victorian age. This room was real, under mellow gaslight. Bill moved into it.

Facing him were two windows, with curtains and blinds. Against the left-hand window showed a painted bust of Sherlock Holmes. Under the right-hand window stood Holmes's desk. Its padded brown desk chair had been slewed round toward Bill.

In the chair, with a large robe of blue silk covering him from the waist down, sat Gaylord Hurst. At least, it was Gaylord as Bill had known him in life.

Marjorie, who had crept in beside Bill, managed to stifle a cry.

"Surely it's . . ." she whispered.

"Oh, no!" said the man in the chair, in so different a voice that both of them jumped. "You never met or talked with the real Gaylord Hurst. *I* took his place, while the real Gay was never even dreaming I was in London. You never even saw him until you saw his dead body. Do you know that?"

Bill was full of sick bitterness.

"Yes, I know it," he said. "That's the best disguise I ever saw. But why don't you take it off?"

The man's hands flashed up behind his head. His wig fell forward into his lap. Down went his spectacles. His right hand made some move at his right eye, then his left; something fell. As he held up his big hands, long legs shot from underneath the robe.

Marjorie could no longer restrain herself. "But that's . . . that's *Larry* Hurst!" she screamed.

22 THE NINE RIGHT ANSWERS

BEHIND Larry Hurst, on the desk, burned a student's lamp. It turned Larry's light-brown hair almost fair. His long face looked older than his age. The wrinkles deepened across his forehead and round his mouth. "God damn you," he said quietly.

Bill stopped himself. He wanted to wade in and kill. But all evening he had been stifling this mood. He would not give way now.

"Oughtn't I to say that to *you?*"

"Why?" Larry's brown eyes were fixed on his face.

Bill was quiet. "I liked you," he said. "I trusted you. When you begged me to settle with Gay, I swore to myself I'd take the job; and I did. And all that time, when you were stinging me with unpoisoned razor blades and camera-guns meant to miss and half-poisoned typewriters and harmless tarantulas, and I was hitting back as best I could . . . all that time, you were the man who'd begged me to do it!"

"Yes," said Larry. "That's the originality." Then his mood changed. "But I had to have Gay's fortune," he added plaintively.

At the same moment he sat up straight, kicking out his long legs. He sat up with that air of flamboyance so likable when he played the good fellow as Larry Hurst, and so detestable when he played the sneering Gaylord.

"Now look, Dawson. I'm snookered. I know it. But I still

can't think *you* penetrated my imitation of Gay, or *your* wits discovered what I was trying to do. If you did find out about me—"

Larry's right hand went behind him. The upper left-hand drawer of the desk was partly open, to show Holmes's derringer. But Larry, fumbling further back, took out the Spandau air pistol.

"—then you're going to tell me how. That was why I deliberately fell for your trick call to Tuffrey. Nobody beats me, old boy. And if I can't learn how—"

"You know," Bill said thoughtfully, "I think I can hit you hardest by telling you just that."

"How do you mean?"

"By telling you, briefly and in order, the mistakes you made which proved who you were, and what your game was."

Facing out from a table stood an elaborate wicker armchair, painted white. Bill swung it round so that it faced more or less toward Larry.

"Sit down, Marjorie," said Bill. "This won't take long. But sit down."

Larry's intense brown eyes fastened on Marjorie as lecherously as had the false blue eyes of the false Gay.

"Yes, my dear," he mimicked Gay's soft precise voice, "*I could have given you a good time.*"

Bill stood with his back to the famous fireplace. Round the fire ran a high fire guard with vertical brass rods and a padded seat.

Bill sat on the fire guard. Larry kept the Spandau trained on him.

"For all I know," said Bill, "there may be nine wrong answers. But I know there are nine right ones, with many clues. Take the first right answer, fitting two pieces of evidence together, and you unlock the box. I did it! But there was so much rush that I couldn't even keep straight the days of the week. So I lost it. But I found it again, tonight, when I looked at the desk calendar on Gay's table."

"Desk calendar?" echoed Marjorie, whose frightened eyes were moving from Larry to Bill.

"Right answer number one!" said Bill. "Take it from the night I wandered into George Amberley's office in New York, and heard voices over an open transom. On the table was a bigger desk calendar. Twice I looked at it. It was Tuesday, June 12th.

"The next night, Wednesday the 13th, I spent in the airliner. The following night, when we went to meet somebody we thought was Gaylord Hurst, must have been Thursday, the 14th. Thursday. That same night, the so-called 'Gaylord' ar-

171

ranged a meeting for a week hence: the 21st, also a Thursday. Now what's wrong with that?"

Larry's eyes turned. In the doorway lounged Ronnie Wentworth, looking his mildest as he did when most dangerous.

"I'm a photographer from the *Evening News.*" He showed the camera. "Mind if I stay?"

Larry hesitated.

"*I* can tell you," said Ronnie, "what's wrong with the notion of finding Old Man Hurst at his flat on Thursday. I'm a member of his club, the Cocoa-Tree. Every Thursday, from morning until night, Old Hurst goes to his club and stays there. If he missed, they'd think he was dead and search for him. And two successive Thursdays? . . . No!"

"Exactly!" Bill said. "Ronnie told me that over the phone, more than a week ago. Somebody was impersonating Gay at that flat, with the assistance of Hatto: the one and very obvious accomplice. But who was impersonating him?

"Second right answer!" continued Bill, reaching into his inside jacket pocket, and shaking rain over the floor as he held up a fairly large old photograph.

"Well?" demanded Larry.

"Now this photograph," Bill showed it, "taken eighteen years ago, shows you and Gay. You gave it to me, of course, to emphasize his small stature; you'd been hammering at that all evening, and also at his blue eyes. Actually, it shows the very strong facial resemblance between you. Even more, it gives a clear picture of Gay's features, the lines in his face, his mop of iron-gray hair. At that time you were sixteen. Gay must have been in his fifties."

Carefully Bill put down the photograph on the seat beside him. "Very well! But at eight o'clock on Thursday, June 14th, the impostor Gay made Marjorie and me wait in his picture gallery, to see what we were meant to see.

"There was one striking, skillful picture, a full-length portrait in oils of Gaylord Hurst. It showed him seated, with emphasis on one short leg. It had been painted recently, and it was signed, *Thompson, '50.*

"And yet," Bill added, "and yet—Gay's face, his features, even the color and shape of his hair, were exactly the same as in a photograph taken eighteen years before! Gay by this time was over seventy. Can anybody imagine that his face wouldn't have shrunken, his hair whitened or fallen out, during all those years? In other words, just as the real Gay's caved-in face looked when I saw him dead tonight?"

Marjorie shuddered.

"Somebody," Bill went on, "had made a bad mistake. It was

172

a natural mistake. When we haven't seen some old relation or friend for years, we always remember him as looking exactly as he did when we saw him last.

"Somebody, perhaps a year ago, had the face and figure copied by a painter. Have we any indication of that?"

Here Bill took out a number of business cards and shuffled them.

"You know, Larry," he said sharply, "you did an admirable bit of misdirection with these business cards. We were supposed to think you kept them because of the amorous comments and telephone numbers penciled on the backs. But why should you keep the card describing the one woman who'd given you the bird? Because you wanted the name and address.

"Somebody, many hours ahead of me, carried that painting to London. On the first Thursday it was substituted for some other picture in Gay's gallery. And Marjorie and I were deliberately kept waiting there, so that we should have a clear reminder of the impostor we were going to meet, and not be surprised."

Bill held up one of the business cards.

"Here you are," he said. "The card of H. F. Thompson, with a studio in Los Angeles. His signature is on that painting. Nobody but you, Larry, could have had that photograph for a painter to copy. You're licked in two answers!"

Larry, moistening his lips, was crouched back. The Spandau was trained on Bill's face, and Larry's finger tightened.

Bill, dropping the card, fished out something else, and held it up before Larry's eyes.

"Third right answer!" said Bill. "It's short and sweet. In my hand I've got an alleged cutting from an alleged American newspaper. It was shoved under my door at the Waldorf, some time during the night after you were supposed to be dead.

"The cutting," he continued, "compressing two heads into one, is a fair imitation of American tabloid style for three paragraphs. But, in the fourth, comes the word j-e-w-e-l-l-e-r-y. But that's the English version. In America, always, it's j-e-w-e-l-r-y.

"Again we get a staggerer. It says: 'No post-mortem could yet be done, but the odour of the death-glass indicated,' and so on. The English is *post-mortem*, the American *autopsy*. Above all, no American reporter would ever write *odour*.

"Plainly, that press cutting was a fake, written out by an Englishman or Englishwoman. A private printer could set up and run off one copy in a short time. At first I thought it must be given to me by Joy. But here, Larry, we have the card of Edward J. Riley, a Greenwich Village printer not far from where you were supposed to have died. When you went there after this supposed death, you wrote out the copy.

"That fake newspaper story was excellent in its own way. It was Larry's ingenuity working again. The story had witnesses giving testimony slightly wrong, like real life. It had, I'm certain, the true explanation of that old man looking through a tear in a newspaper. But everything else was false."

Marjorie spoke out then. "But why?" she cried. "Why should he need it? What was the necessity for a fake newspaper cutting at all?"

"Because otherwise, angel-face," Bill retorted, "I might have backed out of the whole business. I was in a bad position, thinking Larry was dead with my own passport and papers on his body. But, if you read that account as I did, you'll see what it was meant to do. It stressed the supposed dead man was unidentified, everything stolen from his body. It heavily stressed that I, his companion, was not under suspicion.

"You see? It sent my confidence soaring up like a fire. I'd wanted desperately to go on this mission and now I saw I needn't back out. The dangers seemed all gone. I didn't know Larry there had read my mind exactly."

Larry was now sitting up straight, the pistol in his hand. Up swept that charm, that geniality, that seeming frankness again.

"Quite right," he said. "I can read your mind. Or anybody else's. You're not a bad sort, old boy. Only a quixotic fool. But I *was* poisoned. I thought I was a goner. I don't know a damned thing about what happened. You're no detective, Dawson. If I can't work out who or how or why, you haven't a dog's chance of doing it!"

"No," said Bill, "I'm not a detective. I'm only a rather absent-minded historian, filing facts in my head and pulling them out when I need them. —But I can tell you who poisoned you, and how, and why."

The Spandau flashed up.

"You think you can? Let's hear it!"

"Oh, no!" said Bill, and got to his feet. "I'm getting bored with that silly-looking gun of yours; you won't shoot. Now sit and boil in your own conceit while I talk about something more important than poisoning you."

Larry's eyes grew cold and steady. Bill knew that Larry would fire as soon as curiosity and vanity were appeased.

"Right answers number four and five, taken together!" said Bill. "Why should it apparently be impossible for you to play the part of Gaylord? On the other hand, why was it certain long ago that you did?"

Bill calmly sat down again. "Remember, Larry, that in New York I never saw you except in a very dim light. The law library was very gloomy. George Amberley's office, with that lamp shade down nearly to the blotter, was all but dark. It was dark in the passage; you were only a silhouette when you offered me the ten thousand dollars. Downstairs, there was only moonlight. Dingala's was very faintly lighted. Even there, the brim of your hat was turned down, you kept your head averted and spoke with lips almost closed.

"All that evening we never saw your teeth. Your most characteristic gesture was to lift your hand and shake your fist.

"The real Gaylord was short. You're tall, taller than the five-feet-eleven you claimed; I can prove that by a South Kensington tailor. All the talk about trousers, in New York, was not to underline the difference between you and me: it was to underline the difference between you and Gay. You were so enthusiastic that you went too far. You said, 'Lot of my height, d'ye see, is in my legs.'

"Any other difference? Several! Larry's brown eyes, Gay's blue ones. I needn't mention hair or bifocal spectacles or age. Above all, Gay had small hands—see the photograph—and Larry had big hands. It seemed to put imposture out of court.

"And yet, Larry," he went on, "when Marjorie and I spent the evening with the so-called 'Gaylord,' I could kick myself now for seeing but not observing all the curious details.

"For instance! This 'Gay' was supposed to wear bifocal lenses, which magnify the eyes. The painting quite correctly showed the eyes magnified. And yet several times, when I bothered to look at his eyes, I saw they were small. He was looking through plain glass.

"Another instance! When I recovered from radium poisoning, my doctor advised reading glasses. Or those very thin contact lenses fitted inside the eyelid. Unfortunately, before my brain unlocked, the doctor's suggestion went.

"But I had heard of contact lenses. When my brain did unlock, I seemed to remember that on these lenses could be fitted an eye of a different color, undetectable because it moved with the eyeball like its own contact lens. Tonight I tried to ring up an oculist, an acquaintance of mine; but I wasn't sure of his name. So I surprised Marjorie by looking him up in the classified directory and then (at night) ringing his home address. He said I was right, and asked whether the man's eyes seemed to *glitter* near even a dim light. They had; I'd seen it. You'll find both contact lenses in Larry's lap."

175

For the first time an edge of fear showed in Larry's face.

He had said before he was snookered, but he had not seemed really to believe it. His left hand went down to the contact lenses in his lap, but hesitated.

"Still another instance!" said Bill. "When we saw the so-called 'Gay,' he was sitting in something resembling a wing chair, yet anyone could see plainly it was a wheel chair. Round his waist he wore a very large blue silk robe. The first moment I had a good look at him, his hands were plucking and scrabbling inside the robe to pull it further back as though to conceal the wheels.

"But why should he do that? Anybody could see the outline of the wheels. No thank you. This chair was a special chair. It was built fairly long in the seat from back to front; when the impostor sat down, it concealed his long legs from hip to knee. Through two holes at the front went his knees; the legs from knee to feet were doubled up and strapped nearly to the underside of the chair."

Bill bent over. He snatched up the blue silk robe and held it taut.

To the inside of the robe, fairly low, had been fastened the movable knee caps, the lower legs, the feet of a child. They were covered with shoes, socks, half-trousers.

"Sewn invisibly to the inside of the robe and clamped to a high footboard so that they couldn't move, here's the last proof of 'Gay's' small height and weak legs. Grotesque?" asked Bill, flinging the robe and its grisly contents over to a leather sofa, strewn with newspapers, on his right. "Yes! Very grotesque." He glanced toward the tall-backed empty armchair on his left. "But it is only one step from the grotesque to the horrible. As a fourth and final instance—"

"Bill!" Marjorie cried out. She was watching the Spandau.

"But I won't stress the final instance, Larry," said Bill. "Your hands were always under the robe. Your big hands were the one thing you couldn't conceal. Though there was a hand-bell, you shouted to summon Hatto. (You had used that hand-bell only once, to summon us from the picture gallery while you were alone.) When you threw dice, your hands were be-low the tablecloth. It was the reason Hatto always had to push you. When Hatto and I got ready to fight it out to a finish, you kept screaming at Hatto to remove your precious jade chess pieces—or you pretended they were your most prized posses-sion. You could have moved yourself forward ten feet, dragged the table back yourself. Nobody, at that time, would have no-ticed your hands. Why didn't you? Because your balance was too unsteady. You couldn't have gone three feet without up-setting and showing the whole trick.

"With dim lighting everywhere, with your wig and natural wrinkles, you created 'Gay.' But you had one horrible moment, didn't you, when Joy rushed in? Remember, Larry?"

"Joy!" said Larry, in a very curious inflection.

"The sixth answer," said Bill, "is rather interesting. How could you, who boasted to me you'd never opened a book except the adventure kind you liked, hope to impersonate a genuine historical scholar like the real Gay? Yet you told us the answer yourself."

Larry sat up straight, radiating his very real charm. He still wore the blue double-breasted suit in which Bill had last seen him, damp round the lower legs.

"Yes, you're quite right," he said to Bill in his ordinary baritone. "In the role of Gay, I did tell you how his nephew might have beaten him at his own game. And did! Or, rather, I told this sexy young lady here." Larry, the not-very-subtle ladies' man, let his eyelid droop at Marjorie. "Gaylord told you his nephew, whom he had mocked for dullness at certain studies, might try to come back and beat his uncle at the latter's own game. Gaylord told you that's what *he* would have done. Well, that's what I did. What I made Gay say about long waits between hunting or fishing expeditions: that's true. For years I ordered crate after crate of books. It was hard going, for a few years. But I kept on and kept on. Until . . .

"And," again he mimicked Gaylord, "those stilted, rather pedantic sentences of mine? If mostly you read the Victorians or Edwardians, it's easy to fall into the rhythm. Anyway, I did it! You're a historian yourself, Dawson. But I fooled *you*."

"Oh, no, you didn't," Bill said mildly. "But let it go now."

"Let it go?" Larry almost shouted. "By God, we won't! How didn't I fool you?"

"For heaven's sake," cried Marjorie, "no more about old Louis Quatorze!"

"Better do it, Bill," Ronnie advised. "That Spandau can blow your head off."

"Well . . . I thought from the first your so-called learning was a fake. Your French pronunciation, as I told you, would have disgraced a one-day tripper to Boulogne. I gave you fourteen questions about the Fourteenth Louis, and you were so floored you had to dodge them and yell for Hatto.

"Stop!" Bill held up his hand. "I know what you're going to say. At dinner, when you had time to recover your wits, you answered a few of the questions whose facts you could have got from any light biography. It wasn't until this infernal unobservant brain of mine unlocked, completely unlocked, that I saw you were faking all the time. I'll ask you just one

177

thing, and drop the subject for good. —Describe the 'iron mask.' "

"It was a ruddy great iron thing, and bolted together at the sides. Saw it in a film once."

"Nonsense!" Bill said curtly. "That was a legend invented by Voltaire. The so-called 'iron mask' was only a face mask of dark velvet, tied behind the head with strings."

Abruptly he turned away toward Marjorie.

"Let's briefly dispose of right answer number seven . . ."

"Bill, wait!" There was a rattle of china, a movement of mellow glow from a shaded lamp, as Marjorie's wicker chair creaked against the table. "You haven't explained the most important thing of all. We know Hatto was Larry's accomplice. That hasn't even been mysterious. But Larry must have had at least two other accomplices, the fake 'Chief Inspector' in the flat across the street and 'Bartley Somers' in the flat next to yours."

"That, my dear, *is* right answer number seven. If you exclude Hatto, Larry had no accomplices at all."

"But Partridge and Somers . . . !"

"In addition to playing the role of Gaylord Hurst," said Bill, "Larry played the roles of Partridge and Somers; and it was the most practical thing he did."

"What!"

"Larry could use Gay's flat only one day in the week, and not all of that. He needed a place to live, to 'stow his gear: the painting and wheel chair I suspect folded out flat, to be hidden in a flat box. Above all, he needed a place where he could watch and hear my every move.

"Chief Inspector Partridge was mostly a blind to draw my attention from Somers close at hand. But 'Bartley Somers,' the commercial traveler, on the same floor as mine? He needed no disguise. He is described as tall, fair-haired, a reasonable description of Larry when you see him now, with light-brown hair under that lamp; and a pair of plain-glass spectacles.

"Remember: all the flats had been booked far in advance, with impeccable references and cash-down. Larry took an early plane from New York on Wednesday morning, and arrived here in London before I had even started.

"On Wednesday evening, he could have explored all three flats. Because the keys, together with references and money, would still be at the agent's! Hatto could have picked up the keys to my flat, reserved in Gay's name. If Hatto asked for the other keys as well, what agent would be suspicious of the famous Gay? Well ahead, Hatto could have got a duplicate key to my flat.

"Wednesday night, Larry (as Somers) went to his flat to 'look round'. But he had a duplicate key to mine. He's a good man with his hands. It'd take him only a few hours to install two microphones with wires leading to his own flat.

"You were so ruddy careful, Larry, that I wonder"—here Bill whirled toward Larry—"that I wonder you didn't remember at the start what might have dished your whole scheme. George Amberley was suspicious; Joy told you. On Thursday, as Gay, you received a letter from Amberley giving these suspicions in detail. You waved the letter in my face as a threat. Didn't it occur to you that, when the real Gaylord died, Amberley would investigate? No; apparently not. Never mind."

Bill turned back to the others.

"Larry, as 'Somers,' was now impregnable. The next morning, when I went out to perform some errands, 'Somers' nipped in and put the radium paste on my typewriter.

"Afterward, he simply followed me on my errands. The fake Gay said that 'he employed no agents.' No; he was playing everybody.

"Did I say impregnable? Larry wasn't even at Gay's flat when I rang up on Thursday at five o'clock. He couldn't have been, because he was deliberately seen flashing field glasses from 'Partridge's' flat.

"But Hatto was always at the other end. When I rang up, with Hatto apparently turning to his employer for an answer, Hatto merely stepped back and said something indistinguishable. Of course, Larry hurried back and made himself up to meet me.

"Well! Now you know almost everything. You know Larry's motive, his fundamentally simple plan—"

"Motive?" echoed Marjorie, biting at her lip.

"Plan—er—plan?" asked Ronnie Wentworth.

"Good God!" said Bill, "do you mean you still don't know the motive? Very well. Changing chronology, we'll make the next one right answer number eight.

"Larry, many months and possibly nearer a year ago, realized he was going to run through his mother's large inheritance. But Larry, like every murderer of his type, *had* to have money. The only immense source of money lay in his uncle. But he knew Gaylord, who still hated him, wouldn't give him a penny. I knew that myself—Ronnie told me on the phone— it's club gossip.

"On the other hand, Larry was Gay's only relative. And the real Gay had never made a will. I learned that tonight from the report of Sergeant Green. Larry could have learned it from George Amberley.

"Gay wouldn't relent. But suppose he *seemed* to relent? Suppose there came to Amberley a letter with ten thousand dollars and a vague agreement to receive back the prodigal if the prodigal would agree.

"Some months ago, when Larry was in London conferring with Hatto . . ."

"In London?" cried Marjorie. "But he said he hadn't been in England for eighteen years."

"Just a moment, Marjorie!" Bill held up his hand. "I had wondered, from the time Larry told all those hideous and true stories about Gay, why Larry didn't mention Hatto as a menace until nearly the end. I thought it was because he didn't fear Hatto; and that was true. Hatto had been decent. But, in all those years, Hatto had outgrown servility; and he hated Gay's airs almost as much as Larry did.

"So Hatto was ready to listen to Larry's proposition, Hatto still believed Larry was rich with his mother's money. When Larry was in America, Hatto controlled the phone and the letters; they could communicate without Gaylord knowing anything. So, on Gay's stationery, they typed out the letter to Amberley, and on legal paper the contract with an almost undetectable imitation of the real Gay's signature. This was, at Larry's signal, to be posted to Amberley."

"Do you mean to say," demanded Marjorie, "that Larry could forge his uncle's signature so that nobody would recognize it?"

"Couldn't he?" asked Bill. "You should have heard the little lecture he preached on the ease of forgery. But he talked too much and slipped again. He said, 'Done it myself. Why, I've—' He'd almost blurted out that he'd forged his uncle's signature to the papers upstairs.

"I did notice that Amberley had been looking rather dubiously at the third and last page of the agreement. But there was nothing there as yet except the last paragraph, unimportant, and the (presumed) signature of Gaylord. Gaylord Hurst was erratic; his writing had been erratic; he could accept it.

"And now what was Larry's real plan?

"The agreement was a fake of which Gaylord knew nothing. Larry couldn't go back to England as Laurence Hurst. But then he never meant to. He would find some actor who looked rather like him, preferably down in his luck. Larry would offer ten thousand dollars for an impersonation.

"And then, when the impostor accepted? Larry would get to England ahead of him. He would play the same game: insulting the impostor, playing the devil generally, and inviting him to a kill-you-unless-you-can-escape game. If the impostor refused, as most men would, the false Gay could then tell him he knew the impostor wasn't his nephew; he could demand the money back, and threaten arrest on a charge of fraud.

"The impostor's got to play. Mind you, the false Gay *wanted* him to be exposed as an impostor. Well, it worked with me. Furthermore, this first 'six months' and later 'three months' was all nonsense. Larry had to act quickly, or the real Gay might hear of it. Very soon Larry would creep into the flat while the real Gay was there. He'd kill the real Gay, having already established a mountain of evidence against the man posing as Laurence Hurst.

"And then? Naturally the police would arrest the impostor. Larry, having hared back to New York on the impostor's passport, would be shocked and horrified to learn of his uncle's death.

"It wouldn't matter if the impostor swore that Larry had put him up to the whole scheme. With such a weight of evidence, for both imposture and murder, the poor devil wouldn't stand a chance. Who would believe such a crazy story? And Larry would return, with a new passport because clearly the impostor had stolen his, to inherit half a million."

Bill turned to Larry. "A beautiful plan, eh? When you'd even let your passport expire, and got a new one so that nobody could prove you'd been in England before?

"And yet, from the very first, your plan went wrong.

"You'd decided not to approach an actor on the Coast. You were too well known in that district. So, in reply to a wire from Amberley, you flew east with Joy Tennent. She knew nothing about it; you don't believe in confiding in women.

"You were hoping to get the actor in New York. But your plane was grounded for three days. You got to New York on Tuesday, the 12th, and late. All your plans depended on an impostor taking the five o'clock plane next day. I don't wonder your behavior was so wild. I don't wonder your true stories about your uncle rang so true. You couldn't go back! Then as a godsend, I turned up."

Larry would say not a word.

"Or was I such a godsend, Larry? You know what a battle we've fought for just one week and one day. I think you broke first. I can tell you when the climax happened. It was last night.

"I burst into Gay's flat. You were there, decked out as Gay. I smashed up Hatto, and left him unconscious on the chessboard. Then you began to talk to me, and you were thinking very hard. You kept it up until ten o'clock. You must have known you couldn't get a doctor for Hatto—before the real

181

Gay returned from his club. Then that was the time to snaffle Gay, wasn't it? So you told me that I should get my death sentence twenty-four hours from then?"

"Yes, old boy," replied Larry almost cheerfully. "I rang for a doctor, yes. Unsavory chap; but you could trust him. And I snaffled Gay as he stumbled and sneered through the front door."

"Oh?"

"Yes. Funny thing, too. Hated him more than I used to. But I wasn't afraid any longer. Little rickety old swine with white hair standing up in white patches? Bah!"

"But you didn't kill him that night, did you?"

"No, no! Didn't even hurt him," retorted Larry, with the smile that could be so engaging. "Didn't even tie him up, in case the marks showed. Just sat with him all night in the dark —his own style with me—and told him what was going to happen. He's got guts; but he did squeal a little. This evening, about twenty minutes to eight . . ."

"How did you get him to swallow the cyanide?"

"I'd got it from a little brown bottle that belonged to him. Show old Gay some Nazi methods, and be ready to use 'em. . . . I didn't have to. Funny: he was a little crazy by then. He snatched the brandy glass out of my hand and drank the lot; but I yanked back the stem." Larry laughed. "Your fingerprints all over the glass, too."

"You read my mind again, I suppose?" Bill asked softly. "Since you didn't stalk me in the daytime, you expected me to stalk you at night? And come straight to Gay's flat?"

"What the hell else?" asked Larry. "Had to leave Gay's body for you. The old swine died just before Hatto phoned the police. Hatto and I agreed on a story. He hadn't known murder was intended. I left a back window unlocked, and went away with the painting and my folded wheelchair. Couldn't expect you much before dark. Thought you'd meet the police. Sorry if you lost the duel."

Then his voice sharpened and his eyes grew alert. He ran his left hand along the polished barrel of the air pistol. "But you haven't told the most important thing! It's got to be right answer nine." Larry peered up. "Who poisoned me? And how? And why? And how did I wake up in that telephone booth, just as two internes arrived?"

Everyone in that stuffy room could feel death hiding in each corner. Unless Larry could be stopped, he would run amok when he learned what he wanted to know. Casually Bill rose from the fire guard, sliding along the seat toward his right, and his right hand behind him, touched the fire irons, drew out the heavy poker and held it behind his topcoat.

182

Not a sound. But, as he stood up, he realized how tired he was.

"Come on!" snapped Larry. "Who poisoned me?"

"Joy Tennent," answered Bill. "But she meant to poison *me*."

"*What's that?*"

"You've had so much success with women that you can't understand one woman. Joy wasn't interested in your *beaux yeux*. She was interested in your money."

"Be careful, Dawson!"

"Shut up!" said Bill, edging closer with the poker behind his back. The muzzle of the Spandau was within five feet of his head.

"Joy *couldn't* understand why you wouldn't go to England. She was desperate. But would she kill you, the source of income? No! She'd dispose of the obstacle. Me."

"But she was four bar seats away from you, with everybody watching her!"

"When you and Joy and I were in that moonlit corridor, you and I were talking. Joy had turned away. She tore silver paper off the edge of a cigarette pack, and rolled it into a pellet. . . .

"Across the corridor there was a flattish tin rubbish bin, with a back edge above it against the wall. Joy took the pellet between her thumb and second finger. She flicked it with such accuracy that it struck exact center of the back edge, and fell into the bin. In Dingala's Bar, Joy, well away from us, climbed down from her stool, went to the jukebox, and set it going in a ring of colored lights. Everybody in that direction looked at the jukebox.

"Joy's timing was perfect. She went straight back to the bar stool, and almost immediately turned to stare out of the window.

"We turned and looked out at a harmless vagrant. The others were looking at the jukebox. In that moment, with everybody's back turned, she flipped something across into my glass. During the war she was in charge of a department making cyanide capsules for the cloak-and-dagger lads. She kept some as souvenirs. She couldn't have seen us change glasses. When we did it her back was turned. Then she realized what had happened, ran out, and waited across the street. None of us touched you, Larry. None of us saw you die. All we heard, from a crowd which didn't touch you either, was a falsetto scream of 'The guy's dead.' And we went away thinking you were dead."

"But I must have swallowed two and a half grains of the stuff! Or more! Then why didn't it . . . ?"

183

"Because you hadn't swallowed half enough to kill you."

Slowly Bill groped under his soggy topcoat. Murrell on poisons was still there.

With the fumbling fingers of his left hand, he managed to get the book open.

" 'Fatal dose: five grains is usually fatal,' " he read.* "But Joy thought she'd killed you. She forgot that those capsules, manufactured during the war, would have dwindled to half strength. Joy made as bad a mistake as you did, in your role of Gay, when you left me at the door and said: 'You're one of these nervy, high-strung people.' As Larry, you'd said almost exactly these words in America."

Bill flung the book in Larry's lap. "That night of your 'murder' in the bar, Joy wouldn't go near me or take the seat in the plane next day. She was afraid I had spotted her. But she'd seen that schedule of instructions. She knew I would call on Gay on Thursday evening. If she burst in then, I was cornered; I should have to play her financial game . . ."

"Easy, Dawson. Joy wasn't the mercenary kind, at least—"

"I'm afraid she was. You, playing Gaylord, hated her because she might have recognized you. Wife or no, you'd intended to ditch her in New York. Joy even tried her amorous wiles on me; but it didn't work.

"Accidentally, only as a nervous gesture, I kept snapping my thumb and forefinger in front of her. Like this!" Bill illustrated. "She ran away. She thought I knew. That was why I thought she'd never go to the police.

"But she did. She told Scotland Yard the whole story, with a pack of lies to convict me of your 'murder,' but enough about your part so that you'll never get that inheritance. You were right, Larry: I did run into the police tonight, but they never saw me.

"I nearly fell dead when I heard that New York reported a corpse, poisoned with cyanide, had been found in a telephone booth. I'd seen the policeman on the beat hurrying in as I left. He'd take one quick look, catch the talk, and immediately phone a report. Afterward New York either got mixed up or they used that first report and asked for twenty-four hours to check it.

"I knew that within seventeen minutes there would be a cable to say there had been no murder at Dingala's, no corpse, nothing. But, in case the Chief Inspector went off his rocker and turned in an alarm anyway, I must hide for a few hours until I could prove my innocence of this crime as well as Gay's murder. —Still, Joy did go to the police."

* Murrell's *What to Do in Cases of Poisoning.* London, H. K. Lewis & Son, edition 15, 1944.

Larry favored him with a mirthless smile of his wide-set teeth. Again eerily, he fell into the speech of Gaylord Hurst.[9]

"My dear fellow," he murmured, "surely you must be aware I already knew this. That Joy had telephoned Scotland Yard yesterday afternoon?"

"You knew?"

"Naturally. Regrettably, I was obliged to hire a private detective and tap her telephone line. Today my man's report indicated so many indiscretions even by phone. . . .

"Tonight, having disposed of Gay and dropped into a newsreel theater for a time, I returned to my flat in the Albert Arms with my folding wheel chair, oil painting, and other things. While musing, one of my microphones picked up Tuffrey's side of a conversation with you. This included much of what you now tell me: including the fact that you would be at this exhibition, and could prove my guilt. An obvious trap. Yet I answered it.

"But first I phoned my Joy, in my own name and voice, asking her to come here immediately. You, my dear fellow, must have been delayed. I arrived first, and burgled a window. My dear Joy, delighted, sprang out of a taxi. I held down my hands, pulling her up through the window. Her arms went round me. And I strangled her. Slowly.

"I had brought my folding wheel chair," he sighed, "to convey her away without suspicion. Fortunately, too, I had a pair of those blue silk robes. The plain one, I draped round Gay's body to hide the repulsive tufts on his head. This one . . . what matter? My dear Joy, deprived of all wiles, now sits in a wheel chair out among the main exhibits."

Abruptly his voice changed.

"But I am tired of Joy Tennent! If I go, two others go with me. Now!"

Round swung the Spandau.

Marjorie, petrified, saw Bill's right hand with the poker whirl up and slash down at Larry's wrist. The bursting whack of the shot—a shot like that, from a quiet air pistol?—shocked their eardrums amid a mist of heavy, sharp-smelling powder.

---

[9] The attentive reader may wonder whether he has been swindled in text or footnote. He has not been swindled. In footnote number 4 there is a warning that all remarks must be taken literally, meaning no more or no less than they say. Thus in footnote number 3 the author states that Larry had been poisoned with two and ⌣ half grains of cyanide, and not by Larry's own hand. Never does the author say Larry is dead. This occurs only when it is plainly indicated that matters are seen through the eyes of Bill, who does believe it. Similarly, in the scenes with the false Gay, the author himself does not say that here is the real Gaylord Hurst. It is fair to speak of Gay's flat and his belonging, anything which refers to the real Gay. But again, in the many interviews, he is Gaylord Hurst only in the eyes of Bill. Otherwise all is circumlocution: "the so-called uncle," "Mr. Hurst," "the man in the wheel chair," and dozens of terms misleading yet true. Often, too, he speaks only after a stage direction without any reference to his name. This is legitimate mystification. Discard answer number nine.

Then Marjorie saw the gouge of the bullet hole in the window frame between Bill and Larry. She looked back toward Ronnie, whose right hand was no longer hidden.

"Don't try that again, Buster," Ronnie lazily advised Larry. "There are lots of revolvers in this place: all unloaded, of course. But I keep one, and slide it down ahead, in case some visitor doesn't think Holmes and Watson didn't mean business. She's a Colt, made in '91; but she works and fires black-powder cartridges."

Bill's poker had smashed Larry's wrist, deflecting his bullet. With an infinite effort Bill bent and picked up the Spandau. He took it back to the fire guard, stooped over, and dropped it gently inside on the tiles.

"Anyway, Larry," he said, half turning round, "that's my case. If you won't come with me to the nearest police station, I'll drag you there. And who's won the duel now?"

"Not bad, Mr. Dawson!" struck in a new voice. "Not bad at all!"

Bill whirled round. Facing him across the narrow side was the visitors' railing with its full wooden panel underneath.

Up from behind the panel, at one side, rose the burly figure of Chief Inspector Partridge. At the other stood grinning Inspector Conway, notebook in hand. Between them both was a uniformed policeman.

The affable Chief Inspector spoke.

"Mr. Dawson," he said, now genially, "I like your style! Didn't leave that house ten mintues before you phoned Conway. Asked him to make me hold my horses until ten minutes after the reply came from New York; then come on here. . . . Got it all down, Conway?"

Partridge shouldered across the room; he slapped Bill on the arm. "You've got nothing to worry about, son," he said; except maybe this young lady."

Marjorie, her nerve broken, was leaning face down against the table and sobbing. Bill picked her up, turned her round, and held her tightly in his arms.

"What's the matter, my dear? It's all over now."

Though Marjorie was no longer sobbing, she kept her eyes closed as she put her cheek against Bill's and softly seemed to whisper.

" 'Then saith he, speaking but to his squire: Upon this day, by God's grace and my lady's favour, will I do a deed of arms shall . . . shall . . .' "

"Sounds familiar," said Bill. "Can't place it. Never mind, my dear!"